ANGELINA MARIE

Lynda C. Yeates

For Mom,
With Love

Lynda C Yeates

This novel is a work of fiction. Any resemblance to persons, living or deceased, are strictly coincidental.

First Edition- 2015

Published by CompletelyNovel.com

ISBN: 9781849147736

Fiction, Romance, General

Distributed by Lightning Source

This book is dedicated to:

My God, the Author of all creation...

My Donald, for always believing in me....

My Dad, Otis Runyon, who taught me not to wait...do it now.

I dreamed of writing and publishing a novel. I never dreamed I would be the author of two books. The journey of writing has taught me invaluable lessons. Patience. Persistence. Preparation. The three p's of writing a novel. It takes all three to take your book from idea to reality. As a writer it may sound a bit ironic that I find it hard to describe the feeling of holding your dream in your hands. Your story in print, complete with pages and a beautiful cover with your name on it. I promise you there is no other feeling quite like it. There is validation in that moment that is priceless. If you are a writer, a creator, whose dream has always been to write and publish, I encourage you to start today. Begin the journey... today. Don't wait until you're less busy, or your children are grown. The right time, the some days, may never come. Sit down and begin your story today. Do it now.

ONE

Will Biggs sat at the edge of the water watching as it flowed swiftly
by, slowing some as it came to a wider spot in the creek. Beyond
the wide spot he knew it picked up speed again, turning into rapids
farther downstream. Just like the rapids his thoughts seemed to be
swirling, churning, bashing against the rocks. As soon as he began
to believe that all he ever dreamed of was going to come true; his
own horse farm, and Nola; the dream was snatched away. Two
seconds, two words, snatched away a lifetime of living, and
working toward his heart's desire. Angelina opened her mouth, and
poof, the dream vanished. She spoke, and it disappeared like a
vapor.

It seemed to him a lifelong dream was a monumental price to pay for one night of lust. He surrendered to a moment of weakness, and now it was haunting him. Angelina was so beautiful. No denying that. A long black mane, and eyes deeper, and darker, than her hair. Her eyes were almond shaped, with naturally thick lashes and perfect brows. A face that was sculpted by the almighty himself. So it seemed. When she stared into his eyes that night, she was leading him. She took him to a place of no return. A place where he was powerless to stop. The truth was he didn't want to stop. That night in the cabin he did what he wanted to do with Angelina.

He did not care about, or even think about the consequences. Flames of passion grew, until it was a fire that consumed any other thoughts, except for having her. And have her he did. Now his lack of self-control determined he must live with the result of that one union between them. They were going to have a child. The two words Angelina spoke, turned his world upside down, and his dreams to ashes.

"I'm pregnant."

He had a way with horses. Some called it magical. Working with them brought him peace, and a contentment he found nowhere else. Being a horse trainer was not just a job. It was his passion. His drive was to someday own a horse farm. He wanted to train and breed his own horses and cattle. Getting a job at Fair Meadows, and working with Mundy Winks, had been the best opportunity he ever lucked into. The pay was excellent, but even more important to him was the quality of the animals. They were top notch stock, and he loved every minute of his time there. After he met Nola and they fell in love; he wanted to marry her, and take over the business of running the estate. It was not meant to be, or so it seemed.

2

It had been a month since Riley Todd tried to kill Nola at his camp. Will had been there, along with the lawmen, Cash Atkins, and John Goodpaster. Mundy Winks was there as well. Angelina had been secretly following Mundy, and Will, and when she came out of the woods looking ghostly, with her long black hair and white gown, Riley succumbed to a heart attack. In his deranged state, he imagined Angelina was the ghost of the woman he drowned years earlier. Riley died, and fell into the grave he dug for Nola. Such was Riley's fate. Trying to gain total control and ownership of Fair Meadows, cost him his life.

Nola saw a doctor immediately after they got her out of the woods, and back to Fair Meadows. She was badly beaten, and exhausted, but the doctor told Mundy, and Will, she would heal in time. However, the doctor wasn't so sure she would recover mentally, and emotionally. She had been through too much in the last year. The doctor said her mind shut down as a way of protecting itself. There was hope; the doctor told them. The hope was that with much prayer and rest, she would recover.

Will tried to see her. Every day he went to the estate. Every day Mundy would go to her and ask if she would see Will. Every day she replied in a flat unemotional tone "No." Mundy was the only one she would allow near her. Will thought of going against the old man's advice to leave her alone, and give her time. He thought of pushing him aside, and going to her room, forcing her to see him. He wanted to take her in his arms and kiss her face. He wanted to hold her, and never let her go. He went every day hoping that she would see him. Each time she refused, but he would not give up. Today Angelina changed everything. If she were going to have his child he knew he would have to let Nola go. Forever. His heart was breaking. He was in pain, physical pain. A single tear made a trail down his rugged face.

3

He brushed it away with the back of his hand. After Angelina came to his cabin, and told him about the baby, he ran off to the creek. He came to the place where he and Nola had fallen in love. He did not go to the house to try to see her; as he had every morning for the last month. Now it was near dark, and the early stars were out. He stood and picked up his hat, walking up the trail toward the house. When he reached the clearing near the house he stopped, looking up toward the balcony of Nola's room. He could see the French doors open, and in the dim light he could make out her silhouette standing, gazing down at him. He started to call out to her, but it came out a whisper.

"Nola… Nola."

He stood, hat in his hands, tears falling faster now. She saw him but said nothing. They seemed to stay that way forever. Frozen. Waiting. Slowly Nola took hold of the doors, and pulled them closed. Shutting away the night, she closed the doors to love, and any kind of life with Will. He felt a snap in his chest. His heart. He clutched his chest. Breaking. He was breaking. Walking slumped over, and in pain, he made it to his truck, and drove away. He drove back to Pine Point. Back to the woman he detested. Back to Angelina.

On the drive to his cabin Will thought about a life with Angelina. He supposed it would not be so horrible being married to a beautiful woman. She was obviously in love with him. The thought of having a child was a new concept to Will, but one he could get used to. Angelina was an only child, so Pine Point and all its holdings would someday be hers, and if they were married his too. Yes, maybe he could make this work. It was not his dream, but life was sometimes about settling. Nola wanted nothing to do with him. He saw that tonight.

He had to accept it, and move on. He did not know why and maybe never would. Nola was broken; shattered like a delicate vase that had been hurled against the hard unforgiving earth. She might never be whole again. She rejected him, and any help he might have given in putting her back together. She rejected his love. He could feel his pride returning. His tears stopped, and determination began to rise up within his chest. Determination replaced the pain he felt earlier. He gripped the steering wheel, and forced his mind to think about the woman who would soon be his wife.

"Life must go on Nola Rain." Will said aloud. "I must go on..." He turned on the road that led to his cabin.

Angelina sat on the porch steps of Will's cabin. Gone all day, Will ran off when she told him her good news. His reaction was just what she expected. Running off to that Todd woman. What a bunch of crazies they all were. Riley Todd went over the deep end, and tried to kill Nola. He killed Dorian Davis, burying her at the secret camp he owned. She heard that there was a separate investigation going on by the sheriff of Bryce County, and Louisa, into the drowning's at Fair Meadows years ago. Rumor was Riley was behind those two deaths too.

What a lunatic Angelina thought. She'd never been so scared in her life as that night a month ago. But now she was ready to move on, and she wanted Will Biggs to help her with that move. She had a plan on making that happen. It involved a little bundle of joy. She was not happy when she found out she was pregnant. She never wanted a child. She could not stand children. All that crying and constant attention they required. No, mother-hood was definitely not for her, but if it would aid her in getting Will, she would do anything. Getting pregnant was a happy accident. A tool she could use to work her plan. She could figure out what to do with a snotty, crying, brat later. That's what nannies were for. She just needed to

5

be careful, and make certain that no one figured out her little secret. As long as she followed her plan, she knew she could make it all work. Work never bothered Angelina. Patience sometimes got the best of her, but this time she would wait. Wait for Will to see things her way. Wait for him to step up and be a man. Yes she would give him all the time he needed to see things her way.

As he pulled up in front of the cabin he saw her sitting, waiting on the steps. Angelina sat with her arms wrapped around her long legs, smiling sweetly, as he pulled the truck up in the yard close to the cabin. He sat in the truck just staring at her for a few minutes. Trying to collect his thoughts and figure out exactly what he wanted to say, he sat there. She sat staring back at him with a pasted smile, and a look that he decided was one a cat has when it's finally caught the mouse.

He got out, and without a word walked up the steps and into the cabin shutting the door behind him. Angelina let out a scream of rage and frustration as she got to her feet, and followed him inside. "Will Biggs, why would you walk right past me like that as if I didn't exist? And where have you been? Did you go see your little girlfriend?"

Angelina's questions became a little louder with each one she fired off. Her face was red, and her eyes were wild.

Her breaths coming so fast and hard that Will thought she might hyperventilate. They stood this way for a few seconds, and then he couldn't help himself. It started out as a small snicker, which turned into a chuckle, and finally Will was laughing so hard that while holding his stomach he fell back onto his chair. He couldn't stop, and she was furious. Somehow his laughter seemed like the last straw. Without any thought or idea that she was going to do it, she reached out. With all her strength, she slapped him across the face.

The slap landed hard. Will was stunned for a second. He stopped laughing. Standing to his feet, and grabbing both arms, he shoved her across the room to the door of the cabin. Will slammed her hard against the wooden door. It knocked the breath out of her, and she stood gasping, and in pain. Will spoke, in a low tone, through clenched teeth. His anger obvious, and terrifying.

"This is what we are going to do Angelina." He gripped her arms tighter as she sucked in air.

"We are getting married only because you are having my kid. I am going to step up my role in running this farm. You are going to be the dutiful wife, and cook my meals, clean my cabin, and keep my bed warm. Understand?" When Angelina didn't answer Will tightened his grip on her arms. "Do you understand?" Will was shouting now his face just inches from hers.

"Yes…ya…yes," she stammered wincing from the pain.

Will smiled at her then, and released her arms as he stepped back. "You can go now Angelina. I am sure you want to tell your folks the good news. You may want to hold off telling them about the baby. Sometimes things happen, and then… well, babies don't happen. If you catch my drift. Do you understand?"

Angelina didn't take her eyes off him as she reached behind her to feel for the door knob turning it slowly. Her eyes were stinging with tears from fear and pain. Her arms hurt where he grabbed them. Just as she was going down the steps ready to run home, Will stepped out on to the porch, and yelled her name.

"Angelina," she stopped and turned around to face him. "One more thing, if you ever slap me again," he paused, "I will kill you." Flashing her a beautiful smile, he turned and walked back into the cabin. Angelina stood breathing hard trying to process what just happened. When she finally turned to run; the only thing she knew for sure was she didn't doubt what he said. Not for a minute. She knew he meant what he said.

And if he would threaten her because of a slap, what would he do if he knew the secret she carried inside her? She had no doubt he would carry out his threat. She believed him. He could, and would, kill her.

Will sat in his chair before a roaring fire. The autumn air created a deep chill at night, and the fire chased it away. He sipped a cup of coffee held in his hands, and thought about this nasty turn of events. He hated Angelina. Though she was probably the most beautiful woman he had ever known, underneath all that beauty was a black heart. He too had a black heart, and so when the two of them came together, there was no light or love between them. Darkness, only darkness. His life had been a constant struggle of good and evil.

Will could be extremely kind and compassionate, but when triggered he became consumed with rage. Deadly. Some called it hot-headed, or hot-tempered, others had seen and felt first hand his bursts of anger. Today he wanted to snap Angelina's neck. He stopped because of the baby. Now he had to figure out a way to live with Angelina. No more outburst of anger. Will liked being in control at all times. Dealing with Angelina would push him to the limits of control. She was just a silly girl who trapped Will. He felt trapped. Like a wild animal caught in a snare, he was trapped. The only bright side to any of this was Pine Point. The farm was successful and lucrative. Not quite Fair Meadows equal, but close. It would be his pleasure to take it from the Oliver's. He would consider it his payment for marrying their impossible daughter.

He was saving some other poor soul, from a lifetime prison sentence, by becoming her husband. It was late now, but he was not sleepy. He got up and went outside on the small porch. He leaned against the post that held the roof up. Looking toward heaven the stars seemed especially bright, and close. The night was cool, crisp. A full moon cast an eerie glow across the yard. The shadows of the trees fell across the grass, and somewhere in the distance he could hear a dog, or maybe a coyote, howling. Quite a lonesome sound, and one he understood. Alone most of his life Will was used to it. Preferring it at times. But sometimes you just need someone. Some nights a body just aches for someone to be near. He allowed a thought of Nola. Just for a moment. He quickly let go of her, and felt her slip on by. It weakened him to think of her. In the next few months and years, he would need to be stronger than he had ever been. Will Biggs would put on the armor once more. He would wall himself off from the world, refuse to let himself become vulnerable ever again. The love he held, the heart he opened for Nola, was gone. At least on the way out of his mind and life. The door was closing on his heart; just like the one she closed, shutting him out of Fair Meadow, and her life. He stood for just a second more, walked back in the cabin, and closed the door against a chilly night wind that began to blow.

Cash Atkins walked the streets of Monroe smiling at the folks he passed, occasionally stopping to speak. He was walking toward the jail which also served as his office. Breakfast had been good. He was sure getting spoiled on Rosey's cooking. Three squares meals a day, served with a smile at The Red Rose Diner. Served with a smile if Rosey took a shine to you. Rosey was crazy about Cash. Most folks were. Polite and good looking, at times gullible, Cash Atkins was easy to like. Since he landed the job of sheriff here in Monroe, most of his meals were eaten there, or carried from there and consumed in his little office.

After the tragedy involving Riley Todd, Sheriff Elkins called it quits. He said he wanted to go ahead and retire before the big investigation involving the state started happening. In actuality there was no big investigation. A man from the state came and talked to all involved. The body of Miss Dorian Davis was exhumed and sent to the capitol to be examined, as was Riley Todd's. Just as everyone suspected, Riley died from a massive heart attack, a *myocardial infarction* to be exact. There was evidence from his arteries of advanced heart disease, and the Medical Examiner in Charleston stated in his report that "death was inevitable." Cash remembered thinking when he read that part about his death being inevitable, that everyone's death is inevitable.

Poor Dorian's body was so badly decomposed; they were unable to determine her absolute cause of death. They did however see multiple skull fractures so the M.E. was at least able to rule the death homicide; possibly due to blunt force trauma. Her wind pipe was crushed as well, suggesting strangulation. All indications of what happened, but nothing that could be chiseled in stone.

Within a week the man from the state went back to his office in Charleston. Everyone else went back to their lives, doing their best to return to a sense of normalcy. Sheriff Elkins recommended Cash for the position of Sheriff, and he took the job. John Goodpasture was happy for Cash, but told him he would miss him. John was looking to retire soon too, but it still left him without a deputy when Cash left. He was actively looking for a replacement for the deputy turned Sheriff.

Just as Cash made it to the jail he saw a car pull up across the street and park. He stood and watched as Angelina got out of the back seat of the car. A chauffer from Pine Point had brought her to town. She stepped up on the sidewalk making her way up the street looking like she just rode in from Hollywood. She was dressed in a hot pink sweater, cropped tight slacks, large sunglasses and a scarf around her face. She looked like one of them starlets Cash thought. She was about the prettiest thing he ever laid eyes on. He shouted out to her, but she kept walking. When she was out of sight he went into his office.

He sat at his desk, but kept his eye on the window so that he could see Angelina when she came back to her car. His mind flashed back to that night in the woods after Riley fell into the grave and died. Angelina came out of the woods wearing only a long white gown. Her black hair was loose, and flowing all around her. Riley, already near death, thought she was the ghost of the woman he drowned years earlier.

When it was over Cash escorted Angelina out of the woods, and she was so shook up that she clung to him. When he tried to take her home she asked if they could go to his place instead. Even though he knew he should tell her no, and take her home, he didn't. She spent the night with him. He drove her to her truck early the next morning. She drove away leaving him in her dust, and taking with her his heart. Cash fell totally in love with her. He had tried to see her since then; calling her and even showing up at Pine Point, but she would not see him. He just couldn't understand what he'd done wrong. Seeing her today made him more determined than ever to find out.

Cash spotted her returning to her car. Quickly he got up, went outside, and crossed the street. She had her back to him when he approached the car. The driver was opening the door for her, and taking the packages from her hands. When Cash spoke her name it startled both of them. Angelina, and the driver jumped, and turned at the same time. "Angelina, I'm sorry...I didn't mean to startle you," Cash said.

11

"Cash, I uh…,"she stammered, "I uh, well it's good to see you."

He stood staring into those dark almond eyes, and felt as if he were becoming smaller, melting into a puddle of something warm. Her eyes were enticing, enveloping. "I've been trying to see you, to talk to you, since that night," he said shifting nervously from one foot to another.

Angelina spoke to her driver telling him he could get back in the car, and wait for her while she spoke to the sheriff. The man nodded, and smiled at Cash, before getting into the driver's seat and shutting the door.

"Cash, I am a very busy woman, what with the farm and taking care of mamma and daddy. Do you understand?"

"Oh I do understand Angelina. I was just hoping we could go out again. I mean a real date this time. I mean…well I am asking you for a date. You know a real date. I am crazy about you, and I want to see you, I mean date you." Cash waited for her answer, and stopped hopping from foot to foot. He was standing stiffly not even daring to breathe, as if breathing might make her disappear somehow.

Angelina looked at him pathetically, and then smiling a smile that was both sweet, and wicked, she said, "Cash dear, that night after the uh tragic happenings at that awful camp, well I was just scared and shook up. You understand don't you? That didn't really mean anything. Just two friends, comforting each other after a bad scare. Now I must be going, you see I am engaged to Will Biggs, and I just came into town to pick up some stationary, for invitations to our wedding. Oh and you know what? I will be sure to send you one. Congratulations on your promotion."

12

Cash felt like someone kicked him in the stomach as he watched her get in her car. She gave him a little wave of her hand as she and her driver pulled away.

He felt life drain from his body. He could barely hear the sounds of the street around him. His eyesight dimmed. The world became dimmer, duller. What happened? Married? She was marrying someone else? It wasn't supposed to go this way. Why did his life always go this way? He was still standing in the street looking in the direction they had driven, long after they were out of sight.

Angelina was mumbling to herself. The driver kept saying "Ma'am," until she screamed at him that she wasn't speaking to him. She was so angry at that country bumpkin Cash Atkins. Did he really believe that she would want to date the sheriff of Bryce County? Honestly how could he be so stupid? Just because she slept with him one time he thought they were an item? He thought he could come calling on her? What a country bumpkin. It made her queasy to think she spent a night with that overgrown country boy. At least she straightened that out. She was sure he got the message. She smiled thinking about the baby. She should send Cash a thank you card instead of an invitation. After all, that one union with Cash produced the one thing, which helped her trap Will Biggs. Yes she thought smiling brighter, thank you Sheriff Atkins. Thanks for everything, but no thanks.

The driver turned onto the drive that led to Pine Point. Split rail fence lined both sides of the paved road. It had been expensive to have the road paved, but the Oliver's were not the kind of people who worried about money, or how much anything cost. Angelina was their only child. They amassed great wealth in the horse and cattle business by the time she was born. They had believed they would remain childless, until they had her late in life. Both the Oliver's were ecstatic when their little surprise came along. She was a pretty baby, who turned into a beautiful young woman. Spoiled and arrogant, she was very different from her kind, aging parents. They tried to instill a sense of empathy and compassion in her when she was growing up, but she was indifferent to the pain of others. They knew it and tried hard to overlook it. They loved their child and gave her everything. But it was never enough. The best schools, clothes, trips, it was never enough for Angelina. The one common ground for the family was Pine Point. Angelina loved the farm. She worked it like one of the hands, physically doing everything, and anything, the hires did. Cleaning out stalls, breaking horses, even planting and harvesting kept her strong, and capable. Her parents at least had that to be thankful for. She removed some burden and responsibility from her father by overseeing the physical end of the business. That was Angelina Marie, the good child. There was however a totally different side of her that surfaced often. She could be frightening and irrational when life disagreed with her. Known for fits of rage and a smart mouth among the men, no one wanted to cross her. She was however the Oliver's one and only child, their world, and their greatest love.

Grabbing the packages and getting out of the car, Angelina headed inside the massive main house she shared with her parents.

The foyer was opulent, and elegant. Marbled floors, crystal chandelier, a winding staircase, and mahogany wood doors made up the entry. She made her way up the stairs then down the hall to another set of stairs. Her room was on the third floor. The entire floor was hers to use as she wished. She was the only one on that level of the house. There was one more floor above her that served as a type of attic, and storage area. She went into her bedroom, which was actually a suite with two large rooms and a bath. The front room was a sitting area, with a comfy sofa and chair, facing a stone fireplace. The rooms were painted a lovely shade of lilac, and when she was not outside working she spent most of her time here. She threw her bags on the sofa plunking down next to them. Her head hurt from dealing with Cash, His ridiculous idea that she would want to date him left her irritated, and dismayed. Lately she had not been feeling well. She assumed it was from the baby. She could only be about four weeks along and her pregnancy hadn't been confirmed by a doctor, but she knew. A woman knows. She had not figured out yet what she would say about the baby being a ten month baby, but she would figure that out when it happened. With any luck she would have the brat early. Next week she would call and make an appointment with a doctor. For now keeping the baby a secret from her parents as Will suggested seemed smart. Putting her hands on her arms where will grabbed her made her wince. Pushing up her sleeves revealed blue and purple marks. Her anger started to rise within her when she felt the pain from the pressure of her fingers. How dare he, she thought.

If Will had half a brain he would think twice about ever laying hands on her again. Easy for her to be brave from here in her bedroom. Her anger gave way to fear.

A chill ran up her spine as she remembered his threat that night. She shook it off, and laid her head back on the sofa. In a few minutes she drifted off to sleep.

Angelina woke with a start and sat up on the sofa. Her back was stiff and she needed to go the bathroom. Going to the bathroom more often was a growing pattern. She wondered what time it was. Looking out the window she could see that it was getting dark. Her parents should be having dinner by now; sending someone up the stairs to see if she were joining them. She did not feel like eating, but she felt for the sake of the baby she must. After all, she wanted to give Will a healthy child. She didn't quite know how she was going to handle a child at all. Healthy, or not. At least she could hire a nanny like her mother did. Angelina had no intention of being tied down night and day with some crying, snot nosed baby. Better start searching for someone to take care of it, Angelina made a mental note.

She was daydreaming about Will, imagining their wedding which better be soon so she wouldn't be showing. A long white gown, and trailing veil, was how she always pictured herself. She picked up some catalogues at the boutique in town, but Charleston would have a wider variety of gowns and accessories. There was a knock on her door and she called out. "Yes, come in."

"Missy Angelina," said Parker entering the room, "your Momma, and Daddy, sent me to see if you would be joining them for dinner?" Parker, was what the Oliver's called their house boy. He was hardly a boy having worked for them since before Angelina was born. She knew him all of her life, but was never fond of him. Something about him grated on her nerves, and she was never kind to him.

"Tell them I won't be down tonight," she said without looking up from her magazine.

"Yes Missy." Parker quickly turned and left the room closing the door behind him.

After he was gone she stood and went to the window to look out at the stars. It was a lovely crisp night, and she thought of Will. Angelina spoke out loud. "I can make you love me Will Biggs. Just you wait and see. You will forget all about Nola Rain when this baby comes."

Suddenly something in the edge of the woods near the barns caught her eye. It was some distance from the house so she wasn't sure what she saw. Movement. A shadow. It looked like a man staring up toward her window. She stepped back quickly feeling her heart beat quicken and pound a little harder. She moved to the window again, but when she looked out, saw nothing. What is wrong with me she thought? I must be more tired than I know to be seeing things that aren't there. She decided to take a long warm bath, and get a good nights' sleep.

Deep in the woods he crept without making a sound. He had been taught as a child how to move through the most difficult terrain without any noise; like an animal stalking its prey. Angry at himself because he was sure she had seen him; he vowed to be more cautious. He knew better. He knew to keep his distance. He continued on through the woods thinking about the next time. He would not make the same mistake twice. He could not afford to. On the far side of the woods away from Pine Point sat his old truck. Sometime around midnight he made it to the place it was parked. He got in and turned the key. The engine made a dragging sound. It would not start. After two more attempts he sat trying to figure out what to do. It was a twenty mile trek back to his place. He could not make it before daylight. He tried the key once more, and the old truck roared to life.

A sense of relief swept over him as he pulled onto the road following it to the highway. He felt of the rabbit's foot that hung from his keys, running his fingers across the soft fur. Luck was on his side. It had been on his side since he got here and took that job. Finding out about the beautiful, and rich Angelina, was especially lucky. He smiled. A smile that spread from ear to ear. Yes, he was feeling mighty lucky indeed.

TWO

Mundy Winks picked up the letter of recommendation for Maclaine Moreaux, reading through it once more. He hired the man a week ago, but his letter was still on Mundy's desk. The old boss was not very organized when it came to paper, but he knew the inventory of everything stacked and stored in his barns. Keeping up with saddles, bridles, blankets, was part of his job. He had to keep up with supplies so he could order more as needed and not get caught short stocked. He glanced down at the letter as he walked to the filing cabinet. Some bits of information jumped off the page at him. Information he must have overlooked. At the bottom of the letter from his last employer in Simone, Louisiana, Mundy asked the young job applicant to write down next of kin.

Mundy explained he needed next of kin in case of an emergency. If the person Maclaine wanted contacted had a telephone, he was to put the number; if not he was to write an address. Maclaine wrote the name Arlyn Fontenot, and an address in New Orleans. There was no explanation as to how they were related, and Mundy wondered at the difference in the names. Maclaine told him that he was unmarried. The former employer in Simone knew of Fair Meadows reputation as a top notch horse farm, and believed Maclaine would be a good fit. Mundy was looking for another trainer to replace Will. Dave Grimm was a good hand and worked hard, but he lacked the magic, and the passion, for horses. Mundy was trying not to compare because he knew Will was a phenomenal trainer that comes along once in a life time. The letter claimed this young man to be exceptional, and Mundy was willing to give him a chance to prove it. Before he placed the letter in a file he paused again reading the name Arlyn Fontenot. Something about the name caused him stop and think. He shook his head while putting away the letter.

Mundy made his way to the main house to check on Miss Nola. He had been taking care of her since the incident with Riley. More than a month had gone by with no improvement in her condition. She was in a type of shock that caused her mind to shut down to all but the most basic functions according to her doctor. The doctor came to Fair Meadows once a week on Fridays, and Mundy reported to him about her condition.

On his last visit the doctor spoke to Mundy about sending her to a mental hospital for more intense treatment, but Mundy refused.

After the tragedy, he petitioned the court for power of attorney and legal guardianship of Nola Rain Todd, and all her assets. Mundy knew Judge Jacobs and all the attorneys in Monroe, and they knew him. They knew Mundy was an honest man with no ulterior motive. Taking care of Nola was his number one priority. He had no problem convincing them that this was in her best interest. Mundy was the oldest employee of Fair Meadows, having been there long before any of the others. He wanted what was best for Nola and the farm. She was like a daughter to him, and his heart ached for her.

He prayed every day for her health, mentally and physically. She had been through too much, and her mind could not cope.

When he entered the house through the back entrance he made his way to the kitchen first. He could smell bacon and coffee. Naomi was bent over the oven pulling out a pan of golden brown biscuits. He watched as she slathered melted butter on the tops of the biscuits. On top of the butter she drizzled fresh honey from the

20

local hives. The smell was heavenly, making Mundy's mouth water. "Naomi those look delicious, and they smell better than that," he said smiling at the old cook.

"Thank you Mr. Mundy. I will make you up some bacon biscuits, and coffee when you get done with Miss Nola. I was just fixing her tray. Would you like to carry it up to her today?" Naomi stood waiting for Mundy to respond, but before he answered Joseph came into the room, and interrupted them.

"Miss Nola is not in her room," he spoke breathlessly.

"What do you mean Joseph? Maybe she is in her bath, or on the patio." Mundy said, trying to remain calm. Joseph shook his head frantically. His face was pink and beads of sweat were popping out on his forehead. He was near hysteria when he spoke.

"No, No sir, I have looked in her bath, and the patio. She is not in this house I tell you."

Mundy stood for a few seconds as if waiting for his brain to come up with some idea. Like a flash of light inside his head suddenly he knew. He bolted for the back entrance with Joseph doing his best to stay up with him. Mundy was in good shape for his age because of the physical work he did on a daily basis. Joseph on the other hand was overweight, and lifted nothing more than a pen, or his voice. Mundy ran down the path toward the creek. For a short distance he could hear Joseph breathing hard, struggling to keep up. At some point he realized he was alone. Fear crept in as his mind flashed back to the memory of pulling Amanda, and Richard, out of the same creek years ago. "Please God," he began to pray as he ran. All he could utter was "Please God."

Nola sat on the bank talking. "I've missed you so much Mother," she said to her sweetly, as she looked into the old wrinkled face.

"I have missed you too child." Mother gazed back at Nola. A withered hand reached out, and gently pushed a few strands of hair away from Nola's eyes.

"I can't take the pain any more Mother. Please take me with you. Please don't leave me here alone again."

Nola's eyes filled with tears as she pleaded with the old woman not to leave her. They sat still, motionless, and Nola heard Mother sigh. A sigh of resignation, and regret. She stood and reached her hand down to take Nola's. Placing her hand in Mother's, Nola was instantly transformed. Nola was a child again.

Outside her body now, Nola saw herself, and Mother, as if she were watching an old film of their life. Travelling back in time the moment was captured, and displayed for her, in her mind. On the banks of the creek she watched as Mother smiled and pulled her to her feet.

"It's all gonna be all right child. It's all gonna be all right. Mother is here now."

The old woman whispered over, and over, as she held the tiny hand. The two of them started out into the water. Across the bank Nola could see Miss Dominy. And there was Milo with a baby in his arms. Yes of course, it was their baby, Micah. She could see hundreds of people behind them; their faces blurred.

Standing next to Milo, a few feet from him, was a stranger. A beautiful, angelic looking woman. Nola could see her face clearly.

Not recognizing her, she looked questioningly at Mother. "Your Momma, that's your Momma child."

Nola lifted her free hand to wave at all of them. Someone grabbed her hand. Fear, and freezing cold water seized her body. As if her senses were suddenly switched on she was acutely aware of the icy water. She could not breathe. Confusion and panic took over her body. Someone had her, and she was fighting to get away. When her head surfaced she screamed.

"Mother...Mother..."

A man's voice broke through the screams shouting at her. He was telling her to stop. He was shouting at her now, loud and terrifying.

"Stop Nola, stop fighting me. Stop it now. Stop... Stop!"

He was pulling her out of the water. She was doing everything she could to go on to the other side, the other bank, with Mother. At last he gave one final tug of her body. Nola looked across the creek. She got one last look at Mother. One final glimpse at the rest of her world standing on the other side. Just before she blacked out she saw her Momma. As her world grew dim she watched her Momma raise a hand to say goodbye. Mundy could hear splashing and Nola screaming as he approached the creek.

He also heard a man shouting,

"STOP!"

He made it just as Maclaine Moreaux practically threw Nola out of the water onto the edge of the bank. Maclaine crawled out falling onto his back, arms outstretched and gasping for air. Mundy bent down to Nola and lifted her head. He spoke in a soft whisper trying

23

his best to comfort her. Eyes closed, soaked to the bone, she mumbled something over and over.

"Mother, Mo…Mother…"

The boss turned to Joseph who had just made it to the chaotic scene, and yelled at him to find Dave, and blankets.

"Bring blankets." Mundy shouted again.

Without hesitation Joseph turned and started running, back up the trail as fast as his stressed lungs, and chubby legs, would let him. Maclaine regained his breath. His heart rate started slowing some. He was cold, but not freezing thanks to the adrenaline pumping through his veins. He sat up and sort of crawled over to where Mundy was cradling Nola's head. He was trying to soothe her while waiting for help. Mundy looked at Maclaine. With tears in his eyes he said, "Thank you… thank you son. It might have been too late by the time I got here."

Maclaine eyed the old man and the pretty young woman. The affection the old horse man had for her was obvious. "Who is she, boss? Your daughter?"

"I… I am sorry son. I should have introduced you to her when I hired you. She has been ill. That's why I didn't. She's the owner of all that you see here. The sole owner of Fair Meadows. This here is Nola Rain Todd." Mundy looked down at Nola. "She's your boss." Before Mundy could say anything more he heard Joseph and Dave coming to help.

The doctor left Nola's room and gently closed the door. Mundy stood in the hall leaning against the wall with his hat in his hands. The doctor looked at the old boss and thought he looked like hell.

All this drama was taking a toll on an already aged, worn out cowpoke. "How is she doc?" Mundy asked nervously. The country doctor had been practicing medicine for over forty years. He still made house calls but only to an elite few.

If summoned he would come to Fair Meadows, and to Pine Point, but most of his patients he saw in Monroe, at his small office on Main Street. He had been the doctor for the Todd family since coming to Monroe years ago. He reckoned he would be their doctor till they threw dirt in his face.

"Once again Mundy I will give you my best medical advice. Nola is no better, and I would have to say after what she tried today, I feel she is getting worse. There is a facility in Charleston that may be able to help her.

It's my medical opinion she should be checked into the facility there as soon as possible. She won't get better without intense treatment. I can make arrangements as soon as I return to town."

"Doc with all due respect I just don't understand how some head doctors is gonna help her if we can't. She will be in that place with strangers. She won't let no one come near her cept me.

I just don't know. I just…don't…know." Mundy spoke slowly shaking his head. The doctor eyed Mundy sadly.

"Just like a broken leg needs a cast to help it mend, a broken mind needs certain treatments that I am not qualified to give her. She needs special care. You think about it. She will sleep the night with the sedative I gave her. You get some sleep too. Let me know tomorrow. There is a danger in waiting too long Mundy. The mind can escape so far. If it goes too far it may never return to normal." The kind doctor smiled. "Her mind may escape to a place from which there is not return."

He patted the old man on the shoulder and made his way down the hall to the stairs. Mundy stood, the hat he held in his leathery hands, collected the tears that flowed from his eyes.

"God counts our tears." Mundy heard his Mother say. He also heard the echo of the doctor's words,

"…from which there is no return."

Opening the door he went inside her bedroom. He stood watching her sleep, and thought how much she looked like a peaceful child. He prayed for her standing there beside her bed, and then he left her room headed for his bunk house. Tonight he would make up his mind. He was all she had, and he wanted to do everything in his power to help her get well. Tonight would be a very long night he thought, as he made his way across the yard toward the barn.

Nola opened her eyes and stared at the ceiling. She heard the doctor talking with Mundy. She was aware that Mundy was standing by her bed, and she heard his prayers. The walk to the creek began so lovely this morning. The autumn air was crisp, and clear. Bright sunlight filtered through the trees. The leaves were turning, some bursting with color. She just wanted to get out into the sunshine; to go sit for a while by the creek. She was watching the colorful leaves fall from the trees and float slowly to the ground, when she appeared suddenly. Mother was there. Nola felt hot tears sting her eyes as she remembered. The water, the icy water. Milo on the bank with the baby. Her Momma.

And a man. A stranger who pulled her from the creek. He whispered soft words in her ear as she struggled with the water. Who was he? She put her hand to her neck and felt the locket. It was in the shape of a heart. He told her not to open it.

"For healing, Nola. Wear it for healing." Those were the words he whispered to her. Nola touched the locket, and whispered those words.

"For healing." She said those words over and over like counting sheep, as once more she drifted off to sleep.

The Queen had given him the locket with the herbs, roots, and other things she never revealed. He had gone to see her before he left the bayou for his new job. The little shop on Grand Street was a front for the woman's other occupation. She was infamous, yet no one knew anything about her. Old and black, she spoke with a heavy creole accent.

There were many who could not understand her. He understood. He had known her all his life. He did as she said, and tucked the locket away in his travelling case.

"Ya gonta give this to the girl. Ya understand me Shylone?" Slowly as if her tongue were thick and as if he would not understand, she questioned him. "Speak Shy, do ya understand? Dis be for her healing. Without it… she gonta die."

She raised her voice on the word "die" as if to emphasize the meaning.

He understood and was growing impatient. It was hot in the back of the store and he needed air. Feeling light headed and near fainting he waited, and finally she dismissed him. He never left until she told him to go. He stepped out into the cool night air feeling instantly better. He began walking north on Grand Street. He stopped, turning back to the sound of her voice. She was yelling his name.

"She must not open the locket. Make sure she knows. Make sure her dun't. Understand shy?"

"Yes, Mother," he shouted back.

He called her Mother. Everyone addressed the Queen as Mother. She watched him walk out of sight. Her large eyes were as black as the night, and in spite of her age, her vision was sharp. All her senses were intact, and better than people half her age. She mumbled under her breath. Something foreign. The words thick and slow. Slow like molasses running from her tongue. An ancient language only a few still understood. She went inside, closed the door, and locked her shop up for the night.

THREE

Mundy woke early and rolled out of his bunk. He slept in the same bunk house with three other hands. One of them was Dave Grimm. Years ago Riley Todd, built Mundy a nice two bedroom cabin on the back side of the property. He lived in it less than a month. Occasionally he would ride out to check on it, and he kept it maintained, but he just preferred to be with his pokes as he called them. He was a father figure to most of them as well as their boss. His men respected and admired the old man's grit that he mixed with compassion, and occasional advice.

Getting dressed quickly he made his way to the main house. The air was cool, almost cold this time of morning. Soon the snow would be falling and things would quiet down on the farm. Harvest was over.

The barns were full of hay and straw. Fair Meadows grew acres of hay; not just for farm use, but to sell as well. Thanksgiving is just around the corner he thought. Though his heart was heavy, Mundy felt he had much to be thankful for. Today the decision must be made for Nola's care and recovery.

Naomi poured him a cup of coffee. He sipped the black, hot liquid and felt his body begin to come alive. He told the cook that he slept sound last night, which after the incident yesterday with

Nola surprised him. Totally exhausted, and mentally spent, he slept like a rock. "I prayed for that girl hard as I could last night." He told Naomi.

"We all been praying for that child Mr. Winks. Land sakes, I hope we don't have to send her away. She needs to be with people who love her, and we all love Miss Nola." Naomi stopped talking, and swiped at a tear with her apron.

"Well I am going on up to her room, and see how she is this morning. If she aint no better I will have to call the doctor… won't be no choice in the matter." Mundy got up from the table and began to walk toward the hall that led to the stairs.

"I am starving. What's a girl got to do to get something to eat around here," Nola said standing in the doorway of the kitchen.

Mundy, and Naomi, both turned pale as if they were looking at a ghost.

Nola was thin and pale from being sick so long, but she was standing, and smiling. Most important to Mundy was she seemed to be in her right mind. He sank back down in the chair, mouth still open. Naomi backed up to the sink for support. "Naomi I will have one of everything for breakfast. Won't you eat with me… both of you?"

Just like nothing ever happened. Mundy thanked God out loud.

"It's a miracle. That's what it is. A miracle." Naomi whispered.

Staring in amazement as Nola dug in to a plate of eggs and bacon, they listened as she chattered away. Laughing and talking, while shoveling a large amount of food into her mouth Nola seemed fine, and happy. Just like nothing happened Mundy thought. Too good to be true? He wondered, but for now relief washed over him. He could call the doctor with good news.

Angelina, and Will, were in a shouting match. Out by the stables, with a couple of the hands looking on in embarrassment. The men weren't sure if they should walk away, or stick around and see who won. If there was any betting taking place; the hands would have put their money on Angelina. She dressed and came to the barns to do some chores; just like every other morning, when Will approached her.

"What are you doing down here?" He asked through clenched teeth.

"What are you talking about? She asked.

She was standing in front of him looking perplexed, and waiting for an explanation. Will grabbed her by the arm, and tried to pull her away from the hired hands, who were now obviously listening. Will didn't really care what they thought. What anyone thought for that matter. He told her he was not going to have his soon to be wife, down here shoveling horse crap. Reminding her that she was pregnant, and too much physical work might harm the baby, he told her to leave. Angelina was livid as she yelled back. "I will do whatever I want Will Biggs. You don't own me or this baby. This is my farm and I will work it like I have always worked it. Now get out of my way."

Before she realized what Will was doing he picked her up and put her over his shoulder. The men tried hard not to laugh as Will walked with Angelina hoisted in the air, screaming at him "put me down." He didn't say a word. Walking to the big house he went in the back door and down the hall to a study where her parents were sitting enjoying their coffee. He plopped Angelina on the sofa beside her mother. With all the screaming and yelling as they approached the study Angelina's father rose to his feet. He opened his mouth to ask what was going on, but Will cut him off.

"Your daughter is pregnant with my child. We will be getting married next week. I will let you folks decide all the particulars to that union because honestly I could care less how it happens. I wouldn't be marrying Angelina, but that's my child and I intend to do right by it. She was down at the barn getting ready to do some work that I feel isn't smart at this time. You two see that she stays away from the barns. Oh, by the way, we will be living in my cabin not in this house."

When Will said they would be living in his cabin, all three Oliver's gasped in unison. He smiled, turned, and left the house. Long after he was gone they were still in shock. Unable to speak; they sat in silence, wondering what in the world just happened.

Angelina ran up to her room after Will left, and threw herself on the bed. She was sobbing when her mother entered the room. They talked about the baby. What she wanted. A wedding? Did she really want a wedding? Her mom was gentle, and kind. She tried to calm her daughter, but more than anything she wanted her to know she had options. "Will Biggs is a bully Angelina," her mother said. "Why on earth would you want to marry him?"

"Mother, I am going to have his baby. That's reason enough I think." Angelina replied between sobs.

"You don't have to marry him because of the baby. Your father and I will help you raise this child."

Angelina sat up and wiped at her face with the back of her hand. Her mother handed her a handkerchief sighing as she watched her only child struggle to regain control. "Whatever you decide I will stand by your decision. But mark my words, if you marry that man he will make you miserable. I mean the very idea that he wants you to raise your child in that dreadful little cabin…it's, well it's…preposterous," her mother said in a voice louder than Angelina ever heard it.

"Oh, I am marrying Will Biggs. We will see who makes who miserable. Yes, we will see."

Angelina stopped crying and the two women began to make plans for a quick wedding. By days end they had everything set for a small gathering the following week. Angelina would wear her mother's gown. Her father would give her away. Their pastor who had been a family friend for years would officiate the ceremony. The head cook would take care of the cake, and only their closest friends would be attending. Mother said no one would have to know about the baby. Babies are born early all the time she told Angelina.

Angelina stood at the window of her room looking out into the night. She was thinking about the day and the wedding plans. It all happened so quickly that she had no time to think. But she did not need to think about marrying Will Biggs. In spite of their tumultuous relationship she loved him. She had never been in love before, but she knew this was real.

Angelina was willing to live in a tiny cabin for him. Willing to have a child for him.

She would do anything to have him. Now it seemed she would get what she wanted. An added bonus was keeping Nola Rain Todd from having Will. She took great pride in knowing that she stopped that woman from getting him. Angelina won. Angelina always won.

Once again she spotted someone out of the corner of her eye, but when she turned her head toward them there was no one there. Thinking she must be tired, and anxious, and seeing things, she climbed into bed. She thought about Will, and told herself tomorrow she would go see him. She would give him all the details about the wedding plans. Maybe he would be in a nicer mood tomorrow. She would wear a dress, and do her hair, and try not to set him off.

She could act nice when she wanted to. She was imagining a kinder more loving Will as she drifted off to her dreams.

The next morning she woke up and when her feet hit the floor a wave of nausea washed over. She ran to her bathroom. Sitting on the cold tile floor, leaning over the toilet violently vomiting; she held her long black hair with one hand so it would not get in the toilet. Angelina didn't know what it was like to have such a sick stomach for she was rarely ill. A sniffle every once in a while, or a mild head ache, but that was it. She was a strong, healthy woman used to physical activity. She worked harder than some of the men on the farm.

Finally the vomiting subsided. Feeling better she got up and brushed her teeth. She washed her face and pulled her hair back in a ponytail. Searching her vast closet she found a cute flowered dress and slipped it on. By then she was feeling so much better she stopped in the dining room where her parents were having breakfast. They ate every meal in the dining room, treating each one as a formal affair. The Oliver's never came downstairs without being fully dressed, looking as if they were expecting company. Sometimes Angelina wandered the house in pajamas. She would often go in to the kitchen and have breakfast or lunch with Tilly, the head cook. Tilly had been with Paul and Susie Oliver longer than Angelina had been alive. The cook was a surrogate mother to her, and Tilly loved the beautiful, but often impossible child. They were extremely close. Angelina would do just about anything for Tilly. Today she sat and ate with her parents, and while a few minutes ago she felt dreadfully ill, now she was ravenously hungry. She finished off a plate of eggs and toast in no time. She drank her orange juice and strong coffee wiping her mouth on a soft linen napkin when she was finished. She excused herself from her parents and they watched her leave with worried looks on their faces. No one mentioned last night, or Will, or the upcoming wedding. That was the way the Oliver's dealt with most situations. They refused to talk about them, preferring to sweep them under the rug. They only dealt with personal or emotional issues when forced to. For most of Angelina's life bad news or personal information was relayed to her through Tilly or Parker.

The Oliver's loved their daughter, but had no idea how to handle her. They had a child, but in a sense never raised a child. They hired it done.

The air was cool and lovely, making the sun feel wonderful on her arms as she walked slowly to the stables. Autumn was her favorite time of year. She loved to go riding in the early morning sunshine, admiring all the beautiful fall color. Outdoors was where she was most happy, and being near the horses was just icing on the cake. She wondered if Will would allow her to ride, or if he would deprive her of the thing she loved most in the world to do. She was so at ease on the back of a horse. Loving everything about the animals, she would ride for hours. Their warmth, their power and strength, even the way they smelled made her happy. Riding was all she ever wanted to do. She did not care about shopping. No fancy restaurants. No dances or parties. None of that mattered to Angelina.

Will was coming out of the stable barn where they kept most of the horses that were used for breeding. He looked up and when he saw her he stopped in his tracks. He was standing with his hands on his hips as she walked up. "Good morning Will," she said in her sweetest voice. Will eyed her up and down. Seeing she was not dressed to work he spoke gruffly.

"Yesterday must not have been enough of an embarrassment for you. What do you want?"

"I came down here to tell you the wedding is set for next Saturday. It will be small but at least it will please my parents… somewhat." She batted her long dark lashes at him, and he could feel something stir deep in his stomach.

"Is that a fact? Next Saturday. Well I'll do my best to be there," he said with a grin.

"Will," Angelina said softly, "I don't want to fight with you anymore. I want us to be a normal married couple. I…love you Will. I really do love you."

Will still smiling, pulled Angelina against his chest. She could feel his breath hot, and a tingling sensation near her temple. When he spoke his voice was low and sultry, and she felt her body lean and relax into his.

"Trust me Angelina Oliver. There are few things about this union that will prove normal. You will keep me warm when it's cold outside. You will cook and clean. You will take care of my child. That's about as normal as it's going to get. As far as you loving me…I don't believe you've ever loved anyone… except yourself."

36

Will could feel her body tense up as she tried to pull away, but he tightened his grip. He kissed her on the temple. He let her go. Saying nothing more he turned and went back inside the barn, leaving her shaking, humiliated, and near tears.

38

FOUR

Cash sat in his office staring out the window day dreaming. It had
been a week since he saw Angelina. She broke his heart. He wasn't
hurt or angry anymore; heck he always did like a challenge. The
problem was the lie he thought she was telling him about marrying
Will Biggs seemed to have some truth behind it. The big gossip in
town was that she was getting married in a private ceremony in a
couple of days. He was trying to decide what if anything he should
try to do about it. In his fantasy he rode up on a white stallion just
as she was about to say I do. He shouted "No you don't," as he
swept her up on the horse with him and galloped away.

One thing for sure he never got an invitation like she said she
would send him. So, she did lie.

Cash could not figure out what she saw in Will Biggs. From what
he'd observed the guy was a bully. Pushed everyone around, and he
would do the same to her; although he could not imagine any man
getting away with that. Not with Angelina. Some women seemed to
like being dominated. At least that was his impression. That was his
personal and professional observation. Many was the time that he,
and Sheriff Goodpasture, had to intercede in some domestic dispute.

Fighting was a waste of time he thought. He longed for a woman he could love, who loved him back. He sure didn't want to waste time fighting.

Maybe he should leave it alone. Let her go and marry that dude. Could be they would call him out to their place some night to break up a fight, and she would just leave with him. That was how it played out in his young head anyway; always an imagination that ran away with him. Cash wrote his own stories, his own endings. At least in his mind. He got up and went up the street to grab a bite to eat. Good food, Rosey, and the diner's pretty waitress always made him feel better.

Dave Grimm sat on the banks of the creek fishing pole in hand. He watched his bobber go up and down, and he yanked his line a little, but the fish never hooked. He was not much of a fisherman, but he was here to keep an eye on Nola. Ever since the incident, when she came to the creek, Mundy sent one of the guys to fish, or swim. Just to watch over her. They were careful not to let her suspect they were babysitting.

Mundy was sure she would become very offended if she knew they were watching her. He loved that little girl, and had no intentions of allowing anything else to happen to her as long as he drew a breath.

Cash was coming out of the diner when he saw Joseph Camp pull up with Nola Todd in the back seat. He had not seen her since the Riley Todd investigation, but he heard she was not well. He watched her slide out of the car while Joseph held the door open. She started up the street toward him and began waving at him, calling his name. He walked up to her and gave her a quick hug. "Nola it's so good to see you in town. How have you been?" Cash was smiling genuinely glad to see her.

"I am very well Cash. It is so good to see a friendly face. I heard you accepted the Monroe sheriff position. Congratulations. You deserve it. You are so good at your job. More like a calling I think." Nola chatted with him, but he comprehended very little. He could not stop staring into those violet eyes.

"I like it here in Monroe," Cash said, "I'm renting a little house on Kitty Street. Got myself a cat, so I am not too lonely when I do get home. I spend a lot of my time at the jail, but sometimes I bring her with me. Her name is Sassy."

"She sounds adorable. I hope to get to see her someday. Well I won't hold you up. I am on my way to the hat store. I am buying a birthday gift for Naomi, our cook." They hugged goodbye, but as they were walking away Nola turned around suddenly and said his name. "Cash?" He turned toward the sound of her voice. "Would you like to come for dinner, Saturday evening? I mean, if you're not busy. I know this is short notice and all." Nola was holding her hands together looking a little pitiful. Staring at him with pleading eyes as if he might say no.

"Sure. I mean gosh… yes. Try and stop me," he replied laughing.

Nola began laughing too, and the sound of her laughter was melodic, and sweet. "Great. I will see you around seven. Don't dress up. Please come comfortable." Nola smiled, and told him goodbye, walking up the street to the boutique.

Cash stood and watched until she went into the shop. Well, well, well, he thought. Life sure can change on a whim. A few days ago he stood watching from a different direction, and a different perspective, as the woman he thought he was meant to be with drove away. Angelina left him choking on her dust, and aching from the wound she inflicted to his heart and ego. Now it seemed

41

the love fairy had given him a second chance at someone he had always been crazy about. He began to whistle a little tune from his childhood as he crossed the street and headed back to his office. Cash was thinking Nola Rain was probably the prettiest woman he ever laid eyes on.

On Friday before Nola's dinner date with Cash, there were visitors to the farm. Mundy came to see her around noon and asked if she had a few moments to meet Maclaine Moreaux?

She said of course, telling Mundy to bring him to the house whenever he was ready. Mundy also told her that Maclaine's relatives were there to visit him. She said she would be pleased to meet all of them, asking who came to see him. A sister, and a niece, were Mundy's reply. About thirty minutes later Mundy came in with Maclaine ,and his family. When Mundy introduced Maclaine to Nola there was something familiar about him though she knew she'd never met him. "I am so pleased to meet you Maclaine. I hope it is all right to call you by your first name? We don't stand on formality here at Fair Meadows." Nola laughed as she told him that.

"Of course ma'am, please call me Maclaine. Mr. Moreaux sounds like your talking to my father." They all laughed at this. "Allow me to introduce my sister Jolene, and her daughter Gabrielle. They are visiting me from New Orleans."

"So nice to meet you. All of you. Won't you please sit down?" Nola said.

They were in the formal living room.Naomi came in with tea, and slices of pound cake. While they were served, Nola had a chance to look at Maclaine and his family. They were certainly a beautiful group. They all had blue eyes, almost as violet as hers, and dark hair. She noticed that their skin was caramel colored like hers. She wanted to ask about New Orleans, and the people. She had many questions about New Orleans, because she was abandoned there as an infant. She had no idea about her own ethnicity.

Thinking it might be rude she kept the questions to herself. Perhaps when she knew Maclaine better she could open up and ask him about his background. Jolene was speaking and broke into Nola's thoughts.

"Your farm is so lovely. You must be very happy living here. It is so different from our city...from New Orleans." Jolene flashed beautiful pearl white teeth.

"I do love it here. It has become my home. Where will you be staying while you visit Will?"

"We are going to Monroe to look for a room. Maclaine is going to show us the way a little later." Jolene said.

"Oh no, please stay here with us. You are more than welcome, and you won't be far from your brother. Mundy can see to it that Maclaine has plenty of free time to spend with you. Please do stay. I am having a small dinner party tomorrow night, and would love if you could be there." Nola smiled at her guests waiting for an answer. Jolene, looked at Gabrielle, and then turned to Maclaine who nodded his approval. Before she could answer Mundy chimed in.

"You know Nola, I have that nice cabin out back in the woods just sitting there. I keep it clean and ready just in case. It would be fine for our visitors if they wanted to stay in it. Stay as long as they like. What do you think?"

"Well ladies how does the cabin sound? It is furnished with everything you need... and if not I will get it for you. You will need groceries, and other supplies, but Maclaine can help you with that. What do you say?" Nola smiled.

"We say yes…and we say thank you for your generosity. You too, of course Mr. Mundy. We will be leaving in a week, but the cabin sounds very nice and we would not feel like such an imposition there. Thank you so much." Jolene seemed very relieved to have a place to go. "Now if you don't mind I would like to see this cabin. I have been ill as of late and would like to lie down for a while."

Jolene appeared tired, and her daughter Gabrielle looked on with concern. Mundy told them to come with him, instructing Maclaine to get the farm jeep, and his family's bags. They would use the jeep to go to the cabin. It was deep in the woods in a lovely clearing, but it was secluded and difficult to find. Nola told them if they needed anything to let her know. She reminded them about her dinner tomorrow night, saying she looked forward to seeing them then. After they were gone she went to her room feeling a little weary herself. She lay on her bed thinking of her guests. She could not get past how much they looked alike. She found it puzzling how much she looked like them. Was it because all of them were from New Orleans? Were they creole? Was her parents Creole too? So many questions floating around in her head, eventually she nodded off to a very welcome sleep.

The rain was coming down in what seemed like sheets of non-stop water. Occasionally Nola could hear thunder somewhere in the distance. The temperature dropped too. It was a dark, dismal day. Warm food, and a roaring fire in the fireplace should help at dinner tonight, she thought. Dressing quickly she went down to the kitchen where Naomi was busy with breakfast. The cook made breakfast for all the staff and Mundy's cowpokes as well, so it was a big task making such a large amount of food. This morning she was cooking

44

light because it was Saturday. The men did not do as much work on the weekend. She had oatmeal and toast, juice and coffee. Nola helped herself to the oatmeal, and some coffee with cream, and a lot of sugar. "What are you preparing for dinner tonight Naomi?" Nola asked.

"Well Missy, I thought about baking a ham with scalloped potatoes. Maybe some green beans, and of course dinner rolls. How about apple pie for dessert?"

"Wonderful. My mouth is watering thinking about your apple pie. It all sounds delicious." Nola took a sip of hot coffee.

"Everything gonna be ready by seven Miss Nola. Don't you worry none bout that." Naomi pulled another tray of toast out of the oven. She liked to bake the slices of bread with a dollop of butter in the center of each slice. The smell was wonderful.

Nola grabbed a slice of the warm toast and poked the center out plopping it in her mouth. Naomi gave her a disapproving look telling her to eat all of it.

Nola laughed and promised she would. She was just about to leave the kitchen when Mundy came in dripping wet. He always came and picked up the meals for his men. They had a twelve foot table in the large bunk house where they ate their meals.

"Mundy if you wait until I get my boots and coat, I will help you get this food down to the bunk house. It's raining cats and dogs out there." Nola was heading for the coat rack as she spoke.

"No need for you to get wet. I have the small tractor outside by the door. It has a compartment that's mostly water proof. I use it to carry the food when the weather is bad. When it's nice Naomi is

45

kind enough to pack it all in a large basket. Pretty wet out today though."

"All right then. Did our guests get settled in at your cabin?" Nola asked.

Mundy told her about escorting them to the cabin, and how much they seemed to fall in love with it. Nola had never seen it, and he told her all about it. It was in a nice clearing deep in the woods. Deer like to come right up to the little wood porch. There were two bedrooms and a bath. The kitchen and living room were combined, and there was a fireplace. A nice cozy cabin for one or two people he said. When she asked Mundy why he preferred the bunkhouse over the cabin he explained that he liked being near his men, and the horses. Those men were like family to him. Everyone liked each other and got along well. In the evenings they would all sit and play cards, or guitars.

Like family they stayed together to chase away the loneliness of living far from family. The new hire Maclaine Moreaux, seemed to be a good fit for the farm. All the cow pokes liked him. Nola listened intently admiring Mundy, and his passion for the farm and his men. Fair Meadows was blessed; she felt blessed to have him running everything and looking after her. He was like a father to her, and she had grown to love him.

Mundy finished his coffee and loaded up the tractor. She watched as he headed toward the barn and bunkhouse with the breakfast food. Naomi began cleaning the kitchen, so Nola got out of her way. She went up to her room to decide on what to wear that evening for dinner. Standing at the doors in her bedroom she watched as the rain continued to fall from the sky. Relentless. Driving rain. It fell straight down from dark ominous clouds. Beyond the barns and the corral she could see the edge of the woods and a wide trail leading deep into the trees. The trail was more of a dirt road, and it was used by Mundy for reaching his cabin. Nola never ventured that far back on the property, but she stood thinking that in the spring she wanted to cover every inch of Fair Meadows. She suddenly realized she had no idea how big the property was, or how many acres it included. She told herself to remember to ask Mundy that question. Just about to walk away and move to her closet she caught a glimpse of something out of the corner of her eye. Turning her full attention on the road in the woods she could see some kind of movement on the trail. She just couldn't make out what, or who, it was.

Perhaps a deer or other animal she thought, but then she recognized the sweater Gabrielle was wearing today. Or rather the color of the sweater grabbed her attention. It was a very pretty shade of pink.

 Almost a coral color she remembered. She could see the girl, or the sweater, moving round, and round, in the woods. She seemed to be moving in a circle. Whatever was she doing Nola thought? Why would she be out in the rain and walking in circles? She stood and watched for a while longer. The movement stopped. She could still see the sweater, and it appeared to be standing still. Was she looking toward Nola's patio? Could she see Nola watching her? Surely not. The idea made her move away from the doors and sit on the edge of the bed. Instinctively her fingers went to her neck where the locket hung. She touched the cold silver heart. An icy feeling came over her.

A vague familiar feeling of dread, like the feelings she got from Riley. Who were these people? Who was Maclaine Moreaux, and why did she suddenly feel frightened? Very frightened. Calming herself she felt very silly. She felt like a silly, young girl, with a big imagination. Reprimanding herself, Nola continued laying out what she wanted to wear to dinner. Trying hard to conjure up some anticipation and excitement for this evening; she could not. Like the weather outside, a huge cloud now hung low, and ominous over her spirit.

FIVE

Angelina was pouting. How dare it rain on her wedding day. Her mother planned the ceremony inside with only about twenty of their closest friends invited, but still it should have been a gloriously sunny day. It was not just raining. The wind was blowing and the air was cold. It was November however, and it could be snowing. With an hour to go before the wedding she was trying to be positive and happy. Will had been avoiding her since he humiliated her at the barn. Not seeing, or hearing from him for several days, she tried to chase the thought from her mind that he might leave her standing at the altar. Or in this case standing alone in the living room where her Mother fashioned a sort of flowered arch for the two of them to stand under. She was ready except for slipping on her gown. The cake was exquisite. Her parents were downstairs. The guests should start arriving soon. Where was Will? If he failed to show she swore she would hunt him down, and kill him. She thought her father might help her do it. Her parents could not stand him, and Will didn't try to conceal the fact that the feeling was mutual. The only reason they were going along with this farce of a wedding was because of the baby. Of course that was the same reason Will was marrying her. She hoped that someday if she showed him how much she loved him, he would come around. Will would love her back.

Angelina could only hope. She rose from her bed walking over to where the gown was hanging. Near tears, she began getting dressed.

Will changed into his dress clothes even putting on a tie. He had not seen Angelina for a few days. Thankfully he had not been bothered by her plans. All he had to do was show up, and say I do. He would like to say a lot more than that, but he did have some pride. It had been raining buckets and work was slow around the farm. This time of year farm work slowed way down, but would pick back up in the spring. Next week was Thanksgiving, and he supposed his lovely new bride would want to spend it with her parents. He had other plans. Angelina would not be pleased with his ideas on a Thanksgiving celebration, but she would abide by it. He looked in the mirror as he combed his dark hair. All at once Nola came floating into his thoughts.

With a gnawing sense of regret, he wished with every fiber in him that it was her he was marrying today. It wasn't. It was Angelina Oliver. Time to accept that he, and Nola, were never going to be. Time to go. Get through this. Nothing in this world he could do, but go ahead with this union. A legal union was all it was to him.

Grabbing his rain poncho and hat, he opened the door to a downpour, and let the rain drown his thoughts of Nola.

The guests were mingling about the large room. It was quite lovely, decorated with fall flowers and ribbons.

A three tier cake with a traditional bride and groom figurine on top sat waiting. Will, and Angelina, said "I do," and cut the cake. Will was behaving as if this were all his idea. Everyone was having a wonderful time. Will asked if he could have everyone's attention. He said he would like to toast his beautiful bride. The guests who were drinking the very best champagne all turned their attention to the handsome groom. Asking them to raise their glasses in honor of his bride he toasted her. "To Angelina, my beautiful bride, and the most beautiful woman I know." Will raised his glass and took a sip.

"To the bride… to the bride."

Everyone in the room chimed in unison, as they raised their glasses to toast Mr. and Mrs. Will Biggs. Will looked deep into Angelina's eyes smiling his brightest smile.

Later in the evening Will, and Angelina, left what was now her parents' home and made their way to their new home, in pouring rain. In Will's truck they pulled up as close to the cabin as they possibly could. Without a word he got out of the truck and ran to the porch. She sat there for a moment fury rising in her. He never came around and opened the door for her, or offered to help. No carrying her over the threshold, or rain puddles. She opened the door grabbed a small bag she'd packed earlier, and made a dash for the porch. She was drenched within seconds. Will unlocked the door to the cabin, and led the way inside. He lit a kerosene lamp and the room took on an eerie glow. The cabin had electricity but he preferred the lamps. He used the fireplace to do most of his cooking instead of the stove. He liked doing things the old fashioned way.

51

Angelina had been standing in the door all this time, and Will turned around to see her dripping and shivering.

"Best get out of those wet clothes so you don't catch a cold. I wouldn't want my new bride to get sick." He stared at her with hard cold eyes. Those eyes glared at her in hatred. They spoke more truth than the phony concern he verbally expressed. She didn't think he would care if she shriveled up and died right there on the very spot where she was standing, dripping. The only reason he might care would be the baby, but she was beginning to wonder if that really mattered to him.

"Yes, I guess I better change into something dry." She took the bag and headed to the bathroom, but he stopped her.

"Where are you going?"

She turned around and he was staring, and smiling. He had taken his boots off, and was propped up on pillows on the bed.

"I...I'm going to change," she stammered.

"Why so shy Angelina? As I recall you weren't so shy when you stayed with me that one night. One time and got yourself pregnant...hmmm... " Will was a little breathless, as if he were angry.

"Will, I didn't mean..." she didn't get to finish her sentence.

Will was on his feet and grabbed her by the arms forcing her back toward the door. Once again he was hurting her, and she was terrified. She tried to get away, but that only made him angrier.

"You get undressed right here, right now, understand?" Will spoke slowly, and deliberately. His teeth were clinched, and she could see a vein near his temple pulsing wildly. He let go of her and she moved away from him, but never took her eyes off him. "Do what I say. You tricked me into this joke of a marriage, and now you are getting what you wanted. So, you will get undressed, because I am about to take my part of the deal Angelina." He glared at her, and she knew she had no choice. His anger was close to the edge, about to become rage.

Be careful what you wish for rang in her head. Slowly, shaking from fear and cold, she began to undress.

The dinner party at Fair Meadows had been going well until Cash let it slip that Will, and Angelina, were getting married that same evening. Nola hadn't known this. Once the words were out of his mouth Cash regretted saying anything. She could not hide her feelings about Will even after all this time. Nola looked so sad, and both Mundy, and Cash, wished that there was something they could do to take away her pain. It ruined the rest of the party for her; though she tried hard to stay focused, and pretend to be interested.

All she wanted to do was run to her room, and throw herself on her bed. That would come later she knew.

Deep in the night she was still awake. Everyone had finally gone home, and after assuring Cash that she was not angry with him for telling her of the wedding he left. Nola moved slowly up the stairs to bed. She could not sleep. She could not cry. Perhaps she had cried so many tears for Will Biggs that there were none left. At some point while waiting for daylight she got up and went out to her patio. It was cold, but the rain had stopped, and the clouds passed over the moon. She looked toward the woods where Mundy's cabin was, and she could see the faint glow of a fire. At first she felt fear rising up thinking it might be the cabin on fire, but she realized it was small, contained. A camp fire. She could hear voices, the sounds of singing. Chanting. She could not hear well enough to make out what they were singing, or saying, but she knew they were doing something around a fire in the woods. It must be Maclaine and his family. What on earth could they be doing? And why would they be out on a cold, wet night? She didn't know, but she vowed to find out.

A circle of rocks kept the fire inside the ring. Two women, and a young man, danced around the circle. They all chanted. A strange ancient sounding language, sang more than spoken. The pitch seemed to become more intense with every completed circle. The chanting became louder and the dancing more, and more, exaggerated. When the volume reached an almost screaming level the older woman suddenly stopped.

She began to run to the edge of the woods. The others followed, stopping just behind her when she came to the clearing beyond the trees. The three of them stood looking toward the big house. Their faces were sweaty in spite of the cold, and they were breathing hard. Silent and still, they stared at the second floor patio where Nola stood in the cold night air.

Nola was peering hard at the edge of the woods. She could barely make out what appeared to be three dark figures standing at the clearing. Were they looking at her? She rubbed her eyes and looked again. They were gone. Vanished like a vapor. Was it a dream? She felt the hair on her neck stand up as she ran inside, and locked the doors. Again she vowed to get to the bottom of this. Exhausted now, she fell into bed, and tried to find the darkness and escape of sleep.

SIX

The day after the dinner party Nola woke up late, and lay watching the dancing pattern on the wall caused by bright sunshine streaming in through the French doors. Feeling extremely tired, she knew it was from a lack of sleep. Thinking about Will, and his marriage to Angelina Oliver, had been the reason sleep eluded her at first. Later she could not sleep after seeing the troubling fire, and the shadowy figures, in the woods behind the barns. She decided to have Mundy take her to the cabin. Checking up on her guests would be her excuse to nosy around a bit.

Getting dressed she went down to the kitchen to fix a quick breakfast. It was Sunday, and she gave everyone the day off to spend as they wished. She wanted Naomi, and her girls, to go to church, or visit family at least one day out of the week. Lately she had been pondering the idea of giving them Saturday off as well. Farm business was going into the slow season now, and she wanted to let the staff take advantage of being less busy. She of course paid them for their time off. Nola had fallen in love with everyone who worked at Fair Meadows, and considered them all family.

After eating a light breakfast of toast and coffee, she headed down to the stables to find Mundy. Normally he never went anywhere on Sunday. He did attend church occasionally, but most of his time off he spent reading, and writing letters to friends, and family that he kept in touch with.

She poked her head in his office, and finding no one there she walked slowly to the bunkhouse. The sun was shining, and the air was unseasonably warm. Thanksgiving was only four days away, and it felt more like spring instead of autumn. Mundy wasn't in the bunkhouse either. It was empty. It seemed everyone was out and about on this beautiful day. Guess they were taking advantage of the nice weather before the snow started. Nola did not want to go into the woods without Mundy, so she decided to stroll to the creek instead and sit for a while. She knew that soon enough the snow, and the cold, would keep her away from the creek. She decided to do what the others were doing, and enjoy the out of doors.

She sat on the bank of the creek, watching as brightly colored leaves fell from the trees that lined the water's edge. Nola thought about Will, and wondered if he were truly happy. She had no right to want him, or love him, but she did. After the tragedy with Riley she refused to see Will. That must have hurt deeply. Perhaps marrying Angelina was an attempt to get revenge for her rejection of him. Most of her days after that horrific event were a blur. She relied on Mundy to give her details of the time she lost. Mundy was the one to tell her that she refused to let anyone near her. After she was well she tried to call Will, even leaving a message for him. She spoke with Tilly, and she promised to tell Will she called. He never called back. He never came to see her. Now he was married to Angelina, and any thread of hope she held for a life with him floated away. Just like the leaves that fell from the trees, and landed softly on the water, her hope was carried away downstream. Gone.

After a while she got up to leave, wiping tears from her face as she turned to head back up the path. She didn't hear him behind her, and when she turned; she fell into his arms with a scream of surprise. Will was holding her in his arms, and for the first few moments she forgot that he was a married man, and gave herself to his embrace. All she knew in those moments was that he was here, and he was holding her again. "Will…Will," she whispered. Afraid to speak his name too loudly. Afraid he would vanish.

"Nola, it really is you. It has been so long since I've seen you. I… I," Will stammered. "I have missed you Nola Rain."

58

Nola started to say those same words back to him when the present caught up with the past. She suddenly remembered what Cash told her. Will was married only yesterday evening. Now he was here trying to play some game to break her heart again. Was it revenge for not allowing him to see her while she was ill?

She jerked away from him. Seething with anger she stood looking into his face. She put her hand up to her chest in an attempt to calm herself, and catch her breath. "What are you doing here?" She asked him. "What kind of game are you playing Will? You are married and I can't be with you alone this way."

"Nola, I did not know you would be here. I came here to this place, our place. I wanted to be alone, to remember you…to think about us." Will said. His eyes were gazing into hers, begging for understanding.

"It's wrong Will. So wrong. You are married to Angelina. Cash told me about the wedding yesterday. My heart… is broken Will," she said in a whisper. Tears began to fall down her sad pretty face. Her tears seared his already burning heart.

"You don't understand why I married that girl. I don't love her. It's just. Well, I can't explain it to you right now. Please just know that I love you… only you. No matter what Nola." He stood waiting for a word from her, anything that would let him know that she still loved him too.

"I come here too Will. I come here and weep for what I know I can never have. A life with you was only a fantasy. You ended any hope I might have held for us to be together." Nola took his left hand in hers. Will closed his eyes at the touch of her hand against his. She was warm, and soft, and he felt a familiar heat rising up within him. She lifted his hand and traced a circle around the wedding band on his finger. He opened his eyes and looked into hers.

"Nola...listen to me... please," Will pleaded.

"I hope you, and your wife, will be happy together." Nola started toward the path, and stopped. Keeping her back to him she spoke words of finality. "Good bye Will. Please don't try to see me again. I must find a way to let you go...truly let you go." She did not turn around as she continued her walk. A walk that took her away from the only man she knew she'd ever love so deeply. A walk toward a life with no one to love her that way again. He called her name. Keep walking she told herself. The sound of his voice grew faint. "Don't turn around," she whispered, taking another step. Close to the house she realized she could hear him no more. Silence. A fading sun, golden falling leaves, and silence. She went inside, and up the stairs to her room. Walking over to the doors to the patio she stepped outside, and looked toward the creek. The world was still, silent. The air began to cool as the sun drifted lower, and she went back inside. One more look toward the creek, and then she shut the door, closing out the cold. Her heart closed the door to Will Biggs. Feeling as if she could stand no more she fell to her knees. Praying with all the truth and honesty housed within her she cried out to God. "Father God, help me to get on with my life without him. Help me... Oh Father... to let him go. Help me most of all... to want only happiness for him... and Angelina." She stayed on her knees until the sun disappeared. On her knees the daylight faded, and the room grew dark.

The chanting was faint, but she heard it just beyond the doors leading to her patio. Getting up from her bed Nola wondered what time it was, and why Maclaine, and his family, were performing some type of ceremony, or ritual in the middle of the night. Walking out onto the patio, cold night air caught her by surprise, making her shiver. The sound was not coming from the woods. It was coming from the creek. Nola was instantly angry at her new hire. How was anyone supposed to get their rest with Maclaine, and his relatives throwing a party in the middle of the night? The creek was her place. It angered her that they would be there in the spot that brought her so much peace. Irritated, and deciding that she was going to put a stop to this; she got dressed, and went out through the back of the house. Within minutes she was on the path leading down to the creek. The chanting grew louder with every step. She didn't hesitate and she was not afraid; just determined to see who was behind this. And why? Her eyes were growing accustomed to the dark, and she could make out a fire near the water. Four figures were dancing, and chanting. She could not understand the words, even though she could hear them plainly. When she was within 20 feet of the fire she stopped, and stared. The older woman stopped, and the other three followed her lead. Nola could not move as she stood staring at the strange group. Their faces were hidden by the darkness, but suddenly one of them stepped out of the circle and into the moonlight. Nola's breath caught in her throat. She instinctively put her hand up to her mouth to stifle a scream. She could not believe her eyes. Her heart began to pound, and her breath came in short gasps as he came closer, and closer. Trying to turn and run, she could only stand frozen to the spot. Mesmerized. Will stood in front of her, and took her gently by the arms. He placed his mouth on hers, and pulled her slowly down to the grass. She was not aware of the cold air. She did not hear when the others began chanting and dancing again. She was caught up. Caught up with the one she loved, and would always love. She gave herself to him, and in that moment there was no thought of right, or wrong. Being with him was all that mattered. And if this were all she ever had with Will, she would gladly trade the rest of her days for this one night. When at last morning came, she remembered only being with Will, and thought the whole night was just a dream. The chanting, the dancing, the strange people… scenes from a dream.

Angelina woke up the day after her wedding to an empty space beside her in the small bed. After Will terrorized her on what should have been the happiest night of her life, she drifted off to sleep, totally exhausted. He had not made love to her after making her undress in front of him. After she got into bed Will turned over to face the wall, and without saying another word, she heard him snoring within minutes. Frustrated, humiliated, but too tired to fight, she fell asleep. Now it was morning. After sleeping surprisingly sound, she felt reenergized, and ready to deal with whatever Will threw at her. Where was Will? She asked for a real honeymoon, and his answer was no. No explanation, just no. She asked if they could build a bigger house for the soon to be three of them. Again his answer was no, the cabin would do. Where was he, she wondered? Maybe he was at the stables. It would not surprise her to find him working the day after their wedding.

Depression began to sink into her bones making her feel so heavy that she wasn't sure she could get out of bed. What made her think Will would change just because they were legally man and wife. Angelina felt stupid, and frustrated that her plan was not working. It was obvious that he was not going to fall in love with her. All he cared about was this baby that wasn't even his. For a brief moment she thought of Cash, and felt a slight twinge of remorse. Cash would be a great father, and a terrific husband, but he was so boring. Angelina sighed, and managed to get up and dressed. Starving now, she went to her parent's house for something to eat, and for comfort. At least humiliation was not an appetite suppressor; after all she must eat for the baby.

She dug into eggs and bacon, and toast that Tilly made for her. The old cook lovingly brought her meal to the dining room. On the

walk over to the house she looked around for Will, but didn't see
him anywhere. This was Sunday, and the day after their
honeymoon. Surely he was not working. No one worked at Pine
Point on Sunday unless it was an absolute emergency. Occasionally
a cow needed assistance giving birth, or a sick horse that didn't care
what day it was demanded attention. Her parents gave everyone the
day off doing their best to handle any problem that arose on the
Lord's Day. Susie, and Paul Oliver, were faithful to attend their
local Methodist church whenever the doors were open. Angelina
stopped going years ago. Her Mother gave up fighting with her, and
became tired of half dragging her through the church doors. She
was a teenager then and Susie hoped that someday she would
resume going to services, but so far it hadn't happened.

She finished her breakfast, which at this time of day was more
like brunch. Going outside she looked around for Will. She walked
slowly to the main barn that housed the stalls for the best breeding
horses. She could hear them calling to each other in their language
of soft whinnies. Poking her head in the barn she saw no one and
walking around to the back of the huge barn brought no luck either.
Will was not here. His truck was gone too. Angelina's blood began
to boil. Her first thought was that he was with that woman who
owned Fair Meadows. Standing there stewing was not going to
change anything she thought to herself. Well, he better come home
by dark, or she was going looking for him.

If he was with Nola Rain Todd, she would find a way to destroy
both of them. Tired of being the fool in this triangle, she vowed to
change it, or die trying.

It was a long past midnight. Angelina lay in bed alone. She
hadn't seen Will all day, and it looked as if he were going to be
gone all night as well. She tossed and turned, at first trying not to let
it bother her, pretending she just didn't care. But that was far from

63

the truth. She got up, dressed in pants and one of Will's dark t-shirts. She put on heavy boots, and a dark jacket with a hood. Driving her truck toward Fair Meadows she went over in her mind where she might park, and how she was going to get in the house without being caught. As she approached the long drive that led back to the house, she could see the faint glow of what appeared to be a fire near the creek that both the Oliver, and Todd farms shared. Curious as to who would be camping there, and why they would have a fire in the middle of the night, she pulled her truck across the road. Driving into the field that would lead her near the creek, she parked well before she reached the banks. Walking slowly toward the fire Angelina could hear what sounded like singing... no... more like some kind of chanting. Three figures were moving around a ring of fire held in by a circle of rocks. Who were they? What on earth were they doing she wondered? Crouching behind a bush she could hear moaning coming from the path that led back up toward the house. She crawled to her right about ten feet and peered over a bush her eyes seeking the reason behind the groaning and moaning. She stared hard. At first not understanding what her eyes were seeing. Comprehension crept slowly into her brain. She grabbed her mouth to keep from screaming out. Losing her balance Angelina fell backward, and rolled over. She crawled until she felt it was safe to stand and run. Run she did, as fast as her long lean legs would let her. Tears, hot and constant, streamed down her stunned face. She yanked the door open on her truck, and started the engine, not caring now if anyone heard her. She did not care about anything anymore. She hated Nola, and Will. Most of all she hated that she was pregnant. Try as she might she could not get the image of Will's bare back lying over Nola Todd's near naked body. The two of them wrapped up in each other, oblivious to anything and everything around them. She drove straight home. To her home. Not his cabin. She would find a way to get them both. They would pay. Yes, they would pay.

Persistent knocking on her bedroom door caused Nola to wake with a start. The sun was shining through the panes of glass in her doors and she put her hand up to shield her eyes. "Yes," she said, "Who is it?"

"Miss Nola, it is me Joseph. Are you all right Missy?"

"Yes Joseph, I will have my breakfast tray here in my room please," she called out.

"Uh, Miss, it is lunch time." Joseph said.

Nola looked outside a little confused. She never slept that long. After telling Joseph to bring her a lunch tray, she lay back on the bed trying to recall last night, and how long she stayed awake. Like a fog slowly lifting, she remembered the dream. The chanting, the dancing, walking to the creek. She put her hand up to her neck to touch the necklace and felt only bare flesh. It was a dream, she kept telling herself as she tried to get to her feet. Her body was sore all over, and she stared in shock and disbelief at her legs. She was dressed; trousers and a shirt. She had socks on. What was going on? It was a dream. It had to be a dream. Will was there. She and Will had…Was she crazy? Fear pushed her to go down the stairs, and outside. She was running. Running to the creek. She had to see for herself. Nola had to prove that she was not crazy. It had all been a dream. Joseph tried to stop her, but she left him standing with her tray, mouth wide open. He started to call out to her, but she was gone before he could utter a word. She ran as fast as she could. Stumbling at times on roots and sticks she pressed on. Close to the water's edge she stopped suddenly, and stared in horror. A circle of rocks encompassed the faint glow of embers smoldering beneath a pile of ashes. She dropped to her knees. Her hand touched something metal as she did. Glancing down blinded now by sunlight dancing off the chain to her necklace. The necklace that

65

Maclaine Moreaux insisted she wear after he saved her from nearly drowning. Picking it up and holding it she stared at the spot where she found it. The grass was flattened as if someone laid in it, and she knew they had. It was not a dream. She and Will came together here, in this spot. Nola put her hand on her stomach. And she knew. She just knew. She should have felt shame, but she did not. Nola smiled. She got to her feet, and started back up the path, calling out to a panicked Joseph as she went.

"I'm all right Joseph....I'm allright."

SEVEN

Angelina, was having breakfast with her parents, when Will came barging in the dining room of the main house. He was angry, and demanding to know why she was here, and not at the cabin. Paul Oliver stood to his feet and began to argue with Will. "Now see here Will Biggs, my daughter can do as she pleases. Just because you married her doesn't give you the right to treat her like property." Paul's eyes were bulging; his face was as red as Angelina had ever seen it. Her Mother stood up at this point before Will could answer. The two Oliver's creating a tag team of sorts to defend their only child.

"I don't know who you think you are Mr. Biggs, but I won't have you treating my child this way, and in the delicate state she's in. And must I remind you that you created this mess of a marriage in the first place." Susie said.

Will let them say what they had to say. Smiling he sat down at the long dining room table. He looked at Angelina, who sat silent, not uttering a word. Her mouth gaped open and she was near tears.

"Angelina and I... have an agreement. She is to live in the cabin with me, which is sufficient for now. The two of you ..." Will's voice became louder, "The two of you, are going to mind your own business."

"Now see here," Paul started to protest but Will cut him off.

67

"No you need to see Mr. Oliver. I will not tolerate this behavior from Angelina. She has manipulated her way through life, but it stops with me. Understand? Do I make myself clear to all of you?"

"But she is having a baby, your baby. I would think…" Susie said.

"She is not having it today, and as far as I can tell she doesn't have a delicate bone in her body ma'am."

Paul, and Susie, looked at each other. Slowly they sat down in unison. For a few moments they all stared at Will, as if waiting for further instructions. "Angelina, finish your breakfast and then head back to our house." Will said "our house" with a raised voice. Still speaking to his wife he continued with his instructions. "I expect the cabin to be cleaned, and my clothes washed by the time I get home from work. Just like a normal married couple. No maid is to help you. Your mother is not to help you either. Is that clear? Understood? Oh… and I have been wanting a nice beef roast for a while now, so that's what you will fix for your man."

Will glanced at each one of them as he was getting to his feet. They sat in a row, mouths open. Speechless. Stunned. The three of them watched as Will turned, and left the room, slamming the door as he left heading for the stable.

Will was working with his favorite horse; a chestnut mare named Maple. She was so named because her color reminded the former owner of maple syrup. She was a spirited horse. Smart. She was eager to please Will. He was circling her in the corral just finishing up, and about to turn her into a paddock. From there a stable hand would take her and clean her up, before putting her in a stall. This time of year they were putting the horses in stalls for a few hours a day rather than turning them out to pasture. Thanksgiving was a couple of days away, and Will was trying to decide if he wanted to let Angelina have dinner with her parents. He certainly did not want to partake of any Thanksgiving traditions that the Oliver's had to offer. He wanted to be with Nola, and was thinking of going over there this evening to ask her if that would be possible. The other night at the creek was fresh in his mind, and he replayed it over, and over.

He looked up to see Angelina coming across the field to the corral. He walked Maple to the gate and opened it. Talking to her softly, the horse crossed the opening, obediently going into the paddock. Angelina stood on the outside of the fence that separated her from Will. She propped a boot up on the lower fence board, and waited with arms crossed on the top rail.

Will ignored her for a while knowing she was probably growing impatient, and angry. He smiled, and whistled some as he stood on the opposite side of the corral with his back to her. He pretended to be watching Maple, as he waited for the pressure cooker that was Angelina's head to blow. It was near noon, and time for lunch. He was very hungry, so he decided to end the waiting game and walked over to where she stood. "I made lunch and it's waiting in my truck. That is… if you're interested." Angelina said.

"Well…well. Aren't we being the devoted little wifey now. Why this sudden change of heart?"

"Will, I don't want to fight anymore. I want us to be together, and to be a real family. Angelina's eyes were pleading as she spoke to him softly. He felt his heart warm a little with compassion for this woman who was such a child.

"Let's go have lunch." He said suddenly and hopped the fence. The two of them began walking toward her truck.

"Thank you." Angelina said smiling. She continued to smile, and congratulate herself on a fine performance. Perhaps she would get her way after all.

They drove down by the creek that ran through Pine Point. The water then flowed southwest, snaking its way through Fair Meadows property before travelling on. Both farms shared the water and the benefits of the creek.

The Oliver's referred to it as "Pine Creek," while the Todd's never called it by any formal name. Mundy did at times refer to it as "Unpredictable Creek." They got out of the truck, and Angelina carried a small basket, and blanket, to a spot under an Oak tree. She spread it out upon the grass, and she, and Will, sat down to eat. The air was cool but not cold. The sun was bright. It was not typical weather for late November, but Angelina was glad that the snow had not yet begun to fall. They talked mostly about Pine Point, and the work that was beginning to slow now. Will told her that she should make plans for Thanksgiving with her parents. She stared hard at him; a bit surprised that he was being so nice. She asked if he would be joining them; he replied he would let her know. Angelina was glad he had not said a definite no, which was what she expected. After eating chicken sandwiches and potato salad, and washing it all down with sweet tea, she surprised Will by telling him she made the lunch herself. "You are kidding... really?" He asked.

"Why does that surprise you? I can do a lot of things Will Biggs."

Angelina tilted her chin rather defensively. Will smiled at her reaching out to brush a lock of hair from her eyes. Instinctively she jumped when he put his hand near her face. He dropped his hand and started to pack the basket for her. After gathering their things they walked back to the truck. Will told her to go on back without him. He was going to walk back to the barns. She stood thinking of protesting his telling her what to do, but deciding to let it go. She did not want to ruin the lovely time they'd spent together.

 It felt almost dreamlike to her and she felt her guard dropping. "See you tonight," Will said has he walked away. Angelina said nothing. She stood and watched until he was out of sight. Sighing, she got in her truck heading for the little cabin that was now her home.

She made plans for Thanksgiving dinner with her parents. The Oliver's always had a houseful of guests that day. Some relatives came the night before and stayed through the weekend. Angelina hoped Will would play nice and meet some of her family. He kept his distance at the wedding, and even refused to be introduced to her favorite aunt and uncle. The lunch at the creek was so wonderful, and dreamy. She felt her heart begin to hope that she could bring out the good Will. She knew he could be just as kind as he was bullish. The image of him, and Nola, at Fair Meadows was receding, and she pushed it out of her mind when it tried to appear. After stopping at her parent's house and making holiday plans, she went to the cabin and began to clean. She wanted to please Will, and keep him in a good mood. She made up her mind to kill him with kindness. You can catch more flies with sugar, or so she heard. When they fought he always won. Maybe being sweet and agreeable would bring about better results.

Sometime around seven he came home. The cabin was spotless, and she had just taken a roast from the oven when he walked in. A nice fire was crackling in the fireplace, and she had on a cute dress. Her long hair was pulled back on the sides, cascading down her back. Even without make-up she was stunning. They ate dinner, and talked some more about farm business.

It was the one thing they had in common. Will sat in front of the fire with a cup of coffee while Angelina did the dishes. It was quite the domestic scene. Once in a while she glanced at him as she stood washing pots and pans. Never in a million years could she have imagined she would be living in this little cabin, cooking, and cleaning up. Her entire life was spent being catered to, not the other way around. That night they lay in bed. Side by side. Not touching. She wanted to touch him, but feared rejection. She longed for him to turn to her; to tell her he loved her. To hold her in his arms, and say he was sorry for ever being unkind to her. Most of all she wanted to hear that Nola Rain meant nothing to him. But he lay there. She heard him snoring. Angelina turned toward the wall. She buried her pretty face in her pillow so he would not hear her cry. Feeling foolish for dreaming, and wishing that he would show her he loved her, she cried herself to sleep. In her dreams Will was everything she wanted him to be.

Sunlight streaming in the cabin washed her face with warmth waking her from a very deep sleep. She sat up and looked around the room. Will it seemed was already gone. Just as well she thought gloomily. The room felt cold in spite of the bright sunshine, and she shivered as she got out of the warm bed. Grabbing a robe she headed to the bathroom, but passing by the kitchen table she stopped. There was a heart shaped locket on a chain lying on top of a small piece of paper. She picked up the locket, which looked to be made of pewter. Scanning the note she read what Will had written.

Dear Angelina,

Wear this locket, but do not under any circumstances open it. It must remain closed. The locket will protect the baby.

Will

The locket felt icy cold as she traced the heart shape with her fingers. Slipping it around her neck she thought how strange Will could be. Mean, vulgar, and an absolute bully at times, and then this. Insisting she wear a sentimental locket meant to protect the baby he thought was his child. Well she would wear it. After all she was pleased, and shocked, that he gave her anything but a hard time. She stood running her fingers over the cold metal. It felt cold against her chest when she took her hand away. Not knowing why she suddenly thought of the three people at the creek, the chanting. A deep shiver shook her body as she pushed the image from her mind, and walked into the bathroom.

Thanksgiving Day was unseasonably warm, and bright. Nola thought it did not feel like the holiday without some snow. She loved snow, almost as much as she loved the rain. Her guest list for dinner this evening included Maclaine, and his family. They were still using the cabin in the woods, but she did not mind. She thought about that night by the creek. The fire, the dancing, and the chanting. She thought about Will and what they'd done that night. The two of them coming together on such a wonderful, perfect, night. Nola told no one of the ceremonies she'd witnessed.

The bizarre swaying, the trance like chants, ancient and ritualistic. Somehow she felt as if they were responsible for her and Will coming together. She knew that sounded crazy, but she just knew. She also knew she was pregnant with Will's child. She put her hand on her stomach smiling. She wanted this baby more than she ever wanted anything in her life. She did not care if others thought it was wrong. This was her baby. A chance for the family she always dreamed of, and maybe someday, somehow, Will would join her, and their child. She kept everything about Maclaine's family, and that night, a secret for now. She thought of telling Mundy, but as much as she loved him; like a father, she was afraid he would think

73

she had gone mad again. He might even think the whole night and the baby was a hallucination, or dream she'd had. So for now only she, and God, and her baby knew. Will must know too, she thought. Surely he would be coming around to see her; to talk about what happened. She felt a twinge of guilt when she thought of Angelina, but she pushed it from her mind. She got up and quickly dressed eager to get her day started, and happier than she'd been for a long, long time.

Wonderful smells from the kitchen wafted upward, and greeted her nose about half the way down the stairs. Cinnamon, and nutmeg were the spices Nola recognized. Going into the kitchen she saw Naomi busy preparing breakfast for the workers, while starting on pies for dinner this evening. Mundy would be joining them. She invited all of the hands and staff to join her for dinner, but only a few did not have plans to visit family.

Most left yesterday to spend the holiday with families scattered around the state. Mundy's men would not return until Monday, and Nola was happy for them. They deserved to be home with loved ones, and she would pay them as if they were working. Work was slow at Fair Meadows this time of year. There would be much less to do until spring.

She hugged Naomi, and then helped herself to coffee and toast. She decided to take advantage of the beautiful weather and head down to the creek for a while. There was very little for her to do today, and she wanted to be out of the house, and out of the way.

Sitting on the banks watching the sun dance across the tranquil water, Nola closed her eyes and thought about Will. She let her mind go back to the night he was here. The circle of rocks with the ashes contained inside was still here. That was proof of her sanity, and the reality of what happened that night. Hearing movement she quickly opened her eyes. She gasped in unbelief at the sight of Will walking toward her at the water's edge. She tried to get up and lost her balance, but before falling backward Will had her in his arms. He pulled her to him, and placed his mouth on hers, not giving her time to ask any questions that he knew were coming. The kiss was long and hard. Reaching beyond a kiss, wanting, searching for so much more; his kiss seemed to go on forever. Finally he held her away from him so that he could look into her face. Will stared into those beautiful violet eyes that held only yearning and love for him. He loved her. She loved him.

It sounded so simple when he thought of it, but their lives were far from simple. Angelina, and his child, were the stumbling blocks to Nola's love. He vowed to find an answer, for he knew he could not go on living without Nola Rain. He traced his finger around her pretty mouth and then up to her ear brushing back her hair from her face. She leaned into him laying her head against his broad chest listening to the beat of his heart. She was in heaven, and she never wanted to leave this place. They stood together this way for what seemed an immeasurable amount of time. Here in this place, wrapped in each other's arms, this was their world. No one could penetrate the fortress of love surrounding them. Finally Will pulled away, but still held her arms. "Nola, my darling sweet Nola." He pulled her to his chest again, a little tighter.

"Will...I want us to be together. I never want you to leave me again. Please tell me you will stay with me."

"I want that more than anything too Nola. But there is someone standing in our way." Will sighed.

"I know you are married to Angelina, Will. Believe me I have not forgotten. But there are legal avenues to fix all that. I don't understand why you married her in the first place."

Will wanted to tell her about the baby, but fear of driving her away stopped him. He knew that sooner or later he would have to tell her. He could not legally divorce Angelina until after the baby was born. Soon he would have to tell her, but not today. Not here in their special place. "Soon I will explain it all to you, I promise. Not today Nola. I don't want to ruin this moment. This time we have is precious to me."

They sat down on the banks of the creek and talked for hours. It was getting late in the afternoon when Nola told him she had dinner guests coming, and she would have to go. He held her hands looking into her lovely face. Then he kissed her one last time. He told her they would meet again in a few days. She asked him how she would know when he was going to be there, and he answered, "You will know Nola, you will just know."

Dinner was delicious and her guests were interesting. Nola tried to stay focused, but her mind kept drifting to Will, and the situation with Angelina. At one point during dinner Mundy leaned close to her asking if she were all right. She apologized to him, and told him she was a little tired. She asked Maclaine, and his sister Jolene, to tell her about New Orleans. They took turns describing what life was like there. They talked about the music, and French creole dishes. Maclaine described the swamps, and bayous filled with alligator, and craw fish. He said the town of Simone was very different from the city of New Orleans. When Nola asked them about the practice of voodoo all three became stone silent. Gabrielle turned instantly pale and looked at her mother as if for reassurance. Jolene, looked to Maclaine, as if asking for help in answering Nola's question.

"I'm sorry. Did I say something wrong? I was only asking about voodoo because my Mother used to talk to me about it. I apologize if I have offended you. I assure you it was not my intention." Nola said. Jolene, and Gabrielle, looked at Maclaine, as if leaving it up to him to answer Nola.

"No, of course we are not offended. It's just the practice of voodoo is not easily explained. We were caught off guard by your question. You didn't offend us Miss Nola."

Jolene and Gabrielle quickly chimed in that they were not offended, and smiled at Nola. Maclaine told Nola that they should be going now and the three of them rose to get their jackets. She thanked them for having dinner with her, and Mundy.

"The dinner was wonderful Miss Nola, and it is we who thank you. Good night," Maclaine said. Jolene, and Gabrielle, thanked her, and said good night as well. She watched as they walked out to the jeep, and drove across the field to the woods.

"What a strange group Mundy." Nola said.

"I suppose they are Missy, but that Maclaine… is a good hire. Hard working…courteous. How long you reckon his sister and niece are going to stay in the cabin?"

"I've never asked them. Is it still all right with you if they stay? I mean I know it is your cabin."

"Don't make no never mind to me Nola. I don't stay in the cabin anyway. It is up to you girl.

It is your place, and you are in charge like it or not." Mundy said laughing.

"Don't make no never mind to me either Mr. Mundy," Nola said laughing. She hooked her arm in his as they made their way inside to the sitting room.

Angelina's Thanksgiving dinner did not go as she would have liked. Will showed up very late in the day. He ate leftovers by himself at the big dining room table. Angelina sat with him, but they barely spoke a word. Will was acting distracted, and distant. Most of her relatives had retired for the evening, or gone home. He wasn't there to meet any of her family members. Not that he really wanted too.

He was not interested in Angelina, or her family. Will cared about the child she was carrying, and that was as far as his caring went.

Lying in bed that night next to Will, Angelina thought about their relationship. How, or if she could make it better. She wanted a normal married life. She wanted a husband who loved her. She put her fingers on the heart shaped locket he asked her to wear. She thought of it as a sign he was starting to care for her when he left the note and locket on the table. Quickly she jerked her hand away. She was fooling herself believing that he cared about her; and what was all that nonsense about not opening the locket under any circumstances?

He wanted her to wear the locket to protect the child. All he cared about was this baby, and Nola. A baby that wasn't even his, and a woman who was mentally disturbed and weak. Desperation settled into her weary bones.

Tired of feeling second best and tired of fighting for Will, she vowed to do something to change her life. She fell asleep trying to come up with a plan to put an end to Will and Nola's relationship.

78

Getting rid of Nola, was her last conscious thought before she fell off into the nothingness that is sleep.

EIGHT

A few days after Thanksgiving, the weather went from mild to brutal. The temperatures plummeted. Snow stacked up almost two feet. It was hard to get the doors of the house open to the outside let alone try to get anywhere. Nola, could not go down to the creek, and look for Will. The staff and hands were pretty well snowed in; other than getting out for the necessary feeding of the animals. Winter arrived at Fair Meadows with an attitude. Nola loved the snow, but she felt very restless, anxious; for she knew it would keep Will away. The knowledge that he would be snowed in at Pine Point, with Angelina, ate at her.

Nola tried to stay busy. She made a shopping list of gifts for everyone for Christmas, and even a list of baby items she knew would be needed in a few months. Although she realized there was a quite some time before the baby came, she just liked writing down the things he or she would need. Writing it down somehow made it feel more real. She thought the baby was probably a boy. She just felt it was a boy. No evidence or sign, just a feeling. Thinking about a son made her remember Micah, the little boy she lost. A single tear trickled down her cheek and she brushed it away. That life all seemed so long ago. She had a husband once upon a time, and a child that never drew a breath. Sometimes it seemed as if she were remembering someone else's memories.

She longed at times for the simple days, playing in the sunshine, catching lightning bugs at night. Then the reality of her poverty stricken days cast a shadow over any good memories of her childhood. The harshness and grief of burying your young husband,

and next to him your stillborn son, was at times unbearable. But she survived the grief and the pain. Nola was changed forever by loss, but she survived and found happiness again. She found love again, and out of that love a new life would be born. A new life for her as well. A chance for happiness. Real happiness. The family she longed for. Someone to belong to. Nola would be someone's mother. She was so happy these days.

She was having breakfast in the kitchen when Mundy came through the back door trying to stomp off snow from his boots, as much as was possible. He spoke to Naomi, and Nola, when he entered the kitchen. Pulling out a chair and sitting down at the table with Nola, he asked Naomi for a cup of coffee. She was busy getting breakfast ready for the farm hands, and stopped to grab a mug, filled it with steaming hot coffee then handed it to Mundy.

The three of them sat together discussing the upcoming Christmas holiday. Nola asked what days they wanted off. She told them everyone would be paid for their time off, and that included the farm hands. She talked about taking a shopping trip as soon as the weather broke. She ordered many of her gifts from catalogs, but still felt getting out and foraging the town shops would be fun.

She also wanted to see the town decorations, all the bright lights. Mundy said he would be glad to accompany her, or Joseph would take her. She decided to go with Mundy, and said she would enjoy his company. Mundy, helped Naomi pack breakfast into a large basket for the men who were at the bunkhouse. Winter at the farm was basic, and work slowed to a crawl.

There was the holidays to look forward to, and hopefully they would be able to get out to their families. Mundy would be the only one to stay during the Christmas, to New Year week. He always stayed and took care of the animals. Nola went back to her room to work on Christmas cards, and Mundy took breakfast to his men. Naomi was left alone in the kitchen cleaning up. Glancing out the window at the snow she clucked her tongue and shook her head. "Looks like we might be in for a long winter," she said out loud to no one. She then picked up her dish rag, and went back to scrubbing.

Right before Christmas, Angelina began having morning sickness so severe that she became dehydrated, and very ill. Her parents bundled her up and took her to a hospital in Charleston. The roads, and the weather had improved in the weeks following the big snow right after Thanksgiving. She was treated with IV fluids in the hospital for a couple of days, and sent home Christmas Eve. The roads were icy when she was released, and her father was driving. Paul Oliver was being as slow and cautious as possible, inching his way along the treacherous road.

Home was about three hours from the hospital in Charleston, and the highway back to Pine Point was curvy and slick. With her husband at the wheel Susie Oliver rode in the back of the car with her daughter's head in her lap. Angelina was still weak and nauseated, but feeling much better after her stay in the hospital. The three of them talked about Christmases' past, and plans for dinner tomorrow. Anxious to get home to their tree, and presents, and their lives, Paul drove on through a steady stream of sleet and ice. Just two miles from home without warning, the car suddenly began to swerve out of control. The last sounds Angelina remembered hearing was a small scream coming from her mother and what she thought was metal scraping against something. She couldn't comprehend what the scraping metal sound was. Her world went black. She heard someone calling her. What were they saying? She didn't recognize what they were saying. Miss, miss? She tried with all her might to open her eyes, but they would not open. She tried to

83

move her hands, her legs, but nothing of her body seemed to be working. She tried calling out to her daddy first, and when that didn't work she called for her mother. No answer. Panic began to rise up inside her like a giant wave threatening to crash down on her, and take her under. The last thing she remembered before her world blacked out again was the sound of a man, then more men. They were saying that someone kept calling for their mother, and their daddy. She had no idea they were talking about her.

Angelina was that someone.

The day of the funerals was sunny. The temperature had risen to near spring like warmth, and people were commenting on what a blessing the break in the weather was for everyone. The snow and ice that caused the death of two of Bryce County's finest farmers, two up standing members of the community, had moved out of the area leaving beautiful weather in its place.

The funerals were held in what was once a bunkhouse on the Pine Point property. It was now transformed it into a proper place for the funerals of Paul, and Susie Oliver. So many mourners turned out that many stood outside the building during the services.

A platform at the far end of the building served as a podium for the minister, and matching white coffins sat on either side of the lectern. Flowers filled the entire end of the building, and along both sides. There were many arrangements sitting in the main house, because the makeshift funeral parlor could not contain them all.

With an empty seat beside him, Will Biggs sat in the front row. He looked at no one, but instead stared straight ahead. Soft music began to play, and all the chairs were filled. People stood along the walls and across the back of the room.

"We are gathered together to pay our last respects to husband and wife Susie, and Paul, Oliver," the reverend began his sermon, "Lifelong residents of Monroe, the couple passed on to be with their Lord, as a result of a tragic accident.

Their daughter Angelina Marie Oliver Biggs who remains hospitalized as result of injuries sustained in that accident, is their sole survivor. Shall we all send prayers heavenward for the Oliver's only child." Will could hear an occasional sniffle, a whisper, and the reverend's words. He heard, but could not focus on what was said. His mind was with Angelina, and the baby. The baby was still alive; the doctors told him. They could not give him an answer for how long, or if the baby, and Angelina, would survive.

"…and so we have hope, the hope that lives because of Christ our Lord, that one day we shall see Paul, and Susie Oliver again. Not only shall we see them, but we shall be with them in that glorious place called Heaven, never to be separated again." The reverend concluded his eulogy with prayer, and then stepped aside. A young man who worked for the local mortuary stepped up to the lectern telling everyone that the service was concluded, and the grave side service would be private. He thanked everyone on behalf of the Oliver friends, and family, for attending the service.

People began spilling out of the building, some still sniffling and dabbing their eyes. It was a lovely service. Will heard folks whisper, "It was a lovely service." He stood for a moment in the front of the building staring at the coffins. He held his hat in his hands, then turned and went out the nearest door. The sun was bright and the air was warm for December. A few people tried to speak to him, but he kept walking. His truck was parked near the horse stable, and he jumped in it and quickly started it up. Pulling out on to the highway within minutes he was at the spot where the accident happened.

He hit the brakes hard and came to a sliding stop. He sat looking over near the edge of the woods where Paul Oliver's car crashed head on into a massive tree. The tree was scarred; the bark missing from the impact. He felt nothing except gratitude that Angelina, and his baby were spared. He took his foot from the brake hitting the gas hard. Getting to the hospital was the only thing on his mind right now. He looked on the seat beside him at the gris gris Maclaine gave him. He wanted to get to the hospital, and place the gris gris on Angelina's body. It would help her heal, and help the baby to survive. He had to save the baby. The baby was all that truly mattered.

Angelina drifted in and out of reality. She could not yet determine what was real, and what her mind was imagining due to her body's condition, and a lot of drugs. She knew she had been in an accident. She knew her parents were dead. She knew for now her baby was alive inside her. These facts were repeated over, and over, when she would come to the surface for air, and for more drugs. The drugs would drag her back under the water where the world was muffled, and she did not have to fight against everything the nurses and doctors kept telling her. In her world under the water she could float and not feel anything. She was perfectly fine there, and she was angry that they kept trying to bring her to the surface just to keep telling her how her world collapsed. When they withheld the drugs to bring her out of her floating state, she protested loudly.

The medical staff tried to comfort her, but she would not be comforted. They tried doses of reality, speaking loudly about her parents, the accident, and her injuries. She only screamed louder, and so the doctor would order more drugs and proclaim "Mrs. Biggs is not ready yet."

Will Biggs entered the room quietly. The lights were dim and the machines beeped and hummed. Angelina lay on the bed; her hair framed her face and splayed across the white pillows. She looked angelic, peaceful. Will's throat closed up. He felt near tears. Compassion that he never knew existed came rushing to the surface. He felt so guilty, and so helpless. He went to her side and leaned in close to her ear. He whispered to her. "Angelina, please hear me. You must fight. You have to fight to come back. For the baby. For me." A single tear trickled down Will's face, and fell upon her cheek. She did not move. No response. Will stood and took the gris gris from his pocket. He looked at what Maclaine described as a special potion that would bring Angelina back. Looking at her neck he could see the heart shaped locket was gone. Someone must have taken it off. He placed the gris gris inside the sleeve of her gown and folded her arm across her chest. Kissing her on the cheek he turned to leave the room when he heard a sound. Spinning around quickly, and walking back to the bed, he heard her whisper his name.

"Will…Will." Her eyes fluttered and then opened. She looked him in the eye and he could tell she actually was seeing him. Angelina heard Will yelling for the nurses, and she smiled.

Nola returned to Fair Meadows following the funeral service of Paul, and Susie Oliver. She did not want to attend, but felt it was a business obligation. In the past the two farms shared many business deals and she felt she must go as a gesture of condolence. Angelina was in the hospital, and Will Biggs would be taking care of everything Mundy told her. At the mention of Will her cheeks grew hot, and pink. Mundy asked if she were all right. She assured him she was fine. It was all so sad, and morose she told him. Mundy escorted her to Pine Point, and brought her home. She did not see Will, though she heard someone say he was in the front of the building. The crowd was large. She and Mundy arrived very close to the start of the service, so there was only room to stand in the back. The two of them left as soon as the service concluded, and Nola was home now in her room. Although she knew that feeling guilty was useless; she felt it none the less. She hoped to see Will, and to be with him even under those circumstances, but she didn't. Now she was feeling sad, and guilty, for not feeling guiltier. Poor Angelina was in the hospital fighting for her life.

The girl lost both her parents, and had no one other than Will to support her. Nola should feel guilty for wanting to take Will away from her, but she didn't. What is wrong with me she thought? Where is my sense of fairness, and compassion?

She guessed it was buried deep within her. Buried under years of poverty. Years of never getting what she wanted. Going without. Buried under the pain of having a child die, and never getting to hold it in your arms.

Buried under always being the one who loses. She got up from her bed and stared out at the darkening sky. Clouds thick and black were gathering. A storm was coming. She could see it, but there was nothing she could do but watch it come. She bowed her head and whispered a prayer. She asked for forgiveness. "Forgive me Lord for loving what isn't mine to love." She turned away from the sight of the storm, and got ready for bed.

NINE

The winter was long, and brutal. Angelina slowly got stronger. By spring after having been hospitalized for weeks, she was well enough to come home. She called it her Easter blessing, and was looking forward to getting out of the confines of the hospital, and home to start living again. Will had been to see her every day that he could make it, only staying away when the weather forced him too. Her belly continued to grow while she was getting well; proof that the baby was going to be all right. In a couple of months she would have her child, and Will's devotion. She thought about her mother, and father, and what wonderful grandparents they would have been. It made her heart ache to think of them. Their memories came drifting into her mind totally without warning. She never could have imagined how much she would miss them. She lay on her bed and stared out at the falling snow. Even though the calendar said it was spring Mother Nature wasn't getting the message. Winter just didn't want to let go. It kept holding on. But there were days of sunshine, and warmer temperatures hinting at what was to come. Unless the roads were slick and dangerous Will would be coming tomorrow to take her home. She told him not to come if the roads were treacherous. She had taken that trip before, and it cost her too much. Again she thought of her parents. She missed their funerals. She'd not seen where they were buried. She missed them both so much. Poor Will had taken care of everything. She heard from friends who told her how well he honored her parents. She would be forever grateful. For a brief moment she thought about the baby, and felt a pang of guilt for Will, who thought it was his. She could never tell him the truth. How would that be fair to him after all he had done for her? No. He must never find out. Cash Atkins must never know either. She would keep the secret to hang on to Will.

The nurse startled her out of her thoughts, and she turned her head away from the window toward the sound of her cheerful voice. She was carrying a vase of flowers. They were beautiful, and she placed them on the window sill bringing the card to Angelina. Flowers arrived almost daily from people all over the world. Her parents knew so many people because of their business. Angelina appreciated the flowers, but she didn't recognize many of the names from the people who sent them. She saved the cards intending to send thank you notes to each and every one. The nurse handed her the card and told her she had a visitor, saying she would send him in. Angelina thanked her, and straightened herself up in bed, running a hand across her hair to try to make it presentable. She was stunned when Cash Atkins walked through the door looking hesitant, and holding his hat in his hands.

She stared for a few seconds and then warmly greeted Cash. "Cash it is so good to see you. I am a little surprised that you would drive all the way to Charleston to visit me. I am being discharged tomorrow."

"Angelina," Cash began, "I came to see you for a couple of reasons. First because I care about you and...I wanted to see you. I have been calling the hospital on a weekly bases checking on your progress." He twisted the hat in his hands moving closer to her bed before he continued. "I also needed to see if you remember anything about the accident. I am the one who did the investigation. I need to close my report, and send it to the state. I waited of course until you were well enough to talk about it. Do you remember anything? Anything... at all?" He smiled at her and she felt her heart warm a bit towards him. She felt a little sorry for leading him on that night she spent with him. He truly was a decent, and kind man, with a huge heart. She could see that in him now; it made her feel guilty.

"I am sorry Cash, I really don't remember much except the sensation of spinning. There was a sound like metal scraping against something. I heard my mother call out, more of a scream really." Angelina's eyes filled with tears at the memory of this. Cash came closer taking her hand.

"It's all right. You can stop right there. I have my report ready, and I will go on and file it with the state. The insurance company will want a complete report, and it will be ready for them." Cash took her hand in his and looked into her eyes. "Don't you worry about anything...you hear? I am just glad you are getting better."

His eyes moved away from her face and then froze on her bulging stomach. He looked back into her face, and he knew. He dropped her hand and stepped back. "Angelina?"

"Cash, it is not what you're thinking." Angelina looked panicked. She could see the question in Cash's face. "I am pregnant but the baby is Will's. I am certain of it."

"But what if it's mine. That could be my child Angelina."

"Stop…STOP… right there," Angelina said. Her voice was a little higher, and a little louder. Her eyes narrowed. Anger bubbled to the surface of her skin burning away any compassion, any remorse she felt earlier.

"I'm sorry, please calm down. I certainly didn't want to upset you. I'll be going now, but I hope to see you sometime… when you are better. Get well. Get home… Angelina." Cash turned to leave, but stopped at the door of her room, and turned around. "Just so you know where I stand Angelina, I don't believe for one minute that the baby you're carrying is Will Biggs. You are too far along. I ain't no doctor but that belly looks way too big. I am in love with you girl. They say love makes you blind, but I don't believe it makes you stupid." With those words lingering in the air; he put his hat on his head, and walked out into the hospital hall.

"CASH…" Angelina called out. "CASH…come back here." Yelling for Cash brought the nurse running into her room.

"Miss are you all right?"

"Yes… yes I'm fine," Angelina said through clenched teeth. "Please leave me alone now."

The nurse looked at her for a few moments, then turned and left the room without another word. She lay back on the pillows, and stared out the window. Her thoughts were on Will, and how to keep him from finding out the baby belonged to Cash Atkins. He would never understand how she could lie to him about the baby. Cash was so sweet, but she wasn't sure what he might try if he knew the baby was his. Angelina sighed and closed her eyes. As if the child were as restless as she was it moved, and kicked inside her. What ever happened she would not let Cash destroy her marriage, and the only life she had left. No matter what she would find a way to silence Cash Atkins.

The streets of New Orleans at night are different from anywhere else on earth. Night there is a darkness that is alive, penetrating, and full of secrecy. The streets are empty, and foreboding. But empty was an illusion; as someone was always watching. Hiding in the dark shadows observing her surroundings, the old woman was looking for someone. No one moved on the street for several hours. Locals knew better than to be traipsing around this part of town at night. No one who knew better ventured over this way in the dark for any reason.

She moved out of the shadows, and unlocked the door to her shop. The closed sign made a clanging noise as she shut the street and the darkness out. He should have been here by now she thought. Where was he? The woman stood resting against a counter pursing her lips, narrowing her eyes. She looked as if she were trying to see in her mind where he might be. Moving through a door way covered with long strands of beads she entered a small room with a table in the center. Sitting down she picked up a match and struck it against the wooden table. Lighting incense she sat with her eyes closed fanning the smoke with black wrinkled hands. A single word escaped her lips and she repeated it over and over. She was singing the word and getting just slightly louder with every repetition. Her body began to sway back and forth as the chanting became more intense. Suddenly she slammed both hands down on the table and opened her eyes. Her eyes were locked into the eyes of the man who she summoned. He had arrived. She did not hear him as he entered

93

the shop and sat down. She possessed knowledge, and she needed to impart that to him. It was vital… urgent.

They sat staring, neither of them saying a word in the dimly lit room. Smoke from the incense rose between them causing a slight burning sensation in his nose. The reward came from the heavenly sweet smell of it. Breathing it in made him less edgy, relaxed, but dizzy. He gladly endured the burning nose. He waited for Mother to speak. It was tradition and a show of respect to let her begin each conversation.

She summoned him, and he was anxious to know why, but accustomed to the rituals Mother put on at every meeting. There was an order for everything, and a reason for all order, the old woman would say.

"Da girl is keepin a lie." Mother said.

When she spoke suddenly, he felt as if icy cold water had been thrown on him. He sat up straight, his hazy relaxed head now fully alert.

"I don't understand." He felt as if cold water had been thrown on him. Goose bumps trailed up his arms, and he could feel the hairs on the back of his neck stand up. The air was electric, and thunder rolled across the roof.

"Dis baby is a lie. She be keepin a lie."

"Mother, I don't understand. How can the baby be a lie?"

Mother jumped up and pounded her fist on the table. Smoke billowed up in to the air obscuring his view of her for a second. It gave the illusion that she disappeared.

"Ya mus to figure it out Shylone. It be all a lie. Dis baby not be da Queen."

"Is the baby a boy? Is that it? Is that why she is not having the Queen?"

"Da baby a girl. Da baby not be from da King." Mother was shaking now and angry. Her anger made him shake. He could sense her power, and shrank back waiting for further instructions.

"Go now... Shy, ya go."

He got up slowly, and walked out of the room. She followed and the sound of her shuffling from behind made him want to run. He stopped at the door, and turned around nearly bumping into her. She took his face in her ugly rough hands. She leaned in and kissed his cheek. Her breath on his face was hot. It's odor old, decaying. He recoiled, but she did not seem to notice, or care. "Go now Shy," she said. He opened the door and started down the empty dark street. She stood watching, and muttering softly, "Baby a lie, ba... a lie," again, and again, until she could see him no more.

Will picked Angelina up, and took her home to Pine Point. A doctor was hired to come to the farm twice a week to check on her and the baby. Will also hired three nurses who would be on call around the clock to see to her needs. He was busy this time of year, and especially since taking total control of the farm business. Most of his time was spent behind a desk barking orders to everyone else. Occasionally he would get out to the corral, and the stables, if there was a problem with a horse, or the cattle.

95

He was enjoying his ownership, and never complained about all the hours he spent working. This was his passion. Finally Will Biggs, was living his dream.

Angelina looked around the bedroom that her husband remodeled while she was in the hospital. He hired the work done as he was much too busy these days to do handy work. It was her old room but the furnishings had all been replaced. The walls were painted a lovey light blue; even the bedding was new. She wondered who helped him to choose such lovely feminine things. Nola Todd entered her mind, but before she allowed herself to get angry she pushed the woman from her mind. After all she told herself she had no reason to believe Will was communicating with Nola. Angelina walked over to the tall chest of drawers.

The top was lined with framed photographs of her as a child. There were several of her parents. One she picked up was the image of the three of them laughing, happy. She looked to be around the age of five. Tears sprang to her eyes as she held it, looking into the faces of first her Mother, and then her Father. Angelina held the frame to her chest tilting her head toward heaven. "Why Lord?" She whispered. "Am I so bad? Is this my punishment for being a bad person?" She lay across the bed clutching the picture, and cried herself to sleep.

When Will came home that evening he found Angelina lying across the bed sleeping. In her hands she held a photograph. His heart broke at the sight of her. She looked like an angelic child lying there.

He knew she missed parents, but she never spoke of them. He knew it was not healthy to keep all that grief inside, but he was hopeful that now that she was home she would start to open up some. He would take her to their graves when she was stronger. When he felt she was ready to visit them. A beautiful plot of land near a stand of Willows was their final resting place. A statue stood between them; a beautiful white stallion, and markers of marble. Will didn't have an inscription chiseled in the marble. He wanted to wait for Angelina to have some say in that. For a moment Nola Rain swept into his thoughts, but he shoved her out of his mind quickly. Refusing to let the image of her dwell inside his head was how he coped with moving on without her. Since the accident he tried his best to keep his priorities straight, and stay loyal to his marriage. He was trying hard to let his choices be guided by being a better husband, and father to be. Letting go of Nola, one final time, was decision number one.

Angelina stirred, and opened her eyes slowly. Such beautiful eyes that focused on Will standing by the bed gazing down at her. "Are you hungry?" He asked. "Would you like to come to the dining room, or eat here?"

"I think here.' She smiled. She was so grateful that he was being kind and attentive to her. "Will you join me for dinner?"

"Of course. Let me tell Tilly to have two trays sent up. All right?" He leaned down and kissed her on the forehead. He felt a stirring deep in his heart for her at that moment. Was it love or pity? He really didn't know but he did not fight it.

"I...I... love you Will." Angelina's words were soft and husky from emotion and sleepiness.

He wanted to say those words back to her. He really did. Just as he started to say them Angelina's face became Nola's, and he stepped back in surprise. With Angelina staring after him confused and hurt, Will turned and quickly made his way to the kitchen.

TEN

Nola spent most of the winter inside. Her body changing and growing, Mundy, and Naomi, and even Joseph, could see she was pregnant. Her belly was growing rapidly, and she found out in March that she was carrying twins. Though her Fair Meadows family were secretly stunned at her condition, no one questioned her. No one asked who the father was. They did not discuss it among themselves, but they knew it must be Will Biggs child. Everyone knew how much she loved Will. Even if they had asked she would not have told them. Since the funeral she tried to go on without Will, and he made it a little easier by not trying to contact her. Cash Atkins came to visit her and mentioned that he had gone to see Angelina, in the hospital the day before she was released. It was Cash, who told Nola, that Angelina, was having a baby. She had not known until then, and the news took her breath away. It also took away any faint thread of hope she was clinging to. Any idea that she and Will might someday be together, and have a family, was gone. Nola would never come between a child, and his or her father. Her children would never be told that Will Biggs was their father. She was trying hard to concentrate on making it as far along in her pregnancy as possible, so her babies would be born healthy. The doctor expected she would have them a few weeks early, and a month before her due date she would go to the hospital in Charleston to stay until they were delivered.

Excitement, and anticipation, replaced the intense sadness she felt over letting go of Will. Nola truly wished for only a healthy baby for Will, and Angelina.

The weather warmed. Winter finally gave way to a glorious spring. Nola started taking walks down by the creek on days that were fair. The trees were leafing out, and everything was growing. The farm was in full operation these days. Mundy was always busy, and Nola saw very little of him. She could sense somehow that he was not too pleased about the babies. Perhaps it was because his generation frowned on children born out of wedlock. But Nola didn't care what anyone thought. She waited all her life for a family of her very own. Someone who shared her blood, and characteristics. The babies' identity would validate her own identity. She loved her twins all ready, and was full of excitement, and joy, at the anticipation of their births.

She reached down to feel the water. It was icy cold. Clear and moving swiftly she was in awe of its beauty and power. She sat on the bank thinking about what she should pack to take to the hospital in a few days. She felt tired, but happy. Her belly was so large and

100

heavy that walking any distance wore her out. After sitting for a while she stood to her feet ready to walk back and take a nap. She thought lying down might help her fatigue. Just as she took a step toward the path leading back to the house she felt a stabbing pain, and a familiar wet feeling between her legs. Panic set in immediately, remembering the awful night she lost her first child, Micah. She looked down and saw a puddle of what looked like water.

"My water broke," she said. She said it again out loud, to no one. The third time she said it a little louder realizing she better start for the house. A few steps into the walk and another pain. She stopped took a deep breath and let it out slowly. Trying hard not to panic, she knew she had to keep moving. Just get to the house, and you will have help, she told herself with each step.

Maclaine was watching her from a distance. He saw her sitting by the water. He watched as she rose slowly starting for the house. He saw her stop, and could tell something was wrong. Following her, he stopped when she stopped. About halfway to the house he called out to her, and she turned to face him. "Maclaine, help me to the house. My water broke. I…I'm having my babies." Nola said.

Naomi called the doctor, and tried to make Nola comfortable. She was in her room on her bed. She was in agony. More than the pain was the fear of knowing the babies would be born here, and very soon. No time to get to the hospital, no time to wait for a doctor. Panic, and fear, gripped her with every contraction. Naomi did her best to comfort her, and assure her that everything would be all right. Naomi was telling Nola that everything would be fine; something quite the opposite of what she felt. The cook knew the babies would be small. Their tiny lungs would not be fully developed. She had no idea what to do about that. She gave birth years ago with the help of a midwife, but her daughters was full term babies. Naomi said a silent prayer for the doctor to get there before it happened.

Maclaine ran to the barn calling for Mundy. Where was that old man he thought? He needed to tell him about Nola, and he also wanted to get back to the house in case Naomi needed help. Mother would want him to be there to see if one of the twins was a girl. The prediction about Angelina's baby had been wrong. Her baby was a girl, but it was not the King's. Mother had a vision, and saw that Nola Rain was having the King's babies. The vision did not reveal however if they were boys, or girls, or one of both. Maclaine would need to let her know right away.

Jolene, and Gabrielle, suddenly appeared at the barn. He told them to go to the house and help Naomi. They ran as fast as they could toward the house. Unable to find Mundy, Maclaine headed to the house too. As soon as the three of them burst into the house and started up the stairs they heard the faint cry of a newborn child. They stopped on the stairs looking at each other for a moment, before heading up the steps toward the cry.

Jolene burst through the door and saw Naomi swaddling a newborn who was now crying loudly. There seemed to be no problem with the first baby's lungs, and Naomi handed the child to Gabrielle, who stood wide eyed and stiff. She seemed to come to her senses once the baby was placed in her arms. Jolene went to Nola, who was in the throes of having her second baby. Naomi looked at Jolene, and she could see the panic on the old cook's face. This baby refused to come out. Jolene took Nola's hand, and began speaking to her in French. The words were soft and comforting, and Nola seemed to relax instantly.

She felt as if the words were familiar somehow and she opened her eyes to look at Jolene, but it was not Jolene speaking, and holding her hand. Nola did not recognize the old black woman. She was smiling down on her, chanting something over, and over. Nola was not afraid.

She understood as the woman told her in French to push with all her might. Somewhere inside her she mustered enough strength to push the tiny boy out of her body. The women yelled out. Then there was silence. The child was not breathing. The stranger grabbed the baby up, and wiped his face hard. She leaned into him and blew her breath hot, and hard into his face. Suddenly his face began to twitch and turn red, as he squirmed and released a scream that could be heard downstairs; where the doctor was just on his way up.

The doctor came into the room running past Maclaine who was pacing nervously in the hall. After first examining Nola and then the twins the doctor proclaimed all to be doing well. The boys were breathing fine even though they were small. Naomi brought a scale up from the kitchen. Each boy weighed four pounds exactly. The doctor said that was amazing since they were quite early. Nola was exhausted, and rightly so. She kept nodding off as everyone was talking about the boys. Naomi, asked Gabrielle, and Jolene, to clean the twins up so that she could clean up the bedroom. They were glad to help. The doctor said he was confident that Nola would be capable of nursing just fine. He instructed Naomi to call if there were any problems. She saw him to the door then headed back up to Nola's room to clean.

Before she got half way there Mundy came rushing in and stopped when he saw her on the steps. Naomi's smile was all he needed to see, and he happily followed her on up to the second floor.

Nola gazed into the faces of her sons, realizing that she had not known how much she could love another human being. They were

103

from the moment of their births, her very reason for existing. There were no words to describe how elated she was. It was a state of total euphoria. Bliss. Tears of joy flowed freely from her eyes as she held them, one in each arm. Thinking about how long she had waited for her little family, her only regret was that her sons would never know who their father was. She would deny that they were Will's children. It was best for everyone, including her innocent boys. She must protect her sons, and Angelina's innocent child, as well.

The twins were hungry, and nursed without any problems. She fed them and Naomi took them from her, laying them in a bassinet beside her bed. Touching their silky heads she thought they looked like sleeping angels. They brought her joy, and gave her so much hope for a future filled with wonder, and new experiences. She was a mother now. Not just the mother of one son, but two. She thanked God for her bundles of blessing. She would cherish every milestone in her children's lives.

Her thoughts were interrupted at the sound of someone knocking. Come in she said softly, trying not to wake her sleeping angels.

Mundy opened the door cautiously standing with his hat in his hands. Nola smiled, and motioned for him to come close and look at her sleeping babies. He walked over and peered in, the smile on his face growing wider. He felt like a proud grandpa. Nola told him that she wanted him to be their surrogate grandfather. Mundy was touched and tearfully told her he would be honored. Nola made an appointment with a lawyer, who was coming to the farm next week. She wanted to be sure that her children, and Mundy Winks, would be taken care of in case anything happened to her.

Not that she was planning on going anywhere and leaving her boys, but still a person must prepare as best they could for any unforeseen tragedy. Nola knew all too well about tragedy. Life had a way of standing you on your head at times. For now life was wonderful, and she felt beyond blessed. Every night she thanked her God for being so good to her.

She and Mundy went to the sitting area of her room and sat on the small sofa. "How are you feeling Missy?" He asked.

"I have never felt so happy, or so blessed Mr. Mundy." Her smile was so radiant he could not help but smile back. Her joy was contagious.

"I am so happy for you. Those boys are perfect. The thing is; and I don't want to take away from your joy, well I was thinking about their daddy Nola. Will has a right to know."

"Mr. Mundy please," Nola's eyes misted with tears.

"Nola dear, I am not trying to upset you. I just think those boys have a right to know their daddy, and a man should know his sons."

"Their daddy... is married to another woman. I don't want my children to grow up with any moral stigma attached to who they are. Besides... Angelina is pregnant. I would not want to cause that girl any more heartache. She just lost her parents." She lowered her quivering chin as a tear escaped her eye.

"I don't want to cause anyone any pain either my sweet child, but the truth is always the best path to travel. When you try to hide the truth behind a lie, well it's just a road that's bound to make you stumble and fall." He patted her hand and rose to his feet.

"I try hard to please you Mr. Winks. You have become like a father to me, and I love you very much." Nola rose to her feet, and gave him a hug.

"There, there, don't worry. You're a good person. I have all the faith in the world that you will do right by them boys, and Will Biggs."

After he had gone she walked over to the bassinet and stood gazing upon the loves of her life. "I will always try to be honest with you. I promise," she whispered. She lay on the bed thinking about what to do. Without making any decisions she drifted off to sleep, where in her dreams she could escape and not decide anything.

Later in the week the attorney she hired to handle her business, and personal affairs, came to Fair Meadows. Until then she had not given the boys names, but for legal purposes she needed to decide while the attorney was present. Nola, asked Mundy, to be present for her meeting with the attorney, so the three of them met in the library. She asked that Mundy Winks be given full power of attorney should she become incapacitated. The attorney advised her the power of attorney rights Mr. Winks had from when she was ill earlier were still active.

Nola, then asked that her sons, and Mr. Winks, become equal beneficiaries should she die. She named Mundy, the God Father of her children, and the administrator of her estate. The attorney took notes saying he would have the legal documents drawn up and return the following week for her, and Mundy, to sign. He then asked for the children's names and she looked at Mundy and smiled. "William Lee Biggs, and Jackson Winks Biggs," Nola said.

ELEVEN

Cash Atkins sat in his office staring out the window at the bright sunshine. His mind was on Angelina, and her baby. These days it was all he could think about. Since his visit with her at the hospital he couldn't let go of the idea that the baby was his. He knew it as well as he knew his own name. He believed it "all the way to his bones," as his Grammy used to say. He knew Angelina was lying, and yet he didn't have any inkling what he was going to do about it. The first notion to come to his mind was to hire an attorney. He lived frugally. There was a surprising amount of money in his savings account. Financially retaining an attorney to prove paternity wouldn't be a problem. The problem was he loved Angelina, and truly didn't want to inflict more pain on her, especially in light of her recent tragedy.

The sound of children laughing broke through his thoughts, and he went to the window for a better look. Three little girls were walking down the street talking, and giggling as they went. He smiled and wondered what his child would be. A boy... a girl? He thought, and still smiling mumbled under his breath, "Yes, the baby was surely a boy...or a girl."

He ran into Mundy who came into town for supplies, and the two of them had lunch together at the diner. Mundy told him Nola gave birth to twin boys, and Cash nearly dropped his fork. He had not known she was pregnant.

He questioned who the father was but Mundy just stared at him with a "figure it out yourself look." Of course Cash knew the twins must belong to Will Biggs, but it was a real shock to hear about all this baby making. "Will Biggs sure gets around now don't he?" Cash said.

"It would seem so, but he don't even know yet about those young'uns." Mundy replied.

"Well, why hasn't Nola told him? He has a right to know about his sons Mundy." Cash's tone was brisk.

"You're right about that son. He does. Nola will tell him when the time is right. She is tryin not to cause more heartache for Angelina Oliver... er I mean Biggs." Mundy took one last bite of potatoes and putting his fork down, he leaned back in his chair studying Cash. "What's eatin at you boy?"

"I have a lot on my mind Mundy. This job is round the clock with no help. Can't keep help when I hire em. I'd like to have some kind of life besides being the sheriff here in Monroe. Been thinking lately about buying some land, maybe try my hand at farming."

Mundy was silent for a few moments. He was moved by the young man's obvious sadness. He slapped him on the shoulder, and pushed his chair back standing up to go. He pulled a dollar from his pocket for the tip, and another five to cover the bill for his, and Cash's meal. They walked the street in silence back to the jail. When they reached the office Cash thanked Mundy for paying for his meal, and for listening to him talk.

"You are young Cash. You have time on your side. Keep searching until you find what makes you happy." Mundy said good bye, and made his way to his truck. "Keep searching...you will find it," Mundy yelled out to him as he got in his truck. Cash stood leaning against the door to the jail, and watched him go. Find what makes me happy he thought. He already knew what would make him happy. Trouble was she was married, having his baby, and acting like it belonged to her husband Will Biggs. "Try being happy living with all that Mundy Winks," he said out loud to the wind. He opened the door to the jail and went inside.

Cash decided to drive to Fair Meadows, and visit Nola. Curious about the birth of her sons, he wanted to see them for himself. There was one other reason and that was to do some checking on Maclaine Moreaux, and his sister, and niece. He met the three of them months ago at Nola's dinner party, and it seemed the sister, and the niece, were still at Fair Meadows. Why were those women still there? Something about that bit of information bothered him. It seemed they might be taking advantage of Nola's giving nature. As far as he knew they were not renting the cabin, or had any agreement about how long they would stay. Cash was uneasy about the whole deal. Maclaine came off as a likeable guy, but there was just something about him that rubbed Cash the wrong way. Mundy mentioned that Jolene, and her daughter Gabrielle, were still there living in the cabin.

He told Cash that he felt like he should say something to Maclaine about them leaving, but Nola insisted he leave them alone. Mundy said they never caused any trouble, but he just felt as if they were taking advantage of Nola's kind heart. There stay in the cabin was originally to be for a few days. A few days now turned into months. Mundy wondered why they would not need to return to New Orleans, and see to their home and lives there. Maclaine was a hard worker who rescued Nola twice. Mundy felt like he owed the man for saving Nola, so that certainly complicated the issue with his relatives and the use of the cabin. There were a couple of disturbing incidences involving some camp fires in the middle of the night. He'd hid in the bushes watching on one occasion. He watched what seemed to be some kind of strange ceremony involving the fire. The story he told Cash involved them dancing around the fire, chanting, and swaying. Every third circle Jolene threw something in the fire from her hand that caused the flame to flare and spark. It was strange, and mesmerizing. Like some kind of creepy ritual Mundy told him.

Nearly dark when he arrived at Fair Meadows; Cash, did not let Nola, know he was coming. He wanted to do a surprise check. He parked his patrol car in front and walked around to the back of the house. No one was in sight, so on impulse he sat off in the direction of the woods where Mundy said the strangers were living. It was dark when he reached the edge of the woods, and he struggled to make his way through the trees, and thicket.

The woods were dense this time of year and mosquitos were out in full force. He could have taken the road that led through the woods to the cabin, but he walked along side it under the cover of the trees and overgrowth. The moon was full, and bright, providing enough light to propel him forward, and not so much that he could be seen.

He could smell wood burning before he saw the fire. Passing by a few more trees he ducked behind a large bush, and peered over the top. Maclaine, and his sister Jolene, were standing near a small fire. The flames were contained by a circle of rocks. They were talking with a man who had his back to Cash. Something about the man was familiar, and when he turned to look toward the path that went to the cabin, Cash could see that is was Will Biggs. What was he doing here? Will was looking toward the path so Cash let his eyes peer in the same direction. He saw Gabrielle appear from the

112

direction of the cabin. He watched utterly stunned as the beautiful young niece of Maclaine Moreaux walked up to Will, and wrapped her long slender arms around his neck. She said something to him that Cash could not understand. Watching as the two embraced he could hardly believe what he was seeing, as she kissed Will Biggs. The kiss was long, and she ran her hands up and down his back. Cash rubbed at the sweat in his eyes, and strained to hear what they were saying. Just not close enough to hear anything more than mumbling frustrated him.

Maclaine, and Jolene, stood by watching, and suddenly Jolene began to dance around the fire chanting, and singing. She was swaying and moving slowly at first, working herself into a frenzy as she picked up the pace. The others watched for a while and just as suddenly as she had begun this ritual, she stopped. The others looked on as she shouted something totally foreign and raised her arm slowly toward the woods where Cash was hiding. Fear gripped his body and his stomach muscles tightened as she pointed her finger directly where he was. Cash didn't wait for what was coming next. Tuning, and moving as fast as his shaky legs would carry him, he ran from the woods. Running and stumbling he didn't bother to conceal himself. He kept running all the way to his patrol car. Driving at break neck speed he didn't stop until he got to the city limits of Monroe. He pulled over, off the road, and let out a breath that until that moment he didn't realize he had been holding. "What... was that...?" He said out loud as he sat trying to get his head together. He would go back and investigate, but not at night. No, the next time he would go while the sun was up, and let some light shine on the darkness he knew was going on in the woods at Fair Meadows. Dark and evil...he thought...dark and evil.

Joseph Camp noticed Cash Atkins' patrol car parked in the front drive, and after a while he went out to see where the young sheriff was. He looked all around the front of the house, and then walked around to the back. It was dark, and Joseph didn't see as well at night as he used too.

Getting on in years and his health starting to falter, he maintained a strict schedule. He ate well, and tried to exercise, but most of all he minded his own business. After the incident with Riley Todd, Joseph learned to leave people to their own lives and concentrate on managing himself. He did not want to be the next heart attack victim. There were moments when Joseph missed his former boss. Choosing to remember the Riley who was kind and good, he buried the evil one along with the body of his former boss, and friend.

It was dark, and Joseph could not see Cash anywhere, so he went back inside. Standing in the door looking out toward the car he was thinking that perhaps he should go down to the barn and find Mundy. Maybe Cash was talking with Mundy about something. About the time he was going to go, his eyes caught a glimpse of someone running. He caught the movement and turned to see Cash running to his patrol car. Watching as Cash reached the driver's side, he saw him jump in, and start the engine in one motion. He quickly turned the car and sped off toward the main road. "Humph," Joseph said. He thought about what he'd seen for a moment. Then he came to the conclusion that Cash must have gotten a call, some police business in town. Maybe an accident, or a domestic dispute. People could be downright ridiculous, he thought. Turning now to retire to his room he made a mental note to ask Mundy why Cash was here.

He stopped walking, and scolded himself for poking around in other people's business.

That nearly got him killed once and he sure didn't want to go through anything like that again. "No old man," he said to himself as he walked up the steps that led to his room, "Just leave it alone."

116

TWELVE

Angelina was now full term, and she knew the baby could come anytime. Everyone thought she was only eight months along with at least four weeks to go. For now she had the doctors, and Will fooled. When the baby did come they would all think it was just a few weeks early. Babies come early. It was common. They would all believe it. Everyone... except Cash Atkins. He knew the truth. Angelina worried about him spilling everything to Will at any moment. She shuddered at the very thought of Will finding out the baby was Cash's. Lately he had been so kind and loving to her. She didn't know if it was out of pity, or if he was falling in love with her, but either way she was elated. In her marriage she learned early on to take whatever bone Will threw at her. It was late in the evening and she began to wonder where he was. The doctor was coming tomorrow for her checkup, and Will promised to be home to hear what he had to say. They made arrangements for a midwife to come when she went into labor, and the doctor was coming to the house too when the baby was close to delivering. Angelina met with the midwife once a week now, and they were growing comfortable with each other. Will found her living in Monroe, and hired her. She asked the doctor if he knew her, and he said he did not. Will assured Angelina that he checked her references and she came highly recommended. So she was as prepared for her child as she could be, and was eager to get it over with, mainly to get her body back. She missed being active. She missed the horses, and riding. Horses were always her passion, and she longed to go to the stable. But, any day now this would be over, and she could give Will what he wanted. For a moment she thought of her mother, and how she needed her now. Brushing a tear away, she told herself she was lucky to have Will, and her nice midwife Jolene Devoreaux.

Sometime in the night Angelina woke to an odd sensation in her stomach. It felt tight, but she didn't feel pain when she woke up. Just a tight uncomfortable feeling. She rose from the bed and switched on the lamp. Looking at the empty bed she wondered where Will was. It wasn't like him to be gone, especially at night. Worry began to creep into her bones. She paced the room trying to imagine where he could be, and worrying that he could have been in some kind of accident. Her stomach was still tight, but still not in pain she decided to get dressed, and go down to the barns looking for him.

She walked across the yard and the field that lay between the barns, and the back yard of the house. She saw no one. There were no lights on in any of the barns. She noticed Will's truck was gone from his usual parking place. Panic, and fear began to rise up in her body. Remembering the accident that took her parents, her mind was imagining the worst. Thinking he must have been in an accident somewhere she turned around heading back to the house to call the Sheriff. She stopped in her tracks when she remembered that Cash Atkins, was the sheriff now. A different kind of fear grabbed hold of her as she thought about Cash. About halfway to the house something more than an uncomfortable tightness hit her out of the blue. The pain took her breath away, and she stooped over at the waist. The baby was coming. The baby was coming and Will was dead. She knew it. He was dead, and now she would be all alone. Panic made her run to the house. Running made the pain worse, but she didn't care. She had to find Will. Somehow… she had to find him. Focusing hard she was able to remember the number for Jolene. She would call and Jolene would come help her. A man answered sleepily when she dialed the number with shaking hands. "This is Angelina Biggs," she said breathless as another pain gripped her body. The man said nothing so Angelina continued. "I'm trying to reach Jolene Devoreaux." Without answering the man hung up. Angelina sat on the edge of the bed holding the phone, and trying to breathe through the contraction that was taking over her body. She dialed a second time. This time Cash Atkins answered.

"Sheriff's office."

"Cash... I, I," she whispered.

"Who is this? Who's there?"

"Angelina... It's me... Angelina." She moaned, and gripped the phone.

Cash felt a coldness in the pit of his stomach. Brushing his hair back from his forehead he tried to shake himself to be sure he wasn't dreaming. "What's wrong Angelina?" There was no answer. The phone line hummed. She was gone. He grabbed his clothes, and began getting dressed. Within minutes he was banging on the doctor's door. He did not respond. After five minutes of banging, and yelling at the top of his lungs, Cash decided to go without him. Heading in the direction of Pine Point, he prayed for Angelina and the baby, driving as fast as he could to get to the woman he loved.

Maclaine, and Will, stood in a clearing under the moonlight. They were talking low and Mundy strained his ears to understand. Earlier Mundy watched as Cash Atkins went sneaking past the barns on his way to the cabin deep in the woods. Following a short time later Mundy, saw Cash, running in the opposite direction back to the main house. The old horseman had always been curious. He continued walking until just at the edge of the clearing. There he saw a small fire encircled by stones. Maclaine Moreaux, and Will

Biggs, were standing by the fire. They were definitely deep in discussion. At times he could hear Will's voice rise, and he seemed agitated. Mundy never saw the women, but he knew these two men were up to no good. Just when he thought he could trust Will, he finds him doing something that seemed ominous, mysterious.

Well, if he had to stay there all night he was keeping his eye on these two, he thought. He might be old by some people's standards, but just like leather; the older it gets the tougher it gets.

With a push, and a scream, Angelina brought life into the world. Tilly, and Cash, helped her as they waited for the doctor to arrive. Tilly was finally able to reach the doctor by phone, and he was on his way. Angelina's beautiful baby girl however, decided not to wait on the doctor. Audreigh Rose, was absolutely perfect. A heart shaped face, and a head of dark hair, her features were feminine, all girl. Her skin was light and she looked like a doll. She cried a little at first but was now sucking her thumb lying in Cash's arm. He stared at her as if he had never seen another human being in all his life. He was totally in love. She looks exactly like me he thought, and she did. Angelina was exhausted, but happy to have the ordeal of childbirth behind her. She was irritated at Will, but she was also worried about where he might be. She watched Cash with the baby, and her anger began to grow. He looked like a drooling idiot standing there holding the child as if she were glass and could shatter at any moment. "Tilly, take the child to the nursery please." She said briskly. Tilly looked at Cash, and then almost apologetically took the child from his arms.

"Missy, don't you want to hold her until the doctor come?" Tilly said.

"I told you to take her to the nursery. Didn't I make myself clear?" Angelina said angrily.

Tilly looked as if she had been slapped, but she said nothing as she turned and headed to the nursery with Audreigh Rose.

"I don't think you should have spoken to Tilly that way Angelina." Cash said.

"You know what Cash? I don't really care to hear your opinion about anything."

"Angelina, really, I…"

"Shut up Cash. You are not the father of that child, and I won't have you hanging around here acting like you are. Understand? I called you because I can't find Will."

Cash stared at her. Her words stung. He fought to keep his emotions in check. He knew that childbirth could be traumatic, and perhaps she lost more blood than she should have. He hoped the doctor would be here soon.

"I will go find him Angelina, as soon as the doctor gets here. Calm down. I am sure Will is all right." Cash thought about what happened earlier in the woods. He thought about Will with that young girl while his wife was having a baby.

The doctor came bounding up the stairs bursting into the room. He spoke to Cash, and then began examining Angelina. Cash excused himself and stood in the hall. Tilly came out of the nursery, which was next door to Angelina's room.

She smiled at Cash, and he started to tell her he was sorry for the way she spoke to her, but Tilly just smiled, brushing it off. The doctor came out of the bedroom declaring Angelina in fine condition. He then asked to see the baby. Cash, and Tilly, escorted the doctor to the nursery. He looked her over from head to toe, and said she was perfect. He commented on what a beautiful baby she

121

was, stating that most often babies are far from pretty when they are first born. She was an exception he said.

After examining both mother, and baby, the doctor left, again saying they were both healthy. Cash was just about to go into the nursery to see Audreigh Rose, when he heard someone coming up the stairs. He turned to see Will standing on the top step. "What are you doing here Cash?" Will's tone was less than friendly.

"Maybe I should ask you why you weren't here... Will Biggs." Cash said.

"I'm here now, and you can go. There's no reason for you to be here. Is there?"

Cash stood looking him in the eye. The pit of his stomach told him that somehow Will knew about the baby. "I'll be going now. Angelina and the baby girl are fine. The doctor just left and I was just about to go hunting for you. Guess I don't need to do that since you showed up on your own."

Will continued to glare at him until Cash told him he might want to check on his wife. Will walked into Angelina's room and closed the door behind him.

"Well your welcome, Will Biggs. And have a good night. What's left of it," Cash said out loud. He opened the door slowly to the nursery, and walked over to the crib. Audreigh Rose was sleeping with her tiny thumb in her mouth. Not being able to stop himself, he picked her up carefully. Holding her close in his arms he peered into her tiny new face. He saw himself, and his Momma. She had his Momma's features. He wondered about the color of her eyes. He and his Momma had the same blue eyes; the color of a summer sky. He kissed her cheek, and breathed in the scent of her. "I will be back for you Audreigh Rose. I don't know how yet, but I'm your daddy, and I will figure out a way for you and me to be together." A tear rolled down his cheek as he placed the sleeping angel back in her crib. Before he turned to leave he said these words, "You are the single most important person in my life now, and the best thing to ever happen to me. I love you little girl." Fighting the urge to pick her up and run; he rushed down the stairs, past a startled Tilly, and out to his car. He didn't cry until he reached the doorway of his jail, then his tears fell like rain.

Will stood beside his wife's bed watching her sleep. She did not hear him come in, and he was not going to wake her. His mind was racing from what he learned tonight. Maclaine, and Jolene, told him about the baby girl that he thought was his. The old Queen had a vision and told Maclaine the baby was not Will's. So many emotions were running around in his head that he didn't know which end was up. The baby girl would never be Queen. They would try again.

They wanted him to try with Gabrielle. Looking at Angelina's beauty illuminated by moonlight streaming in through the window, he knew he should be furious with her. Strangely he was not. He felt sorry for her. All she wanted was for him to love her, but he could not. She had tricked him into marrying her, and just gave birth to a child that she wanted to be his. But she was not. Now he was left with trying to figure out what to do about it. He walked softly to the door, and opened it. He walked out of her room and into the nursery. Slowly, and as quietly as he could, he walked over to the crib. The same moon that shone on the mother's face was illuminating the sleeping daughter. She was beautiful, just like Angelina.

Will realized that she looked very much like her father. She was Cash's baby, for certain. He touched her cheek, and she stirred pursing her lips. Will smiled. It would be easy to play Angelina's game. It would be easy to let her have her fantasy. For now he must. Until he could come up with a plan, he would swallow his pride, and pretend this child was his.

The streets were dark. Velvet black sky, moonless, still. Humidity hung in the air so thick it felt suffocating. Sweat broke out on his neck, and ran down his back. He walked briskly. His breath came in steady puffs. He was on his way to see Mother. She summoned him… again. The baby girl that was born did not belong to the King. They must allow Mother to come up with another plan. Hopefully one that would not fail. The problem lay in the nonbelievers. Their lust, and pleasure, caused a complete and utter failure in procuring the future queen.

He made the turn on the last corner. This was the street where her shop was and where she lived. Home was a couple of rooms in the back of the store where she slept, and ate. Mother did little of either. She sold trinkets, and what she called phony bologny items. The visitors to the city bought the souvenirs like candy. White Fools she called them, but she was more than happy to take their money.

It was late, but a light still caused a faint glow in the shop. The blind was pulled down with closed written in red on the side of the blind facing the street. Small slices of light shone from the edges of the blind. Mother was up, and waiting for him. He entered and the bell on the door clanged loudly. Looking around the empty shop, he knew she must be in back beyond the doorway strung with beads. Just as he was about to walk across the room Mother came through the beads creating a swishing sound. She smiled at him. He returned her smile. Raising her wrinkled old hand she beckoned toward the back, and when she went back through the beads he followed.

The room was small, and hot. Immediately sweat began to form on his brow, under his arms, the back of his neck. Mother seemed oblivious to the heat. Smoke from incense hung in the air, thick, sweet. The incense made him want to cough, but he suppressed the urge. Mother sat down at the small table in the center of the room. He did the same. For five minutes she sat silent, still. As if praying, her hands were folded, eyes shut. He was silent. She always spoke first. It was customary.

"Da baby wus a lie."

"Yes, the baby is not the future Queen." He said.

"Da baby mus be brung to the city."

"I'm not sure I understand Mother."

"Da baby mus be replaced fo da Queen baby. Gabrielle will have da Queen baby now."

"I understand about Gabrielle, and the King. But what about the baby that is there now?"

Mother looked agitated. She clearly told him what he was to do. Shutting her eyes she began to chant. Softly at first and gradually getting louder, and louder, sounding more distressed. She reached a screaming pitch, suddenly stopped, and stood up. She opened her eyes looking toward the beaded doorway. Pointing she hissed, and when she opened her mouth to speak he recoiled in terror. Her tongue was snakelike; her eyes like slits.

"Bring… da baby… to da city." She hissed the words at him.

Her words made his gut seize. Thinking he might vomit he stood, and she motioned for him to leave. They stood at the door, and he waited for his customary kiss on the cheek from the old woman. She made him stand, and wait for a few moments. She was angry with him, but he was not sure why. Uncomfortable, and hot,

125

he just wanted to get outside. Finally she leaned in to kiss his cheek. Her lips were dry, and cracked.

She had an odor of something old, ancient, a smell he could not quite explain. He opened the door stepping out into the cool air. He had never been so glad to leave her. She was unpredictable, and prone to unwarranted rage. She did not entertain fools, and had zero tolerance of people who were slow to understand. Mother hated repetition, having little to no patience. She did not watch him go, another sign she was still angry. He made it to the end of the street, and turned to wave, but she was not there. This upset him more than anything. He turned the corner, leaned up against the brick building, and began retching. When finally he stopped, he pulled a hanky from his pocket. He wiped his face, walking on through the velvet night.

THIRTEEN

Mundy walked around the barn, stunned to see Will Biggs standing near the corral talking with Maclaine Moreaux. The two men noticed him, both raising a hand to signal hello. Waving back, he went into his office in the barn. The tack room served him well as an office. It was also a place to work on saddles, bridles, and other equipment. Mundy thought about walking out to the corral and asking those two fellows how they knew each other. They were engrossed in conversation that appeared serious when Mundy came upon them. He decided the better thing to do would be to come in here, and get to work. A saddle needed repaired and oiled, so minding his own business, and getting down to work was what he chose to do.

A half hour or so later Will knocked on Mundy's open office door. He looked up smiling at Will. "Enter at your own risk," Mundy said.

"How are you old man?" Will asked.

"I'm well Will Biggs. I'm very well. And you?"

"Never better. Angelina…she had the baby." Will spoke softly as if he were speaking some secret. For a new father he did not look too happy. Mundy thought he might make that comment, but held back.

"Congratulations Will. Is the baby and Angelina doing well?"

"Both are fine." He paused a moment looking off in the distance. Mundy thought he looked absolutely lost. Compassion moved on him for the man he once considered a son. "Her name is

Audreigh…Audreigh Rose. The baby is a girl. Very beautiful like her mother." He spoke as if he were talking about someone else's family. His voice held a sadness Mundy never heard in him before.

"Will, ain't none of my business. And boy you can sure enough tell me that it's nothing to me, but what's wrong? You sure don't act like a man that just became a father." Mundy knew he should leave it alone. Will didn't even know about the boys. Nola's boys. Unless maybe Maclaine had told him. Will continued staring off in the distance. He looked as if he were holding a dam back that was going to burst at any moment. Finally he spoke.

"I didn't Mundy. I didn't just become a father. Cash Atkins just became a father."

"Boy, are you feelin all right? You ain't makin no sense at all. What has Cash got to do with the baby?" Mundy asked.

"Audreigh Rose, is Cash Atkins baby Mundy. I'm not Audreigh Rose's father. But I just found out that I am a father after all."

"Son, I…" Mundy started to explain.

"You should have told me months ago. You knew and didn't tell me. Nola's boys are my sons."

Mundy stood speechless. Not knowing what to say, he had no excuse other than trying to please Nola, by helping her keep a secret. "She tried to keep from hurting you Will. She wanted to protect her children too. That's all she was trying to do. Nola didn't want to hurt Angelina either. Surely you can understand?"

"No. No… I will never understand someone keeping a father from his sons. After all that Nola went through as a child, and she would turn around and do the same thing to her children." Will was shaking. Angry, and hurt, he started out the door.

"Will, all this can be worked out."

"Oh you can count on that old man," he said as he stopped and turned to face Mundy. "I'm getting ready to work all this out. My way. Not your way. Not Cash Atkins' way. Not even Nola's way. It's about time Will Biggs gets his way."

Mundy watched him stomp away. Off in the distance, in the direction where earlier Will had stood staring, storm clouds gathered. Mundy shook his head and went back inside the barn just as huge drops of rain fell like tears from heaven. He thought of Nola, and knew he must warn her of a different kind of storm.

A storm on the horizon that would leave a path of heartache, and destruction, for all those in its path. All Mundy could do was watch and wait.

Will Biggs, and Maclaine Moreaux, met in New Orleans when they were both barely out of their teens. Maclaine, introduced Will, to his culture and his religion. Will became fascinated with Black Magic, and the mysterious culture of that area. The two became fast friends. It was Will who helped Maclaine get a position at Fair Meadows. No one but the two of them, and Maclaine's sister, and niece, were aware of their past history. Maclaine's family took Will in, becoming initiated into their culture and way of living. Maclaine introduced his friend to Mother, and she too became fond of the white boy. Much of what he learned about their ceremonies and rituals came from Mother's teachings. It was Mother who sent him to Fair Meadows to take a job working with the horses. She said she saw a young woman who would inherit Fair Meadows and possibly give birth to the new Queen. The woman Mother said was from New Orleans, and was of the Joubert bloodline. She was taken at birth and the plans for her failed when she was abandoned, and found by someone else. Stolen away twice she was raised isolated, secluded, and hidden. Mother found her in a vision and she sent Will to be with her, but the plan became twisted. Will had failed. Now he must find a way to fix everything. Nola gave birth to Will's children, but they were boys. He had failed to have a daughter with Nola, and Audreigh Rose was not his child.

Will sat thinking about all that was going on when Angelina came into his office. He tried to avoid her as much as possible since she gave birth to Audreigh Rose. The baby would have been acceptable except for the fact that she belonged to Cash Atkins. Angelina did not realize that Will knew. He must keep everything as it was until he could form a plan. Angelina stood looking at Will for a few moments before she spoke. "Where have you been Will?" She asked.

"I have been working Angelina. That's what I do… I work."

"Will you have been gone for three days. I want to know…I think I deserve to know… where you've been."

"I told you. Now get out. I am busy. I don't have time to argue with your imagination."

Angelina stood fists clenched and face red. She was so angry at him. She just knew he was with Nola those three days. She turned to leave his office, but at the door she turned back to face him. Seething, with teeth clenched tight she said in a low voice, "Don't let me find out you were with Nola Todd those three days." She turned and stormed out of his office slamming the door behind her.

"Stupid girl," he spoke the words out loud, and then got down to business.

Angelina was back in her room thinking about Will, and what she could do to make sure no one came between her, and the only man she loved.

The nanny walked into the room with Audreigh Rose and approached her, but Angelina put her hand up to stop her. She told the nanny in a very irritated tone to take the child back to the nursery.

"But ma'am, the babe is hungry and you need to nurse her now." The young woman stood wide eyed and waiting for a response.

Without looking at the nanny or Audreigh Rose, Angelina again raised her hand to shoo the nanny away.

"I won't tell you a third time to take the child to the nursery. Bottle feed her, or breast feed her yourself. I don't care. Just get out of my room." Her voice rose with every word until she was shouting at the girl. The nanny looked obviously distressed, and her cheeks turned crimson when Angelina suggested she nurse the baby. She turned and took the now crying child from the room.

Angelina lay her head back on the sofa and closed her eyes. All she could see in her mind was Will and Nola together rolling around on the ground. The image of the night she saw them together was always near. She saw them when she closed her eyes. She saw them every time Will was late coming home, or when he didn't come home at all. Lately she even saw them in her dreams. She felt as if she were going mad. Didn't that woman know that he was married and had a daughter now? Didn't she care? Well Angelina thought suddenly sitting up and opening her eyes. There was one way of getting answers to her questions. Tomorrow she, and Audreigh Rose, would pay a visit to Fair Meadows.

It was about time that someone put Nola Rain Todd in her place. Angelina Biggs was just that someone to do it.

Smiling she got up from the sofa and began humming a melody to some old lullaby. She kept humming as she made her way to the nursery.

After breakfast the next morning Angelina told the nanny to dress Audreigh Rose for travel. Nanny Arlyn gave her a questioning look. She responded curtly that she was taking the baby to see an old friend. Once they were in the car Angelina told the driver to take them to Fair Meadows, then sitting back she closed her eyes. Since the accident, car rides made her nervous, and sick to her stomach. Nanny Arlyn, and baby, sat on the other side of the back seat. Audreigh Rose was sound asleep, and her nanny stared out the window. Arlyn came highly recommended, and she was from New Orleans. Will had taken great care in hiring her, so he assured Angelina. So far she seemed to be a competent nanny who spent all of her time with the baby. Out of concern Tilly, told Angelina she needed to spend more time with the child, or the baby might think the nanny was her mother. Angelina didn't respond to Tilly, but she kept the thought to herself that she didn't really care. The baby was not Will's; Audreigh belonged to Cash. Every day she lived with the fear Will would find out and leave. The baby was a thorn in her side. She knew it was wrong, even unnatural for a mother to hate her child, but she did. She thought of her own mother for a moment, and guilt rose up inside her. Susie Oliver loved Angelina, and would have given her life for her. In a way she did just that.

"Where are we ma'am?" The nanny asked.

"This is Fair Meadows. It is owned by the Todd family. Recently the Todd's have been reduced to one heir. Nola Rain Todd."

"It's beautiful," the nanny said staring out the car window.

132

"Yes, I suppose it is." Angelina whispered. "A beautiful facade sometimes hides something very ugly, Miss Arlyn." Nanny Arlyn snapped her head around to look at Angelina. She'd never heard Mrs. Biggs use her proper name before. She always addressed her as nanny. It sounded strange to hear her call her Miss Arlyn.

"Yes ma'am, I suppose you are right. But I see nothing ugly here, just beauty all around."

Angelina sighed, and smoothed her hair back. She wanted to look her very best when she approached Nola. She looked across the seat at the silly young girl so easily influenced by the beauty of the Todd estate. She said nothing more as the car came to a stop in the front of the house near the fountain. A statue of two young boys playing in the center of a large pool of water softened the majestic stone edifice of the main house. Enamored of the beautiful fountain, Nanny Arlyn clapped her hands in delight. It was whimsical, and nostalgic, she thought. Angelina broke through those thoughts instructing her to gather the baby, and follow her to the massive oak doors. Beyond those doors lay the answer to all of Angelina's problems.

Today she was finally going to put an end to the relationship between Will, and Nola Rain. With a look of fierce determination she marched up the stone steps and knocked on the door while nanny Arlyn, and baby Audreigh, followed close behind.

Since the strange night in the woods when Mundy witnessed some sort of ritual involving Maclaine and Will, he tried to stay close to the house keeping watch over Nola, and her sons. He heard someone knocking and walked from the kitchen to the foyer opening the door. Mundy was surprised to find Angelina Biggs staring at him. She wore a smile on her face that looked as if she had spent a great deal of time practicing to perfect. Behind her was a very lovely young woman holding a baby that he guessed was Audreigh Rose. "Why… Mrs. Biggs, how nice to see you," Mundy said politely. He motioned for them to come in, and asked them to follow him to the sitting room. "I will tell Nola you are here, and have Naomi bring some refreshments. I must say I am pleasantly surprised at your visit. Was Nola expecting you?"

"Well Mr. Winks," Angelina said flatly, "When did you get promoted to butler?"

Mundy's cheeks grew warm as he looked into such a beautiful face. Before he could answer she continued. "I thought the butler of this house was Joseph Camp. But I see you have taken his position. Congratulations Mr. Winks." Again before he could say anything they were interrupted by the sound of crying.

Angelina jerked her head around trying to detect where the sound was coming from. It was an infant cry. The cry of a newborn. She glanced at her own child, still sleeping in Arlyn's arms. Confused she started to ask Mundy what was going on when Nola walked into the room. She was carrying a crying baby in one arm, and a sleeping one in the other.

Nola entered the room with her head down trying to comfort her crying baby. When she noticed someone was in the room she took a couple of steps backward inhaling sharply, and audibly.

"Angelina," she whispered, "What, what are you doing here?"

She looked from Angelina, to Mundy, and then her eyes came to rest on nanny Arlyn, holding Audreigh Rose. Angelina was staring hard, eyes narrowed at the twins in Nola's arms. For a few seconds there was total silence. Suddenly as if released from some type of trance all of them except for the nanny began to speak at once.

"Nola," Angelina's voice cut through the chaos. As Nola and Mundy grew silent Angelina began again. "Nola, I do apologize for dropping in on you unannounced, and I realize uninvited." She was smiling sweetly. The smile and her speech seemed well rehearsed. "We were just out driving and on the spur of the moment I decided to come show you Will's daughter." When saying the word daughter she sounded as if she were hissing. The smile was gone, and her breathing was rapid.

Nola could see her chest rising and falling with anger that was close to being out of control. Her cheeks were bright red. There was a fire in her beautiful dark eyes that was both terrifying, and mesmerizing. Nola was suddenly aware she had tightened her grip on her sons and she relaxed her arms a bit. So stunned by the audacity of this woman that she was speechless, it seemed Angelina on the other hand had a lot more to say.

"Mundy would you please find Debra and Ruth? Ask them to come take the children to the nursery immediately." Nola suddenly felt as if her sons' safety might be in question. She had no nanny, but she sometimes asked for help from Naomi's granddaughters. Within minutes Debra and Ruth entered the room with Mundy following behind. They took the boys from Nola's arms and hurried away with them. Nola then turned her attention to Angelina. "Won't you please sit down?" Mundy would you ask Naomi to bring some tea…and cookies perhaps?" Mundy nodded and left the room. Angelina sat down on the small sofa. Nanny Arlyn sat in a large chair opposite the sofa and Nola chose another chair opposite the sofa as well. The three women sat in awkward silence until Angelina suddenly began to blurt out the real reason she came to see Nola.

"Mrs. Todd, I came here to ask you to stay away from my husband."

Nola feeling as if she'd been doused with cold water responded. "Angelina, I have had no contact with your husband since he left my employment.

So I really don't understand nor do I really care to understand what you are talking about."

Angelina was livid. She felt as if she couldn't breathe and she struggled to get her words out. "You are a liar Nola. I saw you with Will, and I saw what the two of you were doing at the creek." She stood and stuck her finger in Nola's face. "Those twins are Will's aren't they? Answer me?" She grabbed Nola by the arms, and stood her to her feet. Stunned for a moment Nola who was half a foot shorter stood looking up into the furious face of Angelina Biggs. Without thinking Nola yanked her arms from Angelina's grip, took a step back, and struck her full force in the face. Angelina stumbled falling back on the sofa, but she did not stay down. Rising off the sofa she came at Nola like a raging bull. She knocked her to the floor and was straddled the smaller woman striking first one cheek and then the other. Mundy heard the commotion and came running. Nanny Arlyn had risen from her seat and was backed up to the wall holding tightly to a now squalling Audreigh Rose. Mundy pulled Angelina off Nola, and she turned to attack him. Screaming at the top of her lungs she caught Mundy off guard, and he fell backwards. Hitting the floor with a sickening thud it knocked the wind out of him. Angelina jumped on him pummeling him with her fists. She fought like a man, and with her height, and weight, she had an advantage on Mundy. All he could really do was put his hands up to try to deflect the blows. There was no way he would ever hit a woman even if she did deserve it.

Nola managed to crawl out of the room to the foyer where Naomi stood wide eyed and terrified. "Call Cash Naomi." Nola whispered. Bloody, and breathless she managed to get to her feet, and went

136

back into the chaos. Picking up a lamp she cracked it over Angelina's head.

She watched as Angelina sat straight up, still straddling Mundy, then leaning to the left she fell off him, and onto the floor. Nola was horrified as she screamed at Mundy "I have killed her Mundy. Oh my God… I have killed her."

Cash Atkins could not believe his eyes when he entered the small sitting room. Angelina was lying on the floor, Mundy Winks was standing beside Nola, holding her. The two of them were scratched and bleeding. A young woman who Cash didn't recognize stood over against the wall holding Audreigh Rose. Naomi called him in the throes of panic, and he got there as fast as he could. He went first to Angelina who was coming around. A lamp lay close by her and he could feel a small lump on her head. She opened her eyes and smiled at him. "Cash would you be a dear and help me to my feet?" Angelina asked.

"I think we should call an ambulance Angelina. You know… just to get you checked out." Cash said.

"I don't need an ambulance." Angelina was irritated and she shook his hold from her while slowly standing to her feet. Totally disheveled she tried to smooth her clothes and her hair. Looking around the room from one shocked face to another she finally spoke. "This little visit did not go exactly as I planned. I must be going now but let's…NOT… do this again sometime." She motioned for Arlyn and headed out of the room.

"Hold on just one minute there," Cash said. "We need to find out what happened here. You have a couple of folks that are standing here bleeding all over the place. What is going on?"

137

"I have no idea what happened Sheriff Atkins. Perhaps you should ask those two."

"Let her leave Cash. I am not pressing charges." Nola said.

"Pressing charges," Angelina shouted. "I should be pressing charges against you Nola Rain...you...you..."

"That's enough Angelina." Cash said. "Get out of here before I haul you off to jail whether Nola wants me too or not."

"Well I never..."

"Well I never either girl, now get out." Cash was beginning to lose his patience with her and she knew it.

"Come along Arlyn, these people are starting to bore me." She turned and marched out of the room and out through the front doors. They stood and listened as car doors slammed and an engine started. Once she had gone; the three of them let out a huge audible sigh of relief. They looked around the room, and then at each other.

Nola started it first. A giggle that she tried hard to stifle. As it became louder Cash joined in and then Mundy, until all of them were bent over belly laughing.

When the laughter subsided Nola straightened up and putting her hands on her small hips declared; "That girl is crazy as a Bessy Bug." Mundy, and Cash, looked at each other then suddenly the two of them burst into laughter all over again.

Their laughter would soon fade when Angelina proved just how crazy she was.

FOURTEEN

Angelina returned home acting as if nothing happened. She did not
tell Will about the incident swearing nanny Arlyn to secrecy. Nanny
Arlyn's alliance however did not lie with Angelina. She worked for
Will Biggs. After they arrived at Pine Point, she slipped some
powder into Angelina's tea, which caused her to sleep the rest of the
day, and through the night. While she was sleeping Arlyn went to
Will's office, and reported the whole sordid event. Will was livid.
He could not believe Angelina would attack Nola, and Mundy
Winks. He spent the rest of the day trying to decide whether to go
strangle Angelina in her sleep, or make a trip to Fair Meadows to

check on Mundy, and Nola. Arlyn told him that Cash Atkins was called to Fair Meadows, and she was stunned that he had not arrested Angelina. Will was not surprised. He knew Cash was sweet on Angelina. At the end of the day Will decided to do nothing. If Nola or Mundy were seriously hurt; Cash would have taken Angelina to jail. The Nola he knew probably would not press charges. Tomorrow he would go see her. He had not seen his sons yet, and he felt it was time to let Nola know that he knew about them. As for Angelina, he was so sick of dealing with her. She had to be disposed of, but he knew he must be careful. Any sympathy that he felt for her early on in their relationship was swallowed up in a growing disdain for her ugly, jealous behavior. She could not hold a candle to Nola. Perhaps it was time to disclose that to her.

Maybe that would be the last few words she ever heard. Without realizing he was speaking out loud, he repeated the words he heard in his head. "You cannot hold a candle to Nola Rain."

Angelina woke up in a fog. She tried to sit up but felt so dizzy she lay back on the pillows. Putting a hand to the back of her head she felt the bump. It was small and very sore. She thought the bump must be the reason she felt so woozy. The sun was up. Glancing at her clock she could barely make out the time. The numbers were blurry. She was thinking perhaps a doctor should have a look at her head. Dismissing that idea she got to her feet. A knock on the door startled her and she sat down on the bed still dizzy. "Yes… come in," she said. Arlyn entered the room with the baby in her arms. "Arlyn I don't feel well. Please take her away." Angelina waved her hand back and forth as if she were shooing a fly.

"Ma'am, I may be stepping out of line, but I must tell you. You need to spend time with your daughter. The two of you need to bond. Audreigh Rose will bond with me… and believe I am her mother."

Angelina took her hand away from her eyes. She lifted her head and stared at the young girl. The look in her eyes made the nanny back up instinctively.

"You little twit," Angelina began. Her voice was controlled, hissing. "Don't you ever come in here and proceed to tell me how to mother my child."

"But, but…ma'am…"

"Get out of my room," Angelina was shouting now at the top of her lungs.

Picking up a glass that was on the night stand she hurled it toward the girl as Arlyn retreated. The glass hit her in the back and broke into pieces as it hit the floor. Arlyn didn't stop until she reached the nursery with the baby, and once inside slammed the door shut. After locking it she walked across the room and lay Audreigh Rose in her crib. The baby smiled up at her, and a breathless, but unhurt nanny Arlyn smiled back. "It's all right Audreigh Rose," she said. "Nanny will be your Momma. Nanny will love you and protect you." The baby smiled sweetly up at the sound of Arlyn's voice. She began to coo back at her and Arlyn walked away to the large closet in the nursery. She opened the door and retrieved a small travel bag from a larger suit case. Inside the travel bag was a small velvet tote. Opening the velvet tote she pulled out a small fabric wrapped bundle. Unwrapping the bundle she stood looking at a small rag doll. She would show Angelina Biggs a thing or two. The woman had no idea who she was dealing with. No idea at all. But she would soon learn. Arlyn pulled a straight pin from the velvet bag and jabbed it hard into the stomach of the doll. At that exact moment she heard a scream from Angelina's room. Arlyn smiled. Leaving the pin buried deep inside the doll she placed it back in the tote, and then inside the larger suit case. She placed all of the luggage inside the closet and shut the door. She heard another loud scream, then running as Will and Tilly came up the stairs.

Walking over to the crib she picked up the baby and sat in the rocker singing a lullaby Mother taught her years ago. Yes, she thought, Angelina must be taught a lesson. Baby Audreigh cooed louder as nanny Arlyn rocked and sang.

Will banged on the oak entry doors and stood waiting for someone to answer. He stared out across the yard toward the tree line. Something caught his eye and he squinted in the sunlight to focus on the edge of the woods. A shiny object reflecting the sun blinked from the base of the trees as if relaying some type of signal. He thought of Maclaine, but knew it was not him. Maclaine would approach him directly. Just as he was thinking of walking that way to investigate Joseph opened the door. Will was stunned by the butler's physical changes. He looked haggard and frazzled. His swift decline was shocking and sad. "Mr. Biggs, how nice to see you. Won't you come in?" Joseph stepped aside and Will walked into the foyer. "Is Miss Nola expecting you?"

"No Joseph, she is not. Would you please let her know I am here?" Will said.

"Of course. Perhaps you would like to wait in the sitting room."

"Yes thank you Joseph." Will walked down the hall to the sitting room as Joseph left to find Nola.

Will looked up as Nola entered the room. Her beauty took his breath. An air of maturity and grace, a confidence that she had not possessed before could not go unnoticed now. He found her even more alluring and desirable if that were possible. He cleared his throat to say her name but she spoke first. "Will, I am surprised to see you. I hope everything is well in your world." Nola said. She sat down opposite him. He waited until she was seated then sat down as well.

"Everything is fine Nola, I…well I wanted to see the twins." Will said.

"My sons are sleeping at the moment Mr. Biggs," Nola said flatly. She held back any emotion. Learning to control herself was becoming easier for her. Will stared hard at her.

"Nola," he said softly as his face relaxed. "I know the boys are mine. It is time for me to see them. They need to begin to bond with me. They need to know I'm their father. You of all people should understand and agree with that." For a few moments Nola sat silent, looking at Will as if she were seeing a stranger. Finally she stood to her feet slowly, and spoke.

"You are right Will. They do need a father. And I pray nightly that the Father above will send just the right man into my son's lives."

"Nola, wait, please…"

"Don't you dare interrupt me Will Biggs. I will have my say." Nola was angry now, and barely able to breathe.

All the loneliness and hurt from being used by the man she loved and then discarded like a dirty tissue came bubbling to the surface, and spilling out. Will stood up then and with his hat in his hands started to walk past her to leave. He stopped and stood stiffly and still. "You will never be the father of my children. Do you understand? Hurting me by letting me believe we had a future, and then running back to Angelina…" she raised her head a little higher as tears threatened to spill from her beautiful eyes. "Hurting me was wrong, but I promise you this, you will not get the opportunity to hurt my children. Not as long as I draw a breath." Nola was shaking now, staring at Will's back as he stood in the doorway leading into the hall. Without turning around he spoke to her. Low and soft, and with conviction.

"We shall see Nola dear… we shall see."

The pain in Angelina's stomach eased some overnight, but it was still there. Nagging, and deep, like a tooth ache. She tried to get out of bed, but standing made the pain worse. She was doubled over when Tilly came in the room to check on her. "Missy, what on earth is wrong with you?" The old cook crossed the room and took Angelina's arm to steady her. Through clenched teeth she tried to speak, but the pain was so severe it took her breath. Speaking softly, and guiding her back on to the bed, Tilly told her she was calling the doctor. Leaving Angelina alone to use the downstairs phone, a sense of foreboding hit Tilly like an icy wind as she passed the nursery. She stopped, but did not hear a sound as she stood and listened at the closed door to the nursery. Maybe Audreigh Rose was napping and Arlyn might be resting as well. Miss Arlyn insisted that her bed be in the nursery, and Will gave everyone orders that they were to accommodate her wishes. There was something strange about the nanny that Tilly could not explain. Something about her frightened the old woman, and she tried to stay out of her way. Tilly would have liked to have had more contact with the baby, but Arlyn rarely let anyone hold her, or take care of her in any way. After standing at the nursery door listening for a moment Tilly continued on downstairs and called the doctor.

"I could not find anything obviously wrong with your wife Mr. Biggs. Perhaps it is stress from childbirth, or it could be any number of things. I think just to err on the side of caution, she should come to the hospital for some tests. Just to put her mind and my mind at ease. Actually I think it would ease all our minds to look into this more thoroughly." The doctor had examined Angelina and was in the foyer with Will discussing what he found, or rather his lack of finding anything wrong.

"If she feels the need to have some tests I think that would be a good idea. It is up to her doctor. I will of course see that she gets to the hospital for anything she needs." Will said.

"Good. If she agrees have her come in the morning. We can admit her. It will make the testing more practical if she is admitted. Good day then."

"Yes... good day to you, doctor." Will closed the door behind the doctor and started down the hall to the stairs. He was wondering with every step that he took if this was some pathetic play for sympathy on his lovely bride's part. He would find a way to get to the bottom of all this.

The baby was growing and thriving under the care of nanny Arlyn. Audreigh Rose was beautiful like her mother, but she had a sweet temperament that Angelina lacked. She was a good baby who rarely cried. She bonded to her nanny, and smiled at Arlyn in recognition of her face and voice. She was kicking now and cooing, and would soon be sitting up on her own. Arlyn was very attached to her. Early on in this assignment she tried to get Angelina to bond with her child. She knew bonding with her mother would be detrimental to the child's overall growth and development. Angelina emotionally abandoned her child and refused to be a mother to her. Arlyn stepped easily into that role. She was such a beautiful, sweet baby that Arlyn could not help but love her. Arlyn felt sympathy for the little girl that no one wanted; not even her parents. The one person who did want the child was forbidden to see her. Sheriff Cash Atkins showed an obvious interest in Audreigh Rose.

Arlyn bent over the crib looking into the sweet face of the sleeping baby. She softly sang a few lines from a lullaby she heard her own mother sing. She pushed a lock of dark curly hair off the baby's forehead. She had long thick lashes that touched her cheeks when her eyes were closed in sleep. Her little lips formed a perfect bow. Her features were flawless; like a doll. She had fallen in love with this child.

From out of nowhere Arlyn felt a piercing. Sharp and painful it took her breath away. It was not a stabbing of her flesh, but of the blade of knowledge, and foreboding, plunging deep inside her. The sharpness cut her very soul. She knew that any emotion she felt for Audreigh Rose would get in the way of a future that was already decided for the child. Standing over her now her heart broke at the thought of what was to come. How could she now give the child over, and go on with her life, as if she had never cared for her; as if she had never loved her.

Tears hot and steady fell from her eyes, and landed on the blanket near the child. She heard a voice in her head clear, and calm. "Run with her. Run with her." She sucked in her breath and took a step back, placing her hands over her ears as she tried to stop the voice. Over, and over, she heard it. The voice grew louder, and louder, until she fell on the floor in a sobbing heap.

"Run with her...run with her."

FIFTEEN

Nola's boys were growing like weeds. She smiled watching them cooing, and flailing their arms, and legs, as they lay on a blanket. Earlier she, and Mundy, walked to the creek with them stretching out a blanket on the ground to lay them on. The four of them sat at the water's edge enjoying this bright sunny day. Fall was always a favorite time of year for Nola. She enjoyed the sunshine and cooler temperatures. Nights were clear, crisp, and cool. It seemed the cooler nights revealed so many more stars than what were visible at other times of the year. Star gazing was something she had always loved to do. Someday she would do it with her sons. When they were a bit older.

Mundy broke through her thoughts as she gazed at her cooing twins. "What do you think about Nola? I mean, what do you dream of for your boys?"

"I want them to be happy Mundy. More than anything else I want them to grow up knowing real happiness. I love them with all my being.

Mundy studied Nola's soft pretty face for a moment.

"You are a wonderful mother. How could they not be happy?"

Nola smiled at him, and his heart warmed.

He cared so much for this woman child. He could not love her any more if she were his blood daughter. For that very reason he felt as if he could be candid with her.

"I had a rough childhood. Mother loved me... in her own way, but...well...it was rough. I never had a real Momma. And I certainly never had a daddy." She continued smiling at him. "You are the closest I have ever had to family. You are like a father to me."

Mundy's eyes misted. He cleared his throat.

"That is why Nola, I feel like it is important for these boys to know their daddy."

"Mundy..."

"Wait girl, hear me out. You of all people should understand how it feels to grow up without a mother and father. Think of all the times you longed to belong to someone."

Nola took her gaze off Mundy, and stared at the flowing water.

"Will is married. He has a child with Angelina."

"He has two sons with you."

"It is all so complicated Mundy." She looked down at her sons. Jackson was asleep. William was looking back at her smiling brightly. He was flailing his arms and legs about as if trying to roll over. Her heart melted at his smile.

"Think about it." Mundy smiled down at the baby who was now looking at him. William followed the sound of Mundy's voice. Just like Nola, his old heart melted at the drooling, babbling sight of William.

"I think about it all the time Mundy. I want to make all the right choices for my sons."

Mundy shook his head. He took her hand and held it. So soft it felt in his leathery cowboy hand.

"Love is knowing in your heart that no matter what someone says or does, you will love them anyway. No ifs. No buts. It is knowing they could never do anything to change your love for them. God loves us that way. Perfect love. If we are blessed in our lifetime we will have that kind of human love too." Mundy's eyes took on a faraway look. "I once had that kind of love." He dropped his eyes and looked away toward the water.

Nola's eyes were misty now. She wanted to ask him about that love he mentioned. Who had he loved with a perfect, unconditional love? A slight breeze came up suddenly, and her thoughts turned to Dominy Brooks. Oh how she missed her dear sweet friend. So many times she would have liked to ask her advice, and sink into Dominy's loving arms. She lifted her head and heard Dominy's voice. It seemed to float in with the wind, and then just as quickly it was gone. Gone like the leaf that floated into the creek from a nearby tree. Nola watched as the leaf disappeared downstream.

Dominy's voice seemed to be carried away with the leaf, but she clearly heard her say, "Let the Lord hold you girl. He loves you. Let the Lord hold you in His arms."

Nola was in the kitchen talking with Naomi about Thanksgiving when Joseph interrupted the two women. Joseph informed her that Cash Atkins was in the sitting room waiting to speak with Nola. She excused herself, and made her way to the sitting room.

Cash was standing when Nola entered the room. After greeting each other she asked him to please sit down. He did so, but he never took his eyes off Nola. She looked radiant after spending time in the out of doors. Her cheeks were glowing and Cash thought she never looked prettier. He told her so.

"You look lovely Nola. Motherhood agrees with you."

"Why… thank you Cash. But I am sure the sheriff of Bryce County did not come all the way out here to Fair Meadows to pass out compliments." Nola said laughing.

"You are right. I came to see how you were. I mean…well… after the incident with Angelina."

"Oh Cash, I'm fine. Really."

"Well, there is something else. Something that's been bothering me." Cash fidgeted with the brim of his hat.

"What is it? What's bothering you Cash? You know I understand your position in the county.

I know you're the sheriff but, I also consider you my friend. If something is wrong you can tell me."

"Nola, it's…its Angelina. Her baby, I mean…"

"Yes. Audreigh Rose. She is such a pretty baby. But what?" Nola said.

"Audreigh Rose is my baby. She is not Will's baby. She is mine."

A sensation swept over Nola. She felt like someone had thrown cold water on her. She gasped at Cash's confession. Her first thought was of Will. Did he know? How could Audreigh Rose be Cash Atkins baby? Cash cleared his throat and spoke again.

"That is not the only reason I came to see you. The baby is a personal matter between us…between friends."

"What is it Cash?"

"It's the women staying in your cabin." Cash said.

Nola thought for a second, still trying to wrap her mind around the fact that Audreigh Rose was Cash's baby.

"The women? Gabrielle… and Jolene?"

"Yes. Officially I am here because of them. I saw some unusual behavior involving those women, and your hired hand. Will Biggs was in on it too. I don't know what they are up to but I know in my gut it's not good." Nervous and troubled by what he had seen, the memory made him twist his hat in his hands.

"What did you see?"

"I don't want to talk about the details just yet. I just wanted to let you know I am doing some investigating and well…I just want you to be warned. Be careful. That's all. Just be careful." The way he said the word careful made the back of her neck tingle.

"They have been here nearly a year Cash, and really have been no trouble. They keep mostly to themselves. Maclaine is Jolene's brother you know."

Cash stood to his feet. He looked at Nola and she thought he seemed tired, and out of sorts. Considering all he had told her it was little wonder. He reached for Nola's hand and with a trembling smile he warned her once more before leaving.

"For your children's sake you must be careful. You must be very careful Nola."

Nola stared at Cash's back as he left the room. Then she looked down at her arms which were now covered in goose bumps. "Be careful Nola...for your children's sake," rang in her ears.

Sometime in the night Mundy woke suddenly from a deep sleep. He sat up in the dark bunkhouse and rubbed his old eyes with the back of rough hands. Slowly his eyes became adjusted to the dark and something caught his attention at the window to the left of the room. Why was the window glowing?

He rubbed his eyes again, and throwing the blanket back he stood up, and walked to the window.

"Fire," he mumbled, and then it hit him. "FIRE!" This time he screamed the word. Behind him he could hear the rustling sounds of the hands who were jolted awake by Mundy's scream. Mundy stood frozen staring at the flames that were coming from the woods behind the stables. Men were yelling and pulling on their clothes. They were hurriedly trying to dress and get outside to the fire.

"Call the fire department," someone yelled.

Still Mundy stood looking on in horror until Dave Grimm came up behind him and poked him hard on the shoulder.

"Mundy, come on man. Go up to the main house and call the fire department. I will get the men out there and try to get a line of water to those woods." Dave waited for a response. When Mundy didn't answer he grabbed the old man's shoulders and jerked him around to face him. Dave had never seen such a look of terror on the old boss's face.

"Dave...Dave...the cabin...those women." Mundy managed to whisper.

Dave dropped his hold on Mundy, turning and running out the door toward the woods. As he ran he yelled to the men to get a line of water to the woods.

He could see it would be impossible to enter the woods where the trail led to the cabin. He would have to go left, and enter where the trees had not yet ignited. Mundy ran out the door of the bunkhouse and turned to the right heading for the main house. The fire was massive. They would need all the help they could get. For the moment his fear of what may have happened to the cabin and to Gabrielle, and Jolene, was overridden by his fear of what could happen to the entire farm, and Nola. Reaching the back of the house he tried the door, but it was locked. He banged with all his might while yelling for Joseph. When that failed to raise anyone; he ran around to the side of the house where Nola's second floor balcony was. Old Mundy stood there below the French doors yelling her name.

Mundy was shouting her name over, and over. Nola could hear him in a muffled way. Why did he sound so far away?

"Mundy…Mundy…"

Nola jerked awake. She sat up and listened, straining to hear. She bolted out of bed and ran to the French doors throwing them open so violently that they banged the walls. Mundy was down below her second floor balcony, and he was yelling for her. The glow of the woods to her right and beyond the corral caught her eye as she turned to see a massive fire that took her breath away. All she could do was stand and stare in disbelief. After a few moments Mundy's frightened, persistent, yelling paid off.

"MUNDY…MUNDY!" Nola yelled down to him.

155

"NOLA…call CASH! Tell him to get the fire trucks out here. Tell him it is massive and it is threatening the farm buildings and the house."

"The house? Oh my God. My babies."

"Nola listen to me," his voice grew louder. "Listen to me. After you call Cash get the babies and get out. Wake everyone in the house. All of you get out. Have Joseph drive all of you away from here."

A whimper escaped her lips as once again she stood mesmerized by the blazing woods.

"NOLA?"

"Yes, Mundy. Call Cash…get everyone out of here…I'm going, I'm going." She turned to run back inside and then turned back to tell Mundy to be careful but the old man was gone. She caught a glimpse of him running back toward the woods and the flames. A sudden chill seized her heart as she whispered "I love you Mundy, please be careful." Nola turned and ran into the house screaming FIRE!

Joseph Camp rose from his bed slowly. He did everything slowly these days, and these nights. He stood by his bed and listened. Something awakened him from his sleep and he was trying to determine what or who it was. He froze as he heard Nola scream "FIRE!" Quickly he pulled on his pants and ran out of his room toward the sound of her screams. Joseph and Naomi met in the hall at about the same time the girls came out of their room. Debra, and Ruth, stood clutching each other, and waiting for instructions from Naomi.

"Girls, go get the twins. Joseph go with them and make sure they get the babies and go out the front of the house," Naomi shouted.

"Come on girls. Let's get the babies." The three of them ran down the hall to the other side of the house. Nola ran toward them with a child in each arm. Joseph and the girls reached her, and Debra, and Ruth, each took a crying child in their arms. Naomi made it to the stairs, and stopped when she saw all of them coming toward her. Without a word they started down the stairs. Naomi grabbed Nola by both arms, and told her Joseph, and the girls, were getting the boys, and leaving out the front of the house. She tried to turn holding Nola's arm, and start down the steps behind the others. When Nola would not move Naomi turned back to her confused.

"Oh…Naomi…" Nola struggled to catch her breath.

"Just slow down girl, breathe."

"Mundy… th…the woods…fire."

"Yes, I understand. Let's all go to the front of the house and have Joseph bring the car."

"No. No. **NO**… Naomi."

"What? What do you mean no?" Naomi said as Nola pushed away from her grasp and backed away from the stairs.

"Get my children out of here. Take them into town. Get a room at the Inn where you will all be safe. Stay there until I come for you." Nola turned and tried to take another step but Naomi was quickly on her.

"Girl what are you doing? Let's all go. Let's get the babies and go. Why are you staying?" Naomi asked confused, and frightened.

"I have to go help. I have to try to help Mundy." Nola's voice broke when she said Mundy's name. "Don't argue with me Naomi. There is no time for that." Nola lifted a quivering chin. "Take care of my babies Naomi." Without another word Nola ran to her room to get dressed. Naomi stood for just a second, and then wiping away tears she made her way down the steps and to the waiting car that would carry her and the people she loved to safety. As she fled she whispered a prayer for Nola, and Mundy, asking God to keep them safe for they were her family too, and she loved them so.

Mundy pushed his way farther into the woods. The smoke was so thick it was hard to see and he felt disoriented. He coughed and rubbed at his eyes. Was the cabin straight ahead, or off to the left of the fire? He did not know anymore. He held a bandana over his mouth to filter the smoke, but his eyes stung and tears were constant. Mundy stopped and stood breathing hard, sucking in smoke. He knew he was in trouble. He felt his legs give way, and he knew his body struck the hard ground, but he did not feel any pain. Strange he thought, I don't feel anything.

"Mundy...Mundy...over here."

He tried to see through the smoke. He rubbed his old tired eyes, and then he saw her. He felt his heart skip a beat. Adrenalin coursed through his veins. His pulse quickened to an alarming rate.

"Momma, Mom..." he smiled and tried to get up. She came closer.

"Come on child, it's time to go. Your daddy's watin...you know he don't like waitin child."

"Momma?"

"Come on now. It's time to go." She smiled down on him. A wave of pure joy washed over him. Mundy had never felt such complete euphoria. As if watching a movie he saw his body rise, and take his Momma's hand. He watched as he, and his Momma, began walking away. He saw himself and his Momma disappear. Then nothing. The two became a part of the smoke that now along with the fire consumed the trees surrounding Mundy's body. Mundy was now with his Momma, and Daddy, and the God he loved so much. Mundy was finally, and forever... home.

SIXTEEN

The doctor told Will he could find nothing wrong with Angelina. She had been in the hospital for days now while the doctor ran every test possible to search for the reason behind her pain. When the tests came back normal all he could do was rule the pain psychological. She lost a great deal of weight, and was weak due to not eating. Most of her days consisted of lying in the hospital bed staring out the window. The doctor gave her pain medication, but nothing seemed to eliminate the gnawing ache in her stomach. He discussed with Will the option of exploratory surgery, but he warned that even such a drastic step held little promise of finding anything wrong. Without trying to be harsh he told Will Angelina's problem was emotional. She was mentally ill.

Will mulled over in his mind the doctor's words. He was driving back to Pine Point from the hospital; trying to make some sense of his life. Miserable. The only way to describe his life was miserable. He was married to a woman he did not love. She tricked him into marriage with a child that turned out to belong to someone else. The woman he longed for had his sons, but wanted nothing to do with him. And as if that wasn't enough Maclaine Moreaux lured him into his dark world with promises of power and control.

Will was not emotional, but he felt as if a dam lay just behind his eyes. He blinked and fought to keep the tears at bay. He had tried to stay as far away from religion, and God, as he could. His entire life was based on denying the existence of any supreme being controlling his life. Pain and disappointment followed him, holding him in its dark grip when he was young. There was no one to love. No one who loved him. He grew up believing we make our own destiny. He grew up not knowing how to love. Nola made him feel something he never had before. Just thinking of her caused a pain so intense and sharp in his chest that he instinctively laid his hand over

161

his heart. Then the tears started, blinding him. He pulled the truck off the road and killing the engine he lay over the steering wheel, and let the tears come. "Nola…Nola…" at first her name escaped his lips softly, whisper like sobs of grief for the unloved child, torment for the young man who had no family, and no one to turn to. Finally an animal like sound of distress escaped his body. A wounded cry for the love of a woman who despised him. At last his sobbing subsided. "Go…Ggg…God?" He looked up through the windshield toward the blue sky. "Can you hear me? Are you real?" Will felt small as he stared heavenward. He lay his head back down, and said a prayer as best he knew how. "God, help me. Help me make sense of my life." He sat for a while staring at the sky. Waiting. Waiting for what he wasn't sure. A sign. A feeling. Something. Anything. He started the truck and pulled out onto the road. He drove, and the closer he got to home the hazier the sky appeared.

When he pulled up to the main house at Pine Point, one of the hands came running to the truck.

"Boss, there's a fire at Fair Meadows. They need help."

"Fire?" Will repeated. Without another word he turned the truck and headed out to the main road. Driving as fast as he dared, he made his way to Fair Meadow. He made his way to Nola.

Arlyn held the baby close to her body and took comfort in the warmth that came from the bundle of blankets. She looked down into her sleeping face and smiled. Arlyn could not help smiling every time she looked at Audreigh Rose's angelic face. She looked so peaceful lying in her arms that she hated putting her down. She knew she must, so she rose from the rocker and walked to the crib. As she lay her down she made hushing noises to the child. She

162

stood for a moment longer and then glanced out the window. Arlyn bit her lip and tried to steel herself for what she must do.

She had been instructed to leave with the child and bring her to New Orleans. "Take the baby to Mother," they told her. But she could not. She tried hard to come up with a plan to take the child for herself, but she was smart enough to know that would never work. They would find her and take the baby for certain. Time was running out. She knew the fire was raging. A diversion created to give her time to take Audreigh Rose away from Pine Point. Will Biggs was at the fire.

He had not known that taking the baby was the plan hatched by Maclaine and his sister. All her life she followed orders from the others. Treated like a servant instead of a relative she grew tired of always being the one to give. Besides she became more, and more uneasy, and at times frightened of the dark religion her family practiced. She went to a tent meeting one night years earlier in the city. She sneaked out of the house to go. The pastor and his message were one of hope and light, and the love of a savior. That beautiful message was the total opposite of all she had been accustomed to. Darkness, self-service, potions, and curses, those were the elements of religion she knew. Later Mother caught her climbing in her bedroom window as she returned from the service full of hope, and wonder. There was the devil to pay. She never snuck out again, but her resentment grew, and she never forgot that service. She never forgot the words of comfort, forgiveness, and hope from the pastor. Even as much as she could not stand Angelina Biggs she felt bad for using the doll against her. If only Angelina would love her child. If only she would want Audreigh Rose, but try as Arlyn might to turn Angelina into a mother it was not working. Arlyn could not imagine leaving the baby for Angelina to raise. She tried to focus. Like a flash of lightning that strikes suddenly and illuminates the darkness, an idea came to her. She looked down at the sleeping baby and whispered, "I will take you to someone who loves you and wants you as much as I do. Yes, sweet girl. We are going to see your daddy. Your real daddy." Arlyn smiled and reached down to pick up Audreigh Rose.

Tilly stood in the hall watching Arlyn with the baby. She knew that Arlyn loved the baby. It was evident in the way she cared for her. She was more of a mother to her than Angelina had ever been. Something wasn't right about that girl though. Tilly felt her skin crawl when she came in close contact with her. Something about the way the girl looked at Tilly made her want to run from the room. But when it came to Audreigh Rose, Tilly had no doubt that Arlyn would lay her life down for the child. Problem was though, Arlyn would not allow anyone else to get close to the child. Even Ms. Tilly. That was a big problem for Tilly. She had been with this family for years and took care of Angelina from the time she was born. Tilly was so upset with Angelina for not being the mother that she should be, and could be. Wasn't a thing in this world Tilly could do about that right now, except keep her eye on the nanny.

Standing and watching through the crack in the door she saw Arlyn dress Audreigh Rose. They are going somewhere she thought. She watched a few more seconds and decided to walk away from the door and go down the hall to Angelina's room. She would wait for Arlyn to take the baby out of the nursery and then she was going to search the room. Tilly wasn't sure what it was that she was looking for, but she would look just the same. She wanted Arlyn gone from Pine Point and maybe there would be something in her belongings that would help her accomplish that. She sat quietly on the small sofa in Angelina's bedroom.

Looking around she was filled with sadness for the beautiful little girl she helped raise. How could she grow up so vindictive and full of hate? When did she become so ugly and full of hate? Tilly remembered a sweet natured child who loved to be outside with the "ponies." Even before her parents died in that horrible crash she watched as Angelina turned into a manipulative, spoiled, young woman. From time to time Tilly tried talking to her about where she was headed, but the girl would cut her off. Most of the time she was good to Tilly, but if she wasn't getting her way she could turn on the old woman with a sharp threatening tongue. Tilly sighed and pushed a tear from her cheek with a wrinkled thumb. "No use n cryin Tilly. No ma'am, thas right. No use n cryin," she said. Her voice shocked her and she put her hand to her lips. She was nervous. She was not used to playing detective. There was way too many changes around her lately and change always made her nervous. Tilly liked everything to stay the same. She decided it was time things got back to some kind of normal around here.

Tilly jerked her head from the back of the sofa. When did she fall asleep? Light was fading from the large window in the bedroom and she looked around disoriented. What was she doing here in Angelina's room? Yes, yes... she remembered now. She rose stiffly from the sofa and crossed over to the door. Opening it she stepped into the now dark hall and stared down toward the nursery. Hearing nothing she walked slowly that way and realized the door to the nursery was open wide. Good, she thought. Arlyn took the baby for a walk. But why would she not be back? It was getting dark. She stepped inside the nursery and flipped on the light. She blinked as the room glowed from the lamp. The light hurt her eyes some and she rubbed them hard. Standing in the center of the nursery she sensed something was not right. Something odd. What was it? The baby's travel bag that sat near the crib. That's what was wrong. It was gone. Gone along with all the items from the changing table. The lotions, powders, even the stack of diapers. "What in this world is goin on here?" Tilly quickly walked over to the closet and opened the door. She stood frozen as fear crept into her body starting at her feet and making its icy cold way up to her brain. She whispered, "She done took the baby." She repeated those words out loud now. "She done took the baby." Just as she was about to turn and run from the room to tell someone, anyone; something caught her eye. A small bag lay on the floor near the back of the closet. It was barely noticeable in the dark corner. Maybe Arlyn dropped it in her haste to get away, Tilly thought. She went to the back of the closet and picked up the bag. When she found a doll inside she knew it was no ordinary doll. Her Momma told her all about these kind of dolls. She felt her stomach tighten, and she was afraid she might have an accident in her pants. Staring at the doll she noticed the pin. It was a three inch pin stuck deep in the doll's abdomen. Tilly heard her Momma speaking, warning, inside her head.

"They be folks in da city, in da place Tilly girl. Bad folks. They be out there in da swamps. They do bad things Tilly girl."

"Whacha mean Momma? What bad things?"

"Kings and Queens they be callin each other. Potions and dolls. Voodoo dolls they be callin dem. Don be messin wit any of dem folks. Not dem folks Tilly girl."

Tilly pulled the pin out and dropped the doll and the pin to the floor. She ran from the room as fast as her old legs would carry her. She had to get help, but first things first. Tilly ran down the hall to the nearest bathroom, where the contents of her stomach came out both ends.

The church was old, wood clap boards painted the whitest white. A dark haired little girl in a frilly pink dress with matching pink shoes stood staring at the roof of the church. A large hand rested up on the roof. The hand was closed in a loose fist except for the pointy finger. It pointed straight up to the heavens' as if directing

166

the way for the congregation who gathered each Sunday. The hand held an indescribable fascination for the little girl. She and her Momma had been coming here for as far back as she was able to recall. She always stopped and stared at the finger. She thought it was God's finger though her Momma said it wasn't. But she knew it was. God was pointing the way to heaven. She loved that finger. She loved God. She found what went on inside the church to be stuffy, and boring, and mostly way over her head. But she loved the hand, and she loved God.

She was alone this day. Where were all the people she wondered? She could hear music coming from inside and decided to go in.

Everyone must be in there waiting for me she thought. Up the steps she went, counting each step. Ten steps to the top. She pulled on the massive wood door and it slowly swung open. The church was dark. She tried to look inside but it was so black that she couldn't see anyone or anything. Suddenly frightened she turned to run back down the steps, but a car was blocking her way. The car was a mangled shell of twisted metal. The glass windows were gone. It glistened in the sunlight. The little girl approached the car. "Momma…Momma…where are you?" Slowly she stepped up to the side of the car and peering inside she began to scream. "Momma…Momma," each scream for her mamma became louder as she backed away from the wreckage.

"Momma…," Angelina screamed as she bolted upright in the hospital bed. Sweating and shaking, she began to sob as a nurse came running into the room with a syringe. Over, and over, she cried out, "Momma…Momma."

"There…there…is was just a dream missy," the nurse soothed. She lifted the needle to check it before she injected the pain killer into Angelina's flesh, but her patient grew silent. The nurse looked into Angelina's face and saw her break into an ear to ear smile. Thinking that Angelina must be having a mental episode she started to give her the shot. Angelina pulled away.

"No…no…don't do that."

"Missy, this will make everything all better. You know. It's been helping you, and it will help you now. Just a little stick."

"No…you don't understand. The pain. The pain…it's…it's gone. My… pain…my pain is gone." Angelina began to weep as the nurse stood by and silently wondered if she had just witnessed a miracle, or her patient was so disturbed she felt nothing. She was still wondering about the miracle when she dialed the number trying to reach Angelina's doctor.

Looking out the window at the sun coming up over the horizon her eyes took great delight in the amber dawning against a brilliant blue. The scene picturesque as if from a landscape painting was alive and glowing. She felt alive. She felt an overwhelming sense of peace. She felt grateful. The pain was gone. The maddening ache had been replaced with a calm she had never known. She was thinking about the dream from the evening before. The church was a reality of her childhood. Her mother took her there as a child. The hand that served as a steeple fascinated her. She told herself that once she was out of the hospital she would make a trip to the church. Closing her eyes she could see her mother holding her small hand. They would walk up the steps together, counting out loud together, one…two…three… ten. Her mother would laugh, and squeeze her hand. Her laugh was musical, sweet, and made her little girl laugh when she heard it.

Angelina could not remember much about being inside, but the hand, and that finger pointing the way to heaven; pointing the way

168

to God, were etched in her memory. She opened her eyes to stare once more at life going on outside the hospital. Something warm and wet fell on her cheek. She reached up instinctively and was surprised to find tears. Smiling she let them fall from her eyes, content to let them come, and happy in the realization that she still had her memories. She missed her Momma, but she was finally ready to let her go. She needed to let her go. Her Daddy too. She missed them more than she could have ever imagined she would. Regret seized her heart. She was not always the loving daughter she should have been. But she was ready to forgive herself. She must let go of the pain of losing them. She had to let go of the guilt, and remorse she felt that she survived, and they did not. Her marriage depended on it. She did something then that she had not done in years. She whispered a simple prayer. She looked up toward the heavens and whispered, "Lord help me." She believed He heard the prayer. She believed He would help her. She believed. Her own motherhood depended on it. Her life depended on it. In that moment Angelina made the decision to live. Let go…let God… and live.

SEVENTEEN

Driving as fast as he could safely go Cash made his way along the road to Fair Meadows. A call had come in to the Fire Department, and one of the firemen burst through the door of Cash's office to tell him about the call. A huge out of control fire at Fair Meadows was all he'd said before running off to jump on the fire truck heading out of town. Every possible scenario flashed through Cash's mind as he drove. He saw the main house engulfed in flames, or no, maybe it was the stable. He never thought about the woods. He could smell the smoke from the burning trees a few miles before he reached the drive to the farm. He began to see smoke and by the time he turned on the lane leading to the main house it was hard to see anything. Parking the cruiser in front of the house he jumped from his seat and ran around to the left side of the massive stone house. What he saw made his knees go weak. So weak that he stopped, and stood. He was staring at acres, and acres, of burning trees. Men were yelling, and running everywhere. They had formed a long line with buckets of water. They passed the buckets up the line, and threw water at the fire. This attempt looked futile. Cash stood and stared. "My God," he said aloud. The three fire trucks were there from Monroe. The fire Captain sent out a

171

mayday call to surrounding counties. Only one of the trucks was a tanker, and they positioned it very near the woods and the flames.

The Captain knew that help was on the way. He just prayed they would come quick. If not they might lose the entire farm.

Even from where he was standing Cash could feel the heat from the massive fire. Somehow the warmth woke him from his trance. He started moving closer to the other men. Looking around he recognized Dave Grimm and approached him at a run. "Where is Mundy?" Cash asked.

"I...I'm not sure." Dave choked and sputtered as he struggled to speak. His face was red and streaked with black soot. Cash looked around at the men moving about. He did not see Mundy. The hair on the back of his neck stood up. Looking back at Dave he saw realization slowly moving across the face of the farm hand. Dave turned his gaze to the woods, to the flames, as he slowly spoke. "Last I saw him...he was heading toward the woods. Toward the cabin."

"Which direction is the cabin Dave? I have seen it but I don't remember where it is." The flames and the smoke was disorienting.

"The cabin sets in the middle of this stand of woods you're lookin at. I mean what is left of the stand of trees. A few hundred yards in...right in the middle of the fire." Dave began to shake his head in disbelief. He bent over at the waist, and put his hands on his knees for support. He could barely stand as his legs began to shake.

"What...what are you saying?" Cash looked toward the fire and back at Dave and slowly began to shake his head at what his mind was trying hard to comprehend.

"I know the cabin is gone. There can't be anything left of that cabin." Dave started to weep, softly. "If Mundy was anywhere near that cabin," his crying turned into sobs, his words broken, "If…Mundy was near the cabin…he…he is…gone. Gone. Do you understand Sheriff? Mundy is most likely gone."

He dropped to the ground. Cradling his head as if protecting it from the reality of what he had just said. A scream pierced the air. A scream of grief and heartache. The piercing, anguished scream came from Dave, but it brought Cash down on his knees beside the kind hearted farm hand who loved his boss. The scream exited Dave's mouth as a word. One word. As Cash reached out to offer what comfort he could; Dave kept screaming "Gone…gone…gone."

Nola ran past the men. She looked for Mundy as she ran. She did not see him and knew he must have went into the woods looking for Maclaine's family. She ran along the edge of the tree line trying to find an entrance into the woods as far away from the flames and smoke as possible. The fire was now so huge she ran what seemed like a mile though she knew it wasn't that far. Seeing a break in the trees she turned into the woods and began shouting for Mundy. She made her way to the right toward the direction of the cabin.

Smoke thick and dark choked her, and she kept her sleeve up to her nose and mouth. Pulling her arm away every few steps, she yelled for Mundy. She started to feel light headed, and knew it was from the smoke. She was not getting enough oxygen in her lungs and now was constantly coughing. She kept moving and praying she would find Mundy. He had to be in here. Without warning she tripped. Hitting the ground hard she was stunned, disoriented. Her yelling for Mundy had turned into more of a whimper as she lay on the ground trying to gather her thoughts. Trying hard to focus, her mind became as foggy as the smoke surrounding her. Where was she? Why was she in this smoke? A lack of oxygen caused confusion. Choking, and coughing, she lay on her stomach, and her world went dark.

Will Biggs was moving through the woods looking for Maclaine, and the women. Gabrielle and Jolene were staying in the cabin, but hopefully they had got out when the fire started. Hopefully, Will thought, they were lost somewhere in the woods. He knew Maclaine would be in here looking for them too. And he had not spotted Mundy with the other men so he must be looking for the women as well. Will stopped walking. What was that? A noise, faint and unrecognizable. Was it straight ahead? He wasn't sure. He stood listening, waiting, until he heard it again. Moving quickly he ran straight ahead tripping over Nola's legs. Hitting the ground with a thud, he split his lip on a tree root when his face smacked the ground. Moaning and trying to breathe he rolled over quickly. Getting to his feet he bent to pick Nola up.

She was limp, lifeless, dead weight. Struggling to breathe and carry a lifeless Nola, he moved at close to a run to make it out of the woods. As he ran he whispered to the God whose very existence he sometimes questioned. "Please don't let her die. Please... don't... let her die."

Cash saw Will coming out of the woods carrying a body. Still on his knees beside Dave, he got to his feet and ran toward Will. He quickly made it to the two of them. He watched as Will dropped Nola on the ground, and began to try to breathe life back into her limp body.

Getting on his knees he yelled at Will asking if he could help. Will didn't respond to Cash. So focused on getting Nola to breathe, he was oblivious to everything and everyone around him. Cash did the only thing he knew to do. He began to pray.

174

The firemen were making progress in getting the fire under control. Some of the men moved into the woods with shovels and blankets trying to put out spot fires. One of those men found Mundy's body and yelled for help. Two men carried him out of the woods and lay him on the grass. No one bent to try to help Mundy. There was no need. There was no help for Mundy Winks. He was gone. Just as Dave feared, Mundy was gone. The firemen went back in to keep the spot fires under control. They were told to look for two women, and possibly another young man. They found no one else.

Arlyn made it to Monroe in a car she had taken from one of the garages at Pine Point.

Walking into the large garage that housed cars and trucks the hired drivers used; she searched until finding one with keys in the ignition. She learned to drive years ago when she was barely able to see over the steering wheel and had to sit with a pillow behind her to reach the clutch, gas pedal, and brake. The sun was up and the air quite warm as she drove through town. When she saw Cash's office she pulled up in front and turned off the engine. Nervously she glanced around and was happy to see very few people out on the street. Glancing over her shoulder she checked on Audreigh Rose who was sleeping soundly on the back seat. Biting her lip she knew that soon the baby would be hungry and waking for her mid-morning bottle. Glancing around again and opening the car door quietly, and slowly, she then made a dash for Cash's office. It was locked. Frustrated she rested her head against the door and was leaning there when a voice startled her. She jumped backward almost falling. The stranger grabbed her helping her regain her balance. "Sorry ma'am. Didn't mean to scare you none. Sheriff's not here."

"Er…uh…it's…it's quite all right. No harm done."

"He's at the fire. You know…the fire at Fair Meadows."

"Yes…of course. Thank you for reminding me. I forgot about…um…the fire." Arlyn smiled prettily up at the stranger. He was quite taken with her charm.

"Is that a baby I see in your car? Do you need help Miss…?"

"Arlyn…my name is Arlyn. And no sir, I don't need any help. I was just paying a social call on Cash. I will be going now. I forgot about the fire. Is it bad?"

"Oh it's real bad Miss Arlyn. Real bad. Lot of men out there. I here a few people are missing. Maybe even dead. They may lose the entire farm. Sad, really sad. That Nola Todd is a nice lady. Been to Hell and back I heard. Don't deserve this not one iota. Not one iota. She sure don't."

Arlyn eyed the stranger for a moment. She stepped closer to the car and could see the baby was still sleeping. Without saying anything more she turned quickly and got in the driver seat. The man leaned down to the window on the passenger side. He tipped his hat and smiled. "You be careful there Miss Arlyn." Glancing at the baby then back to the stranger, she thought she saw a look of recognition in the man's face. He stared at the baby as Arlyn nervously started the engine. The stranger stood up and Arlyn pulled the car out on the street driving slowly away. Looking in her rear view mirror she could see the man staring at her as she drove away. "He knows something baby Audreigh, yes he does." Biting her lip she drove on without a clue of where she was going.

Nola came around flinging her arms, and fighting to breathe. Spasms wracked her lungs making her cough until she began to vomit. Will rolled her over on to her side, and waited for the coughing and vomiting to subside.

Still gasping she looked up into Will's face. His face was blurry as if she were trying to see through a thick fog. Then her memory returned. The fire. Mundy. Trying to speak and say Mundy's name caused immense pain in the back of her throat. She began to cough and struggle to breathe again. Will picked her up and carried her to his truck. Cash was following close behind. "Where are you going Will? She needs an ambulance. A doctor." Cash said.

"That's where I'm taking her." Will responded as he placed Nola in the front seat of his truck.

"Maybe you should wait for an ambulance Will."

"I'm not waiting for anyone. Get out of my way Cash." Will shoved past the young sheriff and got in the truck. "It's too late to help Mundy," Will said. He started the engine and pulled the gear shift into reverse. Nola hearing what he said began to moan. "I 'm gonna make sure Nola's fate is different from that old man's."

"Go. Go man." Cash said. He stood with his hat in his hands watching as Will quickly backed his truck, turned around, and headed out toward the main road. "Just go… and God be with Nola," he whispered to the heavens. Turning around Cash made his way back to the fire. He had to do all he could to help end this raging inferno. After the fire was extinguished all that would be left were ashes, heartache, and devastation.

The fire was finally contained. A few small flare ups in the charred woods, and the heavy thick smoke were all that was left. Mundy's body was taken to the bunkhouse and carefully wrapped in a blanket. A couple of hands were waiting with him. Cash called the County Coroner to come and pronounce Mundy here at the scene.

He thought this might be the best way to begin the investigation. No one was able to enter the woods at the location of the fire. From the intense burn and heat in that area the fire chief seemed to think the fire started in the cabin. The cabin was reduced to a pile of ash. Anyone who may have been in there would be "burned to bits," as the fire chief stated to Cash. Walking around the perimeter of the fire Cash concentrated on searching for Maclaine Moreaux.

He asked every hand he came in contact with if they had seen him. He asked when they saw him last. All of them stated they saw him at the bunkhouse the evening before the fire. No one could say if they saw him go to bed there. It seemed they all went to sleep at different times. None of the men saw him after that evening. Cash wondered if Maclaine, and the two women, were in the cabin when the fire started. He would have to wait until they could approach the spot where the cabin burned. There would be remains. Bones, buttons, "little burnt bits." Cash felt his stomach churn at the thought of burning alive. If they weren't there, then his investigation would be more difficult. It would then definitely become a murder investigation. For the moment he was giving everyone the benefit of the doubt, and assuming the fire was an accident.

Tilly had only driven a car a few times in her life. There was a couple of reasons for that. She really never had a need to drive. Having worked since she was a young girl at Pine Point,if she needed to go anywhere one of the drivers always took her. The other reason, and the honest reason was; she wasn't good at it. Years back her and a driver the Oliver's hired took a shine to each other. Thinking of him now made her smile. Jessie Porter. Yes, her Jessie. Oh she loved that man so. He was handsome and strong, always making her laugh. She would sneak out at night to be with him. Over the moon in love with him, she surely was. Tilly would have married him, but he got blamed when some little white baby came up missing. That baby wasn't yet a year old when it happened. Tilly knew Jessie would never hurt anyone, but the man she loved was a stranger to the town folks. Seemed to folks he came out of nowhere looking for work when he turned up at the Oliver's. The law came one night and took Jessie away. There was a trial, and a hanging soon followed. Tilly didn't know where his body was buried. The Oliver's warned her that she might lose her job, or worse if she asked too many questions about that child killer. The baby was never found. The only evidence they had was a missing baby. But Jessie paid the price for somebody. Yes, he paid the ultimate price for whoever took that baby. A tear slid down a weathered cheek, and her smile faded as she remembered how she loved him. She never gave up her heart again. Never again would she risk her world being ripped in half. A part of her died with him.

No matter how many good things she experienced in life since; she always felt half empty. She was never able to be fully happy again after Jessie. She was never whole again. The euphoria of love was not worth the pain of loss. Not to Tilly. She gave her life to the Oliver's. A surrogate Mother to Angelina, she made peace with her lot in life. She kept going. She kept living, but living a lesser life. Seldom did she think about yesterday, and the one love of her life. Today as she drove she was remembering the child that was stolen away, and thinking about Arlyn who took Audreigh Rose.

She drove as slowly and as carefully as she could, trying to make her way to town to find the sheriff. Sheriff Atkins would know what to do about Arlyn, and the baby. She said a prayer as she weaved along slowly. A prayer for baby Audriegh Rose, and another prayer for her driving skills. She knew her God, would answer both.

179

EIGHTEEN

Will looked and felt weary. He drove Nola to the hospital in Charleston and after examining her the doctor decided to admit her. He was waiting in an area for family. The doctor was concerned about the amount of smoke she inhaled, and the fact that she was not breathing when they found her. He did assure Will that he was positive with a few days' rest, and oxygen therapy she would be fine. Weakened lungs however would be a permanent effect of the smoke inhalation. Relieved, but still weary and worn out Will sat in the waiting room. Nola was taken to her room and someone would let him know when he could see her. After seeing Nola he intended to check on Angelina. She would be anxious by now and wondering why she could not reach him by phone at home.

Will felt old. Really old. His mind drifted to Mundy, and pain seized his heart. Mundy was dead. He felt responsible even though he had no idea what was being planned. He was confused and angry. As soon as he saw to Nola, and Angelina, he would get to the bottom of all this. They caused an innocent man to die. Mundy was his friend. He tried to be a mentor to Will. Always kind and patient with him. Will would find them if it was the last thing he ever did.

He felt betrayed. Maclaine was a friend. They were as close as brothers. How could he do this? Will was certain that Maclaine, and Jolene, were responsible for the fire. But why?

He rubbed his face with rough hands. How would he ever tell Nola? Tears stung his eyes at the thought of Nola in pain. Hadn't she been through enough? A soft voice interrupted his thoughts, and he looked up to see a nurse standing in the doorway. She was calling his name. "Will Biggs. Is there a Will Biggs here?"

"Ma'am. Yes…yes….," Will said.

"Mrs. Todd is in her room now. Room 220. You may take the elevator right outside of the waiting area to the second floor."

"Thank you Ma'am." Will stood to his feet. The pretty young nurse smiled and left. Will stood for a moment longer. He knew if Nola was awake she would ask about Mundy. He drew in a deep breath and made his way to the elevator. On his way up he said a prayer, asking God to give him the words to comfort Nola. Funny how it seemed he was praying often these days. The doors opened, and he stepped off the elevator and into the hall, searching for room 220. Searching for Nola Rain.

Nola lay eyes closed, dark hair spilled across the stark white pillowcase. She looked so small and frail. Will approached her bedside slowly. If she were sleeping he would leave her to the oblivion of her dreams. He would not wake her to tell her of Mundy's fate. In her slumber she could keep hope, and Mundy, alive for a while longer. Will stood and stared down into her beautiful face. Even with all she'd been through her beauty would not be denied. There were a few scratches on her cheek and tubes were in her nose sending oxygen to her lungs. Still she was a stunning woman. Being close to her made Will's heart leap within his chest.

She had that effect on him from the moment he laid eyes on her. Will knew she would have that effect on him for the rest of his days on this earth. He loved her. He could not deny that he loved her. But he knew she would never be his. The thought that she would never be his to love and cherish made him feel as if his very life was draining out of him. He felt numb and unable to move. A tear he didn't know was coming slid down his cheek. He let it go. He let it go and knew somehow he must find a way to let Nola go. For the first time in his adult life Will felt a desire to do "the right thing." Angelina needed him. They had a child. Audreigh Rose need never know that Will was not her father. He would keep Angelina's secret. Will could learn to love the baby if he let go of Nola and the belief that someday they would be together with their sons. Let it go. "Let it go…" he whispered, and reached out a hand to touch a sleeping beauty. He drew his hand back quickly. Standing up straight he turned and headed for the door. He was going to see his wife. He was going to Angelina. He whispered to himself as he left Nola's room. "Let it go. Let Nola go."

Angelina heard Will's boots in the hall before he got to her room. She knew it was him. She recognized the sound of his walk. Sitting in a chair by the window she had been anxiously waiting some news from Will.

Just on the verge of calling Cash because no one would answer the phone at Pine Point, and she was beginning to worry; relief washed over her at the sound of Will's footsteps. Angelina drew in a sharp audible breath when Will walked in. He was covered in what looked like soot. He reeked of smoke. She sat staring at him with her mouth agape. "Angelina, I know I'm a mess." Will said.

183

"What…what…happened. The farm…Will?" Angelina sat up now panic rising in her chest.

"Not Pine Point."

"Oh my…" Relief washed over her and she sank back in the chair. The dizzy feeling beginning to subside. "Then what happened. What happened to you?"

"There is a massive fire at Fair Meadows. The woods. Mundy Winks…he…" Will lowered his head. He couldn't bring himself to say it out loud. To speak it would make it more real. Angelina sat for a moment waiting. Then like a curtain separating night from day, realization began to sink in as the curtain lifted.

"Mr. Winks is dead? Is that it? He died in the fire Will?" Angelina's words were soft, and soothing. Will nodded his head. He needed to sit down but his clothes were so filthy from the ash and soot of the fire he knew he should go home and clean up.

"Angelina, I uh…well I want to talk but I need to go. I need to get out of these clothes." Will said.

"I know Will. I am sorry…about Mr. Winks. Really. I really am sorry Will. I know you cared for that old man." Still standing with his head down Will made a noise. A grunt of agreement. He did care for that old man. He did at that.

"I will be back tomorrow. We'll talk then." Will turned and hurried out of the room. Angelina wasn't sure if he just wanted away from her, or if it was because she was about to see a bit of humanity in the man who tried so hard to be tough all the time. Will was close to breaking down. Angelina sat amazed. Just when she thought she had Will Biggs all figured out he showed real compassion. Angelina never saw compassion in Will. Ever. She felt hope burn inside her and well up. It came to the surface as tears. Tears that flowed and washed away all the anger and hurt of the past. She was ready for a new life. A new life with a new Angelina, and a new Will. A life of goodness with their baby. The thought of her baby made her cry more. For the first time true maternal feelings kicked in and she longed to hold her child. She vowed to make it up to her husband, and her daughter. Looking out the window toward heaven she vowed to God to be a better mother…a better wife…a better human being. She cried until there were no more tears left. Then she sat waiting. Waiting for tomorrow. Waiting for her new life to begin.

When Will walked through the door of the main house at Pine Point he was met by silence. Total silence. The house was dark and empty. Where was Tilly? Climbing the stairs to the second floor he called out to the old cook. No answer. He moved down the hall and opened the door to the nursery. Calling Arlyn's name as he entered he stopped, and stood in the center of the room. Something was off. Something was not right. Then it hit him like a moving train. He reeled and stumbled back a few feet. The baby. Looking at the empty crib Will could see not just the baby was gone, but her things as well. Walking over to the closet he yanked the door open. Arlyn's bag and all her things were gone as well. Lying on the floor of the empty closet he saw the doll. Will knew what it was. Maclaine, taught Will many things about the dark religion they practiced in the city. Maclaine, and his sister, tried to pull Will into that same darkness with seduction and lofty promises. He picked up the doll and another realization sent a shockwave through his body causing him to stumble once more. Dropping to his knees he saw the pin lying on the floor and looking at the doll that resembled Angelina he broke out in a cold sweat. Shaking and swaying he understood they had tried to kill Angelina, and now they had Audreigh Rose. Where was Tilly? What had they done to Tilly?

Feeling as if he were at a breaking point Will began to weep and cry out to God for help. This was how Tilly found Will when she returned from town. Looking up and seeing the old woman unharmed, he felt as if God was beginning to answer his pleas for help.

Tilly sat down on the floor beside him, and held his head rocking Will back and forth while whispering, "It's gonna be alright now…we'll find the baby… it's gonna be alright son."

NINETEEN

Angelina sat stone faced; her hands in her lap. She was staring out the window of her bedroom. Will picked her up at the hospital and drove her home without telling her of Audreigh Rose's disappearance until she was upstairs in her room. She listened as he explained that Arlyn, and Audreigh Rose, were gone. He didn't know where they were. He assured her the baby was not in any harm stating as evidence the love and protection Arlyn showered on the baby. The nanny doted on her little charge, and Will was certain she would never harm her, or allow anyone else to do so. Angelina sat not moving or interrupting Will, as he told her all he knew. Will spilled everything. He explained his relationship with Maclaine Moreaux, Jolene, and Gabrielle. He knew Arlyn was related to the Moreaux's and hired her as a nanny at Maclaine's insistence. "Did you hear me Angelina?" Will said softly.

"Please leave me alone Will."

"Angelina...we...I...

"Please. Leave me alone for a moment. Give me a moment... please." Angelina turned her face from Will and stared out the window.

"Yes. Yes...I know this is a shock. But I will find her. I will find Audreigh Rose." Will stood waiting for some response. "Cash is on

187

his way here to talk to us. He has a witness. Someone who saw Arlyn in town yesterday." No response. "Did you hear me?" No Response. "We will find them."

"I heard...just please....leave me alone for a few moments." Angelina was struggling to speak. She felt like someone was standing on her chest. Closing her eyes she placed her hand over her heart as if to slow its pounding. Will took a step toward her wanting to comfort her in some way. Dropping his hands to his side he turned instead, and left the room quickly. Once alone Angelina sat and stared out at the blue sky. The sun was shining. She could hear birds singing and the breeze blowing through the tops of the cottonwoods. A beautiful day. It was all deceiving she thought. It was an ugly day. Arlyn had stolen her child. Tears began to fall but Angelina did not try to wipe them away. She was frozen. Remorse and regret began to swell within her heart, and she felt as if it might burst open. Sobbing now, wracked with guilt she began loudly calling her child's name. "Audreigh...Audreigh...AUDREIGH...," she screamed. Holding a pillow to her face she tried to muffle her screams.

Then remorse settled like a blanket enveloping her mind, and the ugly truth came to the surface. That truth escaped her lips just as Will came running back in the room. "Arlyn didn't steal my baby, I gave her away Will.

I gave her to Arlyn long ago. My baby doesn't know I'm her mother. I threw her away Will. I threw Audreigh Rose away." Will held her in his arms and did what he could to comfort her, much the same as Tilly did for him.

"We will get the baby back. It's gonna be alright Angelina. We will get her back."

Cash was driving to Pine Point. His heart was heavy as he tried to concentrate on the road. Miss Tilly came driving into town and found the exhausted sheriff sleeping on the cell bunk in his office. Cash was in such a deep sleep that it took Tilly several minutes to get him fully awake so she could talk to him. Now he was going to see Angelina, and Will, to begin an investigation of the disappearance of Audreigh Rose, and nanny Arlyn. Tears stung his eyes thinking about the baby, his baby. Tired of keeping this secret that ate at him every day, he pondered whether to bring all this out into the light. Words from the Bible, the truth shall set you free, kept tumbling in his mind. He knew he wanted to be free of the burden of secrecy. Audreigh Rose was his daughter. He wanted a relationship with her. Now she was gone. Arlyn had taken her, but he vowed out loud to "find her." If it were the last thing he did on this earth he would find his child. Cash thought of Angelina.

Sympathy tugged at his heart softening him. He would find her for the woman he loved. He would find Audreigh Rose.

Nola was home with her sons and her staff. Joseph had picked her up and brought her home. She was weak and had a lingering cough, but she insisted on coming home. Her beloved Mundy was gone. His body was discovered in the woods. His death certificate would say he died from smoke inhalation according to the medical examiner. Dave Grimm, gave Nola all the details, as much as he knew. He told her Cash was investigating the fire as possible arson. If that was proven Mundy's death would be ruled a homicide.

Nola was shaken to her core. She felt unsafe, and wondered whether to take her children and her staff far away for a while. She knew that first she must settle Mundy's affairs and give him the proper burial that he so deserved. Alone in the small sitting room, her sons asleep in the nursery, she let the tears come for Mundy. He was the only father she had ever known. Her sons loved him like a grandfather. How would she go on without him? But she knew she must. She knew she must be strong for her boys. Mundy would want that for her. She closed her eyes against the pain, and tried with all her might to pull herself together. Sensing someone in the room she turned to see Dave in the doorway. His head was down and he held his hat in one hand and a small box in another. Nola stood up quickly, and as she did she lost her balance. With one step he was by her side. Nola reached out to him and grabbed his arm steadying herself. "Sor…sorry…Dave. I got a little dizzy. I think I stood too quickly." Nola smiled up at him.

"It's alright ma'am. Maybe you need to take it easy for a spell. Doc says you breathed a lot of smoke. Maybe you should sit ma'am."

Nola sat down and so did he. "That's better. I'm fine now." Nola continued smiling through her tears.

"Ma'am…" Dave spoke softly, "I have a box of papers. They were Mundy's. He always told me if anything happened to be sure you got these papers."

"Thank you Dave," Nola said.

Gingerly, as if reaching for something fragile and priceless; she took the box. It was made of wood and Mundy Winks' name was burned in the lid. She held it tight, wrapping her arms around it as if it contained all the love she felt for Mundy. Holding it close to her she closed her eyes and began to weep. She wept uncontrollably. A noise raw and primal escaped her lips and filled the room. Nola heard the noise and wondered for a moment where it was coming from. As Dave reached out to hold her in his arms she realized the grief, the tormented noise, was coming from within her. The pain of losing Mundy was trying to escape her frail body. Dave Grimm could do nothing more than hold her. Let it come. Nola was used to

190

loss. She always found a way to overcome and go on, but this loss felt unbearable. As much as she loved those who worked for her at Fair Meadows there was really no one to share her grief. Suddenly Dominy Brook's words came floating to the surface speaking to her heart and soul.

"The Lord will help you if you let Him Nola. You give it to Him. He will help you. Let God have the pain Nola Rain. Let God have the pain."

Cash sat on a small sofa in Angelina's bedroom looking around the room at everything but not seeing anything. She had excused herself when Cash came in to speak to her. She told him she needed to wash her face and regain her composure. Softly he told her to go on; he would wait; take all the time she needed. Will escorted his wife without saying a word to Cash. Soon they both came through the door and sat down together on a sofa opposite the sheriff. Cash started by asking when they last saw the baby. He wanted to know who hired Arlyn, and how she came recommended. He asked about her last name and where she was from. Will answered all the questions explaining he came to know her through Maclaine Moreaux. He further explained his relationship with Maclaine, and how close he had once been with the Moreaux family. Arlyn Fontenot was a cousin of Maclaine. Cash told them Henry Benning saw Arlyn yesterday as she stood at the door of the sheriff's office. Henry spoke with her and told her Cash was at the fire at Fair Meadows. Henry did see the baby in the back seat of the car and saw her drive out of town toward Louisa.

Cash rose to his feet to leave leaning down to Angelina, and whispering that he would find Audreigh Rose.

Looking up into his face Angelina managed a weak smile as she whispered back, "I am counting on you Cash."

191

Downstairs Cash and Will stood together each hoping the other might have a plan. Will finally spoke up, and said he would go to New Orleans where the Moreaux's last known address was before they came to Fair Meadows. The family originated from a small town not far from New Orleans, and Will planned on going there as well. "If they had anything to do with the fire they won't be easy to find." Cash said.

"Well we don't know they started that fire. I can't believe they would go that far."

"You know em better than anybody I guess. But I think the fire was a diversion to give them time to take the baby."

Will sucked in air. He exhaled slowly trying to calm his fractured nerves. "I know them as deeply spiritual. They are traditional people who believe in rituals passed down through generations. I know of their practices, but I have never known them to harm anyone."

"Maybe they haven't. Maybe they didn't...but Mundy is dead. Nola came close to dying, and a baby..." Cash choked on the words, "Audreigh Rose is missing." Cash fought back tears as he continued speaking low and purposeful. "Kidnapping and murder are serious offences Will. Maybe you don't know your friends as well as you think." Will looked deep into the young sheriff's eyes. He had no answer. "I hope that is the truth here Will." Cash turned to leave, but Will stopped him.

"What are you saying? You hope what is the truth Cash?"

"If they kidnapped a baby, and murdered an old man...I hope you didn't know they were capable of such heinous acts Will. If you knew anything at all about any of this that makes you an accessory. I hope you didn't know them as well as you thought you did." Cash

192

turned again and made his way to the patrol car. Will stood and watched as he backed the car and sped down the drive toward the main road. He felt drained. Numb. Old. Leaning his head against the door he stood trying to catch his breath. Thinking about New Orleans, he climbed the stairs to tell Angelina he was leaving. He was going to find the baby.

Three days after the funeral Nola sat at the edge of the water. The day was warm, sunny; a perfect day. Its beauty was lost on her as she sat on the banks of the creek eyes closed listening to the sound the water made as it flowed by. This creek, this spot had always been her favorite escape, but she could not escape this pain. She could not escape the reality that Mundy was gone, and she would never see him again this side of heaven. She was thinking about the last time she was here with him, and her babies. Her grief had taken on a life of its own, paralyzing her and robbing her of any joy. She could barely get out of bed each day, and for the first time she needed help with even the easiest tasks of caring for her children. Her heart broke anew each time she looked at them and realized they would grow up never knowing the man who loved them so much.

She held the box in her lap and opening her eyes she looked at the name burned in the wood. Taking her finger she traced each letter and was surprised to find it brought a smile to her face. She brought the box with her today to open it and reveal the things that were important to Mundy Winks. Although Dave gave her the box before the funeral she waited until now to open it. Trying a few times to open it something inside made her wait. She felt as if it were in some way a finality. An acceptance that he was really gone. Forever gone.

Ready now to face that cold fact she raised the lid to peer inside. On top face up was a photo of a woman. She was beautiful and familiar looking. Staring down into the face made her feel a little dizzy, so she held the picture out in front of her at arm's length. The photo was black and white but it didn't conceal how stunning the stranger was. Turning it over Nola read the words "Together Forever." It was signed Felice. Strange she thought, Mundy did speak of having the perfect love once. Could this be that love? He never shared much of his personal life with Nola, or anyone else, as far as she knew. Who was this woman? Nola picked up another picture of a baby. The picture was fuzzy but the child looked to be just a few weeks old. On the back were the words "My daughter." Nola felt the hair rise on her arms and neck. Staring hard at the picture of the tiny baby she wondered if she was hallucinating. Maybe losing her mind.

The baby resembled her sons. No she thought. This baby looks exactly like my sons. She lay the pictures back in the box and closed the lid. What was going on she thought? Not wanting to look at anything else in the box she picked herself up from the bank and began to walk the trail to the house. She kept saying the words, "I am not crazy…I am not crazy." She was sure she could convince herself if she just kept saying it.

Naomi stood in the kitchen staring at the photos. One hand was on her ample hip and her brow was furrowed as she looked hard at the beautiful young woman in the picture. Pursing her lips and clucking her tongue she lay it down on the table and picked up the photo of the baby. Nola sat drinking coffee and looking up into Naomi's face. "Tell me I am not crazy Naomi. That baby looks like my babies. And that woman…well she looks like me." The old cook didn't answer. She kept clucking her tongue and squinting her eyes as she continued to look at the picture of the strange baby. "That's Mundy's writing too. On the back of the picture of the baby. I know that is his writing Naomi. See…he wrote 'My

Daughter." Naomi stayed silent. "Why wouldn't he tell us he had a child?" Nola was waiting for Naomi to say something. She wanted some logical reason to explain it all away. Finally in frustration Nola raised her voice, "Naomi…say something."

"Missy,"…Naomi looked hard at Nola, she raised her dark brows then lowered them scowling.

"Calm down. I see some resemblance, but land sakes chile we can't be jumpin to no conclusions here." She said without taking her eyes off the photo of the baby.

"I'm sorry Naomi…but I can't get past how much that child looks like my sons."

"They do some at that. But you know all babies look much the same whens they is first birthed. This here baby is probly a few weeks old." Naomi squinted at the photo again.

"Why would Mundy hide the fact that he had a child? You have known him for years and you never knew? Of course you didn't or you would tell me." Nola poured more coffee and then sat staring into the black liquid.

"What else was in that box Missy?" Naomi asked.

"I don't…don't know. I never looked at any other items in the box after I found these photos."

Naomi stood with both hands on her hips now and a disapproving look upon her face. "Well you needs to keep looking. Might be more clues in that box to help figure out who these folks is…land sakes alive girl." Picking the photos up once more and staring at first one, and then the other, Nola agreed. "Yes, I suppose you are right. Yes, I will keep looking."

"Land sakes alive…what next around here?" Naomi said as she turned back and began to wash the dishes in water that had gone from hot to lukewarm.

Nola heard her repeating those words as she left the kitchen and went to get the box. Hopeful that she would find some answers in the items of Mundy's past.

TWENTY

The first stop Will made was to the shop that Mother owned in the
heart of the city. The front of the store was filled with souvenirs,
and gadgets. Pens and magnets with New Orleans imprinted on
them. Real alligator heads, jars of potions, and lotions, lined the
shelves. It resembled most of the other shops in the area; except
Mother was not like the other shop owners. A lot of the "got-cha"
shops were owned by folks just trying to take the money of the
curious and gullible. People who came seeking some mystery, and
excitement, and wanted some memento to remember their trip.
Something to show the friends back home and prove they'd been to
New Orleans. Mother was Louisiana born and raised. She grew up
in the swamps and held fast to her family's traditions and rituals.
She was the Mother of her clan. Her people came to her for advice.
They came when they were sick, or whenever they were troubled.
"Troubles always was," Mother would say. Yes, troubles always
was.

Will entered the shop just as the old woman was getting ready to
hang the closed sign on the door. As he turned the knob and entered
she stood silent and still just a few feet from him. Mother smiled

from ear to ear as she recognized Will. Her eyes black and large flashed and blinked as she said his name. "Will…well…Shylone, es gud to see ya now." She said.

"Mother…it's been a long time."

"Ta long Shy…ta long. Ya gots troubles for Mother, ya?"

"I gots troubles Mother. Big troubles. My baby is missing. My daughter." Will spoke slowly and with a deliberate tone.

"Ya beez wrong Will Biggs. Ya gots no dawter. Dat baby not beez yorn Shy." Mother's smile faded as she spoke. Will stood still for a moment thinking before he replied.

"That baby is mine. Audreigh Rose. Maclaine has something to do with her disappearance and I need to know where to find him. I need to know now Mother. Where is Maclaine?" Will demanded. "Where is Jolene, and Gabrielle?" Mother was silent. She narrowed her eyes until they looked snakelike. She twisted her mouth into a grimace and raised a bony hand. Pointing to the door she hissed at Will.

"Ya git out. Mothers es clost. Ya git back tomor…tomor…"

Will looked toward the door where her gnarled finger pointed. Looking back at her, as steady as he could keep his gaze he told her he would be back. "I will be back tomorrow Mother. Tomorrow, and the day after that. And the day after that. Until I find them I will be back every day. Until I get my child back I will be back every day Mother." Turning to open the door he could hear sounds escaping her lips. Hissing sounds. Snakelike sounds. He opened the door without looking back; he stepped out into the night air feeling drops of sweat rolling from his brow. Something cold ran up his spine, a chill. He shivered. Tired and scared, he began to walk to his hotel. Frightened or not he vowed to himself he would be back tomorrow. One way or another he would find Audreigh Rose. Mother was wrong. Audreigh Rose was his daughter, because he wanted to be her father. Mother was definitely wrong.

Arlyn held the baby on her lap making a soothing sound as she gently rocked back and forth. Audreigh was fussy and warm, but the nanny wasn't overly concerned with a fussy baby. More than likely she was cutting teeth. No, Arlyn had greater concerns. For the moment she was safe, and the baby was safe, but she knew that they would be looking for her. Not just Will Biggs and Cash Atkins, but Maclaine, and his women folk. She was more concerned about the Moreaux's and what they might do to her for messing up their plan. She was scared about the fire. Knowing they were going to start a fire as a diversion made her an accomplice to arson. But she knew a lot of things she wished she didn't.

Tomorrow she would try again to see Cash, and try to make everything all right for Audreigh Rose. More than anything she wanted the baby to be safe and loved. Maclaine, and Jolene, would not harm her she knew. They had special plans for the baby. If Mother accepted her. But Arlyn knew she needed to be with her own people. She needed Angelina. Angelina was her mother after all. Arlyn was smart, and figured out on her own that Will was not the baby's father. Cash Atkins was. She could see it every time he looked at her. Reaching down and touching the soft hair of the now sleeping baby, she breathed a sigh as she whispered, "Don't worry baby...Arlyn will get you to your Daddy, and maybe he and your Momma will raise you right. You deserve that Audreigh Rose. Yes, you deserve that."

Will entered the shop the bright and early the next morning. The front of the store was empty, but he could hear noise in the back of the shop. Someone was humming. Will called out to Mother, and waited, but she didn't come. He listened and thought he could hear voices. Barely audible, but it was more than one person speaking. He called out once more and hesitating to walk through the doorway, he waited. Finally becoming impatient he started toward the strands of beads that acted as a curtain over the door that led to the back of the store. Just after a couple of slow steps Mother appeared. Making an entrance fit for royalty she sauntered into the room with an ear to ear smile. Will greeted her warmly. "Mother, good to see you this morning. How are you this fine day?"

"Shy...ya comed back ta see Mother. Me has gud news for ya. Maclaine es in da back." She smiled and pointed toward the back of the store. "Go on now. He beez watin for ya Shy."

Will stood frozen for a moment. Wary, and feeling trapped he wasn't sure if he wanted to go to the back of the store. Mother lost any patience she had, speaking sharply to him.

"What ya watin for? Iffun ya wan to see Maclaine go. Mother don gots all day. I not playin wit chu."

"Yes Mother. I'm sorry." Will made his move toward the back. The old woman followed close enough behind that he could hear her ragged breathing. His knees felt weak and the hair on the back of his neck stood up.

The beads made a swooshing sound as he parted them and let go once he was through the door way. Entering the room he squinted straining to adjust his eyes to the dark. No windows and the glow of a small lamp made the room dismal, dim. His eyes quickly came to focus on a small wood table with two chairs. The room was smoky, thick. A burning smell of incense made breathing difficult. Will coughed and rubbed his burning eyes. Will fastened his eyes on Maclaine sitting in one of the chairs. Frazzled, and old looking, Will barely recognized his friend of many years. Sitting down opposite

200

him, and staring into his face Will asked first about the baby. "Where is Audreigh Rose? And where is Arlyn?" Maclaine shifted in his chair and put a hand up to his eyes.

"I…uh…look Will…," he said nervously, "I don't know where the baby is. Arlyn either."

"Maclaine I swear, you best tell me where Audreigh Rose is…or so help me…," his voice trailed off.

"I'm tellin you Will. Arlyn was supposed to bring the baby to Mother. But…but she didn't show… Shy. We have someone working on locating that silly girl. Someone else will bring the baby."

"What in the world were you all thinking? Why did you take that baby to begin with?" Will was getting louder with every question. "I want my baby Maclaine. Now…here….now. This sick game is over. Where is Arlyn?"

"I done told you…I don't know…I'm sorry Will. It wasn't supposed to go down like this."

"You all killed that old man. Did you know that Maclaine?" Will was wild eyed and red faced now. He banged the table hard with his fist. "You killed Mundy Winks when you set that fire."

"What? What are you talkin about man…we didn't kill anybody?" Maclaine looked genuinely confused. "The fire was meant as a diversion Will…I swear to you Shy. That's all…not to kill Mundy. If he's dead Shy…it was an accident."

Will leaned back in the chair, and closed his eyes.

Trying hard to think of some way to get through to Maclaine, but he couldn't focus. The smell, the thick smoky air, and the heat of the room made him dizzy, nauseated.

When he opened his eyes he jumped in his chair and almost turned over backwards. Standing behind Maclaine were Jolene, and Gabrielle. Where had they come from? Why had he not heard them come in the room? Feeling faint Will banged his fist on the table lamely. "Listen to me…all of you," his voice was weak and barely audible. "I want…want…" Will began to sway, "I want my baby…now." He rubbed his eyes and before he could say another word he felt his world fading out. Everything began to glow white, and then nothing. Will fainted, falling to the floor from his chair. The four of them did nothing at first. Looking from one to another they waited for instructions on what to do next. Finally, the orders came from Mother.

"Pick dat boy up. Take em to de ottur ruum."

Maclaine, and the two women, did as they were told. They always did what Mother demanded. Always.

TWENTY ONE

Nola opened the box with Mundy's name on it for the second time. Among financial papers there was a will with the beneficiaries recently updated. Surprisingly, but then not so surprising; everything was left to Nola, and her sons. Mundy was financially well off, but he was frugal so this came as no surprise either. A newspaper clipping lay folded among the other papers. Unfolding it she read the story of a man who was hanged in Monroe after being charged with the kidnapping of a child. The baby, just a few months old, was never found. A man who worked for Pine Point was accused of taking the child, and investigators ruled the crime a homicide. Homicide was never proven, but the kidnapping charge stuck, and Jessie Porter was hanged. There was a faded picture accompanying the article. It was a baby. Nola sucked in a sharp breath. It was the same baby picture she had found in Mundy's possessions; the same picture with the words on the back "My Daughter". How could this kidnapped baby be Mundy's child? Naomi would know about that. She should remember that.

As Nola sat thinking about all the information in the box Dave Grimm came to the door of the sitting room.

Not wanting to reveal too much too soon she closed the lid on the box when Dave entered and sat down opposite her. She looked into his usually smiling face and saw such sadness. It was the same look that everyone was wearing since the funeral. The loss of Mundy would take a long time to come to terms with. Not just the farm itself would miss the boss, but all who knew him loved the old horseman. Dave had a ruggedly handsome face. Dark brown hair that spilled over boyishly on his forehead. His eyes were green, and dimples on each side of his wide grin framed his face, making him look mischievous. Tall and well built, he was muscular from all the physical work on the farm. His personality fit his looks. Country to the core. Laid back, and soft spoken, he smiled often. His smile was contagious. Nola liked him. She was starting to depend on him more, and more, since the fire.

Nola sat the box to one side as she greeted Dave. "Thank you for coming in so soon. I know you are busy, but I had Joseph ask you to come in and talk with me today. I'm glad to see you…and I appreciate how prompt you are. Nola said.

"Yes ma'am. I tried to get here as soon as I could. We, I mean the other hands and I are trying to clean up some. Cash doesn't want us near the cabin. Or what's left of it. But we are moving the horses back to the stable and picking up near the woods."

"Yes, I know. I just want to thank you Dave. Really. I don't know what I would have done without you these last few days.

I depend on you now. With…well…," Nola choked and cleared her throat. "Well with Mundy…gone." It was so hard to say those words. She wondered if she would ever be able to say he was gone without her heart seizing, and tears stinging her eyes. Dave looked at her and felt his own heart tighten. She was so pretty. It hurt him to see the pain in her stunning eyes.

"Ma'am, I will do anything I can for you and Fair Meadows. I am not Mundy…," Dave stopped and smiled, "God only gave the earth one Mundy Winks, and then God wanted him back." Dave stopped and sat back on the sofa. He brought his hand up to his brow as if he were thinking of what to say next. He could think of no words to comfort Nola. He knew it would take time for the pain to ease. "I just want you to know I am here for you. However you need me."

Nola smiled through tears and sniffed a little. "Thank you. Thank you Dave, that means everything to me. I wanted to see you because I want to offer you Mundy's position." She paused to let that sink in. Before he could answer she continued. "I believe if Mundy were here he would agree with me that you are the man for the job. Please say you will accept. Of course the position of Manager comes with a raise in salary and housing… if you want to rebuild the cabin." Nola held her breath waiting for what seemed an eternity for Dave to answer.

"I accept your offer. I am sad that the offer comes in lieu of tragedy, but I accept it." Dave said smiling.

"Good. It's settled then. Run this farm as you see fit. Mundy had free reign and you will too." Nola said.

"I will take care of it much the way Mundy did. He was a good boss and a great teacher. We…all the guys…miss him." Dave stood to his feet.

Long after Dave had gone Nola sat thinking about the gentle young man. So mature and sensible, she knew he would take good care of the farm. The next thing on her agenda was sorting all this information out about Mundy's past. She wasn't sure where to start but she picked up the box and made her way to the kitchen. Surely Naomi remembered some of the story about the man that was hanged and the missing baby. The story of the missing baby made her so sad. Perhaps because of her own past and the fact that she was kidnapped, or abandoned, and found in a rain soaked alley. She vowed to figure out what this was all about. "Oh Mundy," she said out loud, "what's this all about?"

Arlyn pulled the car off the street and parked it in front of the sheriff's office. It was early. The sun barely up and she was already tired from a lack of sleep. Glancing in the back seat at Audreigh

Rose she noticed the baby didn't seem to have a sleeping problem. She looked so peaceful and pretty. Not a care in her little world. Looking at her brought tears to Arlyn's eyes. She turned around and placed her hands on the steering wheel shutting her eyes against the tears.

She wanted to shut the world out. When had this become so complicated and wrong? "You all right miss?" Arlyn jumped out of her stupor and made a noise resembling a muffled scream. "Whoa…whoa. Sorry Miss. I didn't mean to scare you none." The man was leaning down into the passenger side window which was cracked a few inches.

"No…it's…I mean, I'm all right. Thank you for asking. Just here to see Sheriff Atkins." Arlyn said.

"Well I believe he is here. Want me to go check for ya?" The man started to turn and head for the door to the office.

"No wait. Sir…I will go. I'm going now. Thank you for being so thoughtful, and kind. Really. I'm getting out now." With those words Arlyn got out of the car and opened the back door to take the baby out. She so hated to wake her up knowing she would be cranky. She glanced up into the face of the nice man. Arlyn recognized him from the other day. He was the stranger who had talked to her when she was looking for Cash. He had told her about the fire. As she reached in to get Audreigh the man placed his hand on her shoulder. She stopped and stood up facing him. Brushing a lock of hair from her eyes with her hand she waited for the stranger to speak.

"No use waking your baby Miss. I can stay right here beside the car while you go talk to Cash. He knows me ma'am. My name's Henry…Henry Benning." Henry gave her a big smile, revealing bad teeth.

"Your baby is safe with me. Go on now. I will wait right here."
Arlyn looked at the sleeping baby and back into the kind eyes of the
stranger. It was true she told herself they were not exactly strangers.
She had talked to him before. He seemed so helpful, and the thought
of waking Audreigh and making her fussy did not appeal to her in
the exhausted state she was in. Hesitating for a second longer she
made a decision. A decisions that would live with her the rest of her
life.

"Thank you sir. I will be right back. Thank you so much. I really
didn't want to wake her." Arlyn smiled at the stranger.

"Go on now. I'll be right here. Go on Miss." The stranger with
the kind eyes smiled back. Arlyn stepped away from the car and
walked to the door of the office. Looking back over her shoulder
she saw the man still standing there smiling. Turning the door knob
to the office she let herself in, and closed the door behind her.

Arlyn barely had a chance to get inside Cash Atkins' office
before she heard the enjine of the car parked she'd parked outside
roar to life. It took a few seconds for her brain to compute what she
was hearing, but when her mind comprehended, she bolted for the
door with Cash on her heels. He was calling out to her as she
opened the door. Standing on the sidewalk watching the car with
baby Audreigh speed away Arlyn began screaming at the top of her
lungs.

Everyone within the sound of her screams froze where they were
and looked to see where the sound was coming from. Cash grabbed
her harshly and shook her. She began to mutter trying hard to catch
her breath. "The baby...the baby...in the car...," she beat her hands
on Cash's chest. "Henry...the man took her...Henry....Benning."

Arlyn was trying desperately to make him understand. Looking into her horrified face the reality of what she was saying sank in.

"The baby? Arlyn…is the baby…Audreigh. Is Audreigh Rose in that car? Who is in that car girl?" Cash was shouting at her now.

"I…don't know. He told me he knew you. Henry…Benning. He offered to keep an eye on her. She was sleeping…," Arlyn could hardly breathe. Cash released her and ran to the cruiser. He jumped in and went speeding off praying he could catch the car. His mind was racing trying to sort all this out. One thing he knew for sure; nanny Arlyn was going to jail. She started all this by taking the baby. It seemed like the world was falling apart. First the fire, then Mundy dying. Now someone, the town nut, was speeding away with a baby. His baby. He hit the gas harder, and gripped the wheel tighter, determined to find the car that had his Audreigh Rose.

Henry Benning drove with a smile on his face. Henry was always smiling. When he was a young boy folks would often ask Henry's Momma if he was simple.

Afraid that folks might be right she had him checked out by a doctor who assured her that he was not simple. Just a happy child.

Henry was feeling happy right now. His plan to take the baby worked out better than he expected. He thought he would have to take the child by force, but as luck would have it he didn't have to. That made him happy. That made Henry's smile a lot wider. He sure didn't look forward to hurting that itty bitty Miss Arlyn, but money was… well money. Henry was offered a deal he couldn't pass up. Too good to be true, almost. Deliver the baby, collect ten grand. That was more money than Henry could count. He had a no fail plan. Deliver the baby, collect his money, start a new life in a new place. After all there wasn't much of anything or anybody that he was leaving behind in his old life. Momma was dead, and Henry was never much good at farming. No reason he could see to staying in Monroe. When Maclaine approached him with this deal it felt like he struck gold. He just hoped that baby stayed asleep. He had no idea how to care for a baby. With that thought in his head he hit the gas harder and smiled a little wider. "New Orleans, here I come," Henry whispered into the air.

TWENTY TWO

Cradling his head with both hands, Will tried to sit up. His eyes were open, but not focused. The world was a blur and his head was pounding. What happened? He tried to remember, but he wasn't sure where he was, or what day it was. He lay still for a moment with eyes closed willing his head to stop pounding. After a moment he tried sitting up again. Feeling with his hands he realized he was lying on the floor. Foggy, and breathless, he sat up and rubbed his eyes. The room was dim and musty smelling. No window and no light made it almost impossible to see with his failing eyesight. After sitting still for a few moments longer his eyes began to adjust to the darkness of the room. He was in a storage room, but nothing was stored there. It was empty. Totally empty. He remembered then. Mother's. He was at Mother's shop. But everything, and everyone, was gone. He stood shakily to his feet and stumbled into the main room of the shop where the shelves should have been lined with gadgets and trinkets. Nothing. Gone. Swept clean. Suddenly he felt ill and stumbled through the door to the outside. The air smacked his face and he breathed deeply. He felt somewhat better out on the street.

He turned around and saw the sign hanging over the door was gone too. Without any clue as to where to look for Maclaine, and Mother, Will began making his way up the street to the place he thought he'd parked his truck. Hoping his was memory was still intact, he walked as quickly as his shaky legs and aching head would let him.

Angelina sat nervously looking around the nursery as if she might find some overlooked clue as to where Arlyn had taken Audreigh Rose. Tilly stood nearby staring into the closet with the same intent stare. The women were searching and willing something, anything to give them a direction. They needed a starting point. At times Tilly would repeat out loud what she remembered from the last time she saw and spoke with Arlyn. Every few minutes Angelina would throw out a question. "Did Arlyn seem nervous Tilly? Did you notice any bags packed and waiting?

Was there anything out of the ordinary in this room?" Tilly would think hard, and answer, but nothing new was revealed. There were looks of despair, and unbelief, after every failed attempt at coming up with anything relevant. After a few hours they were exhausted. Tilly suggested they start over in the morning. A good night's rest and a fresh start in the morning might bring a new perspective, at least that's what she hoped for. Angelina retired to her room. Heart sick, and weary, she was sure sleep would not come, but she was blissfully wrong. Within minutes of lying down she was whisked away to a deep dark place. Tilly on the other hand laid awake for hours.

When the first light of dawn began to glow along the edges of the drawn curtains she was awake to see it.

 Getting up and going down to the kitchen she was surprised to find Will, and Cash, setting at the table drinking coffee. Both men looked aged and haggard. Tears welled up in Tilly's eyes as she realized that neither of them brought any good news home. Her heart ached for Angelina, and for now she would let her sleep on in ignorance. Soon enough she would have to face another day not knowing where her baby was. How many days would Angelina have before she found Audreigh Rose Tilly wondered? Her mind drifted back to another time, another baby gone missing, and a man she loved. Jessie had paid the ultimate price for something Tilly was sure he had not done. She hoped folks got it right this time. She hoped with all her heart they got it right.

Tilly eyed the two men who sat in silence staring back at her. She poured herself a cup of coffee and sat down at the table. No one spoke for a few minutes and with questions swirling in her head Tilly broke the silence. "Well gentlemen, what is going on? Do you know where the baby is? Where Arlyn is? Do you two know anything?" Cash, and Will, looked at each other, as if neither one had an answer.

"Tilly," Cash began, "All we know right now is Henry Benning has Audreigh Rose." Cash put his hand up to stop Tilly. "Arlyn had her, and Henry took the baby and the car Arlyn took from here." Cash knew it was Henry who drove off with Audreigh Rose.

 Henry had told Cash of Arlyn's visit to the sheriff's office when Cash was at the fire. He had seen Henry hanging around outside minutes before he drove off with the baby.

213

"But...I don't understand Sheriff...how did Henry get the baby? What in God's green world is goin on with people round here?" Tilly interrupted.

"Arlyn came into my office and Henry was out by the car. She left the baby in the car and that crack pot drove off with her. I chased him, but couldn't catch him. By the time I got back to my office Arlyn was gone too." Cash rubbed the back of his neck. "That's all I know at this point."

"I saw Maclaine, in New Orleans, but he claimed he didn't know anything about the fire, or the baby missing. Thing is... I blacked out and when I came around Maclaine and his family were gone. Disappeared. That's why I came home. I had no idea where to look for them. But I can guarantee they had something to do with all this," said Will.

"Well I'm gonna head over to Fair Meadows and see if the fire chief is still there. I want to see if he knows what started the fire. Guess I will know how to continue this investigation after he rules on arson or accident. Tilly please tell Angelina that I chased after Henry, but he had too much of a head start on me." Cash looked so despondent.

"But you tell her we will bring Audreigh Rose home. She can count on that. Will you tell her that for me...please?"

Tilly's eyes filled with tears as she reached across the table and took Cash's hand. "I will tell her for you Cash... for certain I will...child."

Cash stood at the edge of the still smoldering woods with the fire chief from Monroe. He could not believe his ears when the chief told him the fire started as the result of an accident. Near the cabin the arson team found the remains of a tree that had been struck by lightning. Checking the records for the night of the fire the chief discovered a storm blew through and so it was deemed likely the fire was officially of an accidental origin, or an act of nature. Cash scratched at his face contemplating what he was told. He thanked the chief and watched as the men gathered up equipment ready to move off the farm. The fire would soon become a bad memory and new trees would grow in place of the charred remains. Cash thought of Mundy and was glad that the old man had not died as a result of someone purposely setting fire to the cabin and woods. He guessed Maclaine's relatives moving out when they did was purely coincidence. Had they still been in the cabin they would have perished along with Mundy. Cash thought about the lightening, and wondered if that too were purely coincidental. The fire, and the baby missing at the same time seemed a bit much even for Mother Nature.

He turned when hearing his name spoken softly. Facing Nola he was struck with how frail and small she looked. She was pale and her eyes were red as if she had been crying. Cash smiled at her and took her arm. As they walked back toward the house and away from the woods he told her of the chief's findings. She stopped walking and looked at him in amazement. "An accident?" Nola said. She paused and then said those words again, but this time as a statement not a question. "An accident."

"Yes, Nola. The chief said lightning started the fire near the cabin. It struck a tree. Lucky that Maclaine's family were gone. Did they tell you they were leaving? Did Maclaine tell you he was quitting and leaving?"

"No…no…not a word about leaving from any of them. Don't you find that strange Cash?" Nola asked.

Cash smiled and took her arm to begin walking again. "These past few days have been strange Nola. Angelina's baby is missing. Maclaine and his sister are gone. Suddenly gone. Mundy…," he let his voice trail off. Angelina's eyes stung with tears at the mention of Mundy. When, she wondered would she ever be able to hear his name and not feel her heart breaking?

"I have asked Dave to take Mundy's position. He accepted. No one can ever fill Mundy's shoes…," she smiled, "or boots I should say. Dave is a good man. He will be a good manager for the farm. He has been a life line for me these last few days.

I would have been totally lost without his help." Nola thought for a moment before adding, "You have been there for me to my dear Cash."

"Just doin my job ma'am." He smiled down at her and she noticed for the first time how handsome he was when he smiled. A wide easy smile, and a dimple in his chin made him an extremely attractive man. Why had she never noticed this before, she thought? The two of them walked along the side of the house and then they stood at Cash's cruiser.

He told her he would be back soon, and she told him that she would say a prayer for Audreigh Rose. "I appreciate that Nola, more than you know." Nola watched as he drove down the long driveway that led to the main road. She whispered a prayer right then as she watched. A prayer for Audreigh and Angelina. And one for Cash. Then turning to go into the house she said one last prayer that she would figure out why Mundy never told her he had baby, and what happened to her. She carried her weary body up the steps, and the very last thought on her mind was to lay down and rest. Let sweet

216

sleep carry her away to a world where everything was as it used to be, and Mundy was still alive. Yes, in her dreams he was still with her, and not even death could steal him from her there.

After talking it over with Naomi, Nola decided it might be a good idea to pay a visit to Pine Point. Even though she and Angelina were not exactly friends, she did feel as if she could at least reach out to her and offer to help her, or at least support her somehow. It was a cool crisp morning with endless blue sky and bright sunshine. Joseph was driving her to Pine Point and she found herself enjoying the country side. She tried hard to put everything out of her mind and concentrate on what she might say to Angelina. Nola had another reason for the visit. She wanted to talk with Tilly about the man who kidnapped the baby years ago. Naomi, told Nola, that Tilly was involved with Jessie Porter. There was some connection between the baby that was kidnapped, and Mundy. When Nola pressed Naomi for more information she simply did not know the baby that was kidnapped was Mundy's. Naomi reminded Nola once more how private Mundy was. He never talked about his personal life. Naomi surely didn't know anything about a woman and a child. Nola was speculating that the baby was Mundy's daughter, but she believed the kidnapped baby, and Mundy's child, were one in the same. She hoped that Tilly would talk to her, and perhaps shed more light on the mystery. She could only hope. At this point Nola's investigation was at a stall.

Parking the car, Nola told Joseph she would only be half an hour or so. Perhaps he could just stick around rather than drive back to Fair Meadows. He told her he would of course wait for her. Knocking on the massive oak doors of the main house Nola felt queasy and uneasy. She tried to calm her nerves by taking deep breaths. The door opened and Tilly greeted her warmly. She led Nola to a large living area and asked her to have a seat.

217

She then left saying she would get Miss Angelina, and also bring some refreshments. She looked around the large room. It was elegant and upscale. The furniture was heavy and imported. She recognized some of the art work and was sure it was original. Her eyes landed on some framed photographs. Paul, and Susie Oliver, in a gold frame, a little girl that Nola knew must be Angelina. Then a picture caught her eye and made her heart skip a beat. She took a sharp breath and got up to look closer. It was a picture of Will holding a newborn. Will holding Audreigh Rose. A voice behind Nola startled her causing her to nearly drop the frame, which was fragile sea glass.

When Nola turned around she still had the frame in her hand. Quickly she turned back to the mantle and placed it carefully on the ledge. "Angelina," she said, crossing the room to greet her.

"Nola, how nice to see you." Angelina put her hand out to Nola. Taking her hand in her own she noticed how warm and soft Angelina's hands were. This surprised her as she heard the woman liked to work the horses like a man.

"Angelina, I am so glad you would allow me to come see you. I heard about the…well…your baby, and I just wanted to extend my hand to help you." Nola searched Angelina's face. She saw a woman in so much pain trying with all her might to hold it together.

"Yes…the baby is…well we will get her back. We will…very soon. Cash promised."

"Oh yes, I know you will. Cash is working very hard on getting her back. And he will." Nola smiled. Still holding her hand she continued speaking softly to Angelina. "I just want you to know if there is anything I can do. Anything. Please don't hesitate to call." Nola's voice faltered, near tears.

"Nothing can be done except Cash finding her and bringing her home. And he will. Any moment now." Angelina dropped Nola's hand and sat down on the large sofa. She looked so small and she was not a petite woman. Very thin and pale, it was obvious the toll this was taking on her body. They continued to talk for a few minutes while Tilly made herself busy around them. She poured tea for Nola, and there was warm biscuits with butter, and honey. Nola took one and tried to eat it. She was hoping Angelina would take one as well. It was obvious she was not eating. It did not work as Angelina touched nothing, not even the tea. She sat staring off into space. After a few minutes Angelina rose and apologized to Nola telling her she must go lie down saying she was exhausted. Nola told her she understood. After she said goodbye and left the room Tilly returned. Nola then asked if she could speak with her for just a few moments. Tilly looked surprised, but said "of course, Missy." She sat down opposite of Nola on an overstuffed chair. Tilly looked a little uncomfortable as if she were about to be accused of something. Accused of what, she did not know. Nola smiled and sat her tea cup down, while clearing her throat.

She was stalling trying to figure out where to begin. So she thought of the newspaper clipping and pulled it from her pocket and handed it to Tilly.

Tilly stared down at the paper and her hands shook slightly when she handed it back to Nola. She raised her chin slightly, looking as if she felt a little indignant. She folded her hands in her lap and finally spoke. "What do you want Missy. Why show me that?"

"Oh Miss Tilly, I don't want to upset you." Nola struggled to find the words. "I am trying to find out about the child that was kidnapped. You see, well…I think the baby might have been Mundy Winks daughter." She reached in her pocket to take the picture out to show Tilly. When she looked back up Tilly was on

219

her feet. Agitated and upset, the old woman stood wringing her hands.

"I don't know nothing bout that Missy. All I do know is Jessie never took nobody's baby. But they hung him anyways. Now if you escuse me I have work waitin on me." Tilly turned to leave the room, but Nola called out to her.

"Tilly, wait…please…wait. I don't mean to upset you it's just…well I loved Mundy so. I just want to know what this is all about. You are the only one who can help. You are my only hope." Tilly slowly sat back down looking at Nola long and hard.

"I don't know what I can say Missy, everythins bout been said that can be said."

Her lip quivered and she gazed out the window before turning her eyes back to Nola. "Jessie Porter was a fine, Christian man. He never took nobody's baby. I will be sayin that till they throw dirt in my face. Yes, ma'am I will."

"The article…it says the baby belonged to a woman from New Orleans. It says she was staying with relatives in Monroe. Do you know who they were?" Nola waited feeling breathless and dizzy.

"I only know that she was visiting her kin that owned a farm near Louisa. The farm was Pleasant Ridge. The folk's last name was Benning." Tilly thought for a moment before she spoke. "The lady that had the baby was named Phyllis…no… that's not right. Felice or something like that. Yes,I believe it was Felice. I don't know her last name. Maybe Benning like her kin. I know she was from somewhere round New Orleans. After her baby got taken she left and went back there. Never heard no more bout her." Tilly looked out the window shaking her head. "Jessie was the love of my life…and they hanged that love and left me with nothing. I never had any interest in no other man my whole life." Looking into Nola's face with quivering lips and eyes puddled with tears Tilly sighed. "You see Missy...part of me died with Jessie. But I have hope we will be together again. That's whats kept me goin all these years. Jessie's watin for me."

She looked away again, staring out the window at the trees blowing in the soft breeze.

When she looked back at Nola she seemed so sad. It broke her heart to think she had caused Tilly so much grief by asking about any of this. She stood to her feet, and Tilly did the same. As Nola got in the car and Joseph pulled down the drive she thought about what she learned today. Tomorrow she would find out where Pleasant Ridge Farm was and pay a visit there. Perhaps someone still lived there that knew the story of the missing baby. Nola lay her head back on the seat and let the vibration of the moving car soothe her frazzled nerves. Her need to find out who Mundy's daughter was grew every day. It was now an all-consuming desire to know. She could not let it be. Some unexplainable force was driving her to find the answers to this mystery. Nola vowed she would get the answer she was looking for. She would, she must. There would be no rest for her until she knew the truth.

TWENTY THREE

Henry Benning got a bright idea about half way to New Orleans. The idea was so good it even surprised him. He never came up with much of anything that turned out to be any good, at least not until now. Maybe he was getting a little wiser with age. He slowed the car and with one smooth move turned it around in the road and headed north. He was going back to the farm. Or maybe somewhere around the farm. Back to Bryce County. It came to him sudden like that he could get more for the baby on his own. Those New Orleans people only wanted to give him a few thousand dollars. He should be able to get 100 grand from Angelina Oliver. Everyone knew the Olivers' were filthy rich. Henry heard his Momma say that many times. "Yes siree bob," Henry was right proud of himself. After all this was not the first time he had cashed in on a baby. Years ago he'd stolen away another baby that belonged to his cousin. He never got any money that time. Alone and spooked in the dark alley of a city he was unfamiliar with, Henry panicked and left the baby. Rain was pouring down in buckets that night. He laid the baby down in the street, and ran. Over the years he revisited that same dark street, in his sleep. His nightmares started after that botched "get rich quick" scheme. Henry sighed. He was thinking about that other baby. He was thinking about how sad his Momma had been when the baby went missing. His cousin Felice eventually went back to New Orleans.

Henry never told anyone that the baby was there somewhere in New Orleans. The only remorse Henry had was the pain he caused his Momma. Hard as she was on Henry, he sure loved his Momma. But it worked to his advantage. His momma softened a little after that. At least where Henry was concerned. She didn't nag him so much to find work. She was easier on him as if someone might come and steal her grown son. Henry considered that ordeal a practice run. He intended to get his money this time. Anyway Henry never liked Felice. A loose woman. She messed up; had a baby out of wedlock. Getting rid of it was probably doing her a favor. Now those same people want this baby. But Henry knew where the real money was, and he wouldn't have to go to that dark, scary, city again. He just needed a place to hide out, and in a few days, he would be on his way to Paradise. He chuckled. He laughed out loud. His laughter made the baby cry. Henry stopped laughing. He would need to find a store and buy milk. He felt his anger start to surface. Henry couldn't wait to get rid of this kid. Concentrating hard on his thoughts of Paradise, he tried to drown the sound of her crying. Henry never liked taking care of anybody but Henry. Just a few days, he thought. Just a few days and he would be on his way to Paradise.

He came out of the store carrying a screaming Audreigh under one arm, and the sack with milk and cigarettes in his other hand. He was muttering under his breath at the baby telling her to "hush up that crying."

He sat the sack on the hood of the car and opened the door to the back seat. Laying Audreigh down he tuned and almost bumped into the lady who ran the store. "Oh I am so sorry," the lady was short, fat, and more than annoying Henry thought.

"You forgot your change." The lady looked into the back seat at a screaming Audriegh Rose. Instinctively she started to reach in to comfort the baby, but Henry grabbed her by the wrist. Startled she tried to pull her arm from his grasp, but Henry held it for a moment. When he let go she rubbed her wrist with her other hand and before she could say anything Henry quickly apologized.

"Sorry ma'am," Henry smiled his kindest smile. "I didn't mean to grab you so hard. It's just…well me and the young-un, well I have to protect her. Being her daddy… you know. Sorry."

"Well I was just going to see if I could quiet her down. Are you travelling alone? Where is the child's mother?" She stared hard at Henry. His smile had no effect on her.

"Her mother is back home in West Virginia. We are on our way to meet up with her. She had to leave us and see to her sick Momma. Her Momma didn't make it so we are going to be with her, and make the funeral.

The lady eyed him carefully. She could spot a liar from 50 feet away. She had her late husband to thank for that skill.

He lied to her their entire married life, but because of that she had picked up an invaluable skill. She became adept at knowing when someone was not speaking the truth. This man was lying and she knew it. She however became extremely skilled at getting people to believe anything she said. She smiled sweetly at the stranger. "I am so sorry to hear that. I just wanted to give you your change and let you two be on your way. She is just the most beautiful baby I've ever seen. You and your wife must feel very blessed, I'm sure." Henry relaxed. He said nothing as he poured milk into a bottle and stuck the nipple in Audreigh's mouth. Instantly the child stopped crying as she noisily sucked the bottle. She was hungry.

"Thank you ma'am. Got to be goin now. Thanks for bringing me my change." Henry never glanced her way as he got in the car.

"Drive careful." The fat lady called out as Henry drove off. He never looked back. He never gave the lady another thought. That was one of several mistakes Henry would make.

The glow from a full moon illuminated the highway that stretched out in front of him as Henry made his way wearily to his destination. He remembered a cabin deep in the woods not far from Monroe. He stumbled upon it once when he was poaching deer on private property. No trespassing signs ever deterred Henry Benning. No one told Henry what to do and when to do it. "No siree bob." He knew he must be near the turn off to the property so he slowed the car.

The baby was asleep and he didn't want to make any sudden turns or stops and risk waking her. Henry was so tired he didn't trust what might happen if she started crying again. He saw the narrow road and slowly turned on it. The road was rough, and overgrown with grass, and weeds. It was obvious no one had been here for a long time, which was exactly how Henry was hoping it would be.

Cautiously he drove at a snail's pace down the narrow rough road that was nothing more than a pig trail now. After what seemed an eternity the woods surrounding the cabin came in to view. He knew that he would have to park and walk a quarter of a mile to the cabin. Henry stopped the car and turned the engine off. He sat still listening to the night sounds for a few minutes. Tired and weary from driving and no sleep, he thought about sleeping in the car. Another thought crossed his mind. Not wanting to carry Audreigh Rose, he thought of leaving her in the car and returning to fetch her in the morning. He quickly dismissed that thought. Fear of her screaming, and alarming someone, made him decide to take her with him. He looked around and doubted that anyone would be able to hear a sound from this remote place, but he wasn't taking any chances. After all she was his golden ticket to Paradise.

He picked her up as gently as he could and breathed a sigh of relief when she didn't make a sound. Gazing at her in the moonlight he felt something close to compassion cross his troubled mind. Brushing it away Henry started walking toward the cabin.

It took all his concentration to keep from stumbling in the tall grass and thicket. In the distance he heard the call of an owl. The land was lit up and for that he was glad. He could not imagine trying to find his way if not for glow of the moon. As he walked up the few steps to the porch of the cabin he nervously looked around. The place was overgrown. Obviously no one had used this place for a very long time. Still he moved warily. He tried the door and was startled to find that it opened. The fact that it was not locked made the situation seem too good to be true. Henry knew from past experience that when something appeared too good to be true it usually was. He stood peering through the open door into the darkness of the room that lay beyond the threshold. Listening, and hearing only the sound of the baby's light breathing, he finally got his nerve up and stepped inside. Feeling the wall for a switch and finding it, the room exploded with light. Henry cringed and squeezed his eyes tight. He was temporarily blinded by the stark light after driving in hours of darkness. Looking around and simultaneously rubbing his eyes; he noted how neat the cabin was. The furniture was covered with fabric drop cloths. The floor was immaculate and there was no dust anywhere. Turning from the living room he crept down the hall and stopped to see a small bedroom with a single bed to the left of the hall. To the right was a much bigger bedroom and larger bed. A bath was at the end of the hall with large closets on both sides. Henry placed the sleeping child in the smaller room. He lay pillows around her so she would not roll off the bed. Crossing the hall he fell across the big bed.

Within seconds he was snoring, standing on a beach, talking with a pretty, dark haired girl. In his dreams Henry had made it. Henry Benning was living in Paradise.

TWENTY FOUR

Nola sat on a blanket watching the gentle water flow by. Dave sat
next to her and they were both deep in thought. The two of them
walked to the creek together discussing what she learned from the
papers in Mundy's box. She asked Dave, if Mundy ever mentioned
that he had a child. Dave said he had not. Mundy never talked about
personal matters with his hands. At least not to Dave's knowledge.
They sat now watching the creek, wondering what all of this meant.
Nola felt as if she could not quite make the pieces of the puzzle fit
together. Talking with Tilly helped some, but now she knew she
must visit the Benning farm. Hopefully someone would have more
information and be willing to share it. "The Benning farm, Pleasant

Ridge, it is not far from where I grew up in Louisa. But I don't recall any mention of it. Of course my mother was not very social. She kept to herself." Nola said, wincing at the memory of Mother's paranoia.

"Well now that you know where it is…the farm I mean…I would like to go with you. I mean…uh…when you go talk to them. Just let me ask Cash if he knows anything about them. About the Benning's." Dave smiled at her.

"Yes, I would love for you to go with me…I could use the company. You know what they say," Nola said as she pushed hair from her eyes, "two heads are better than one." Dave laughed a little at that statement. His laugh made Nola laugh. The sound startled her. It had been quite a while since she had heard her own laughter. The laughter stopped, and they found themselves staring. Nola was suddenly aware of how masculine Dave was. It was if she were discovering that fact about him for the first time. She had always thought him handsome, but never saw such masculinity in him. Dave was held captive by Nola's incredible eyes. She made him feel lost, vulnerable, and he forced himself to look back at the water. This broke the spell and Nola felt her cheeks grow hot with a sudden embarrassment. Dave stood to his feet, no longer trusting that he could sit with her another minute and not take her in his arms, and kiss her deeply. His mind was racing, and he was trying desperately to stop the silly pursuit of this woman. He knew Nola would never be interested in a cow poke, and he felt angry and disappointed for letting go of his feelings. He had always been one to bottle up his thoughts, keeping them to himself. Nola had a way of bringing his emotions to the surface, and he was not liking this game at all. Nola stood and reached out to touch his arm. Dave stepped back and mumbled that he had work to do. He turned and left Nola standing, watching him walk away. She felt embarrassed, and confused about what just happened. How had she offended him? Sighing she made her way to the house. Her thoughts turned once again to Mundy, and the mystery of the child he never revealed.

These days no matter what she did her thoughts always returned to Mundy, and his child.

She wanted to make a call to Cash, and tomorrow visit the Benning farm. Where would all this lead she wondered? Maybe tomorrow she would find the answers that haunted her nights and days.

Cash and Will were driving to New Orleans together. Cash was officially off duty. He had managed to get the sheriff from the neighboring county to cover Monroe while he investigated the kidnapping of Audreigh Rose. A couple of detectives from the capitol had been in town and asking questions, but with no leads and no evidence that the baby was taken out of state, they grew frustrated and went back to Charleston. They did tell Cash they would likely return in a few days, and demanded that the young Sheriff keep them up to speed on any new information. Cash assured them he would do just that.

Somewhere in Kentucky, Cash was becoming uncomfortable by the silence in the car. His attempts at any conversation with Will had been futile. Cash was a talker, but he needed a recipient of his words, and Will wasn't receptive. Will was driving and a little too fast, while Cash sat as far over in the passenger seat as possible. Cash spotted a roadside Mom and Pop grocery store up ahead, and broke the silence by asking Will to pull into it. He needed to get something to drink and stretch his legs. Will didn't answer, but he pulled off the road and parked in front of the store. Both men got out slowly, stretching and trying to move on stiff legs.

Will entered the store with Cash following close behind. An older lady sat on a stool behind a counter. She greeted the men warmly when they entered. "Good afternoon gentlemen." She eyed them closely as she did all strangers who walked into her store. "Can I help you fellers find anything?" She asked smiling. Will ignored her and stood looking around at nothing and everything.

"Ma'am I just need me a soda water. Grape if you have it." Cash smiled at her politely.

"Oh sure…I got grape. And orange. But you said grape. Want me to open it?" She pulled the bottle of soda out of a large tub of ice and water. Not waiting for his answer on whether he wanted it open she wiped the dripping bottle with a towel and quickly opened it. Handing it to Cash she took the dime he held out to her. "What brings you fellers this way? Don't think I know you two."

"On our way to Orleans ma'am. Official business you might say." Cash said.

"Lands sake. Official business. You some kind of lawmen?"

"Yes ma'am. I'm the sheriff of Monroe. We are trying to find a baby that was kidnapped. A little girl a few months old." Before he finished the last sentence he saw the woman's face completely drain of color. She swayed a bit and reached for the counter to steady herself. Placing her hand to her chest she tried to speak but found it hard to breathe.

"She…Sheriff," she said between gulps of air, "There was a man…a man…"

Cash and Will both instinctively moved to either side of the woman and took her arms. They led her behind the counter to a stool and sat her down gently. The hair on the back of Cash's neck stood up

232

as he realized God had sent them to the right place at the right time. "Go on ma'am…a man…you saw a man with a baby?" Will was asking questions now.

"Yes. Yes… he was in here yesterday buying milk. He had a baby with him. A little girl…beautiful…screaming her head off. I followed him to his car because he forgot his change. I knew that baby was not his. I've lived with a liar for years and I can spot me a good liar. This man wasn't even a good liar. He fed me some story about the child's grandma bein sick and all." She closed her eyes and looked as if she might faint so Will took the rag she used to wipe the bottles and dipped it in the tub. Wringing it out he placed the cold, wet rag on her face, and she began to feel better. "I watched him drive away with that baby. What could I do?"

"Which direction did they go ma'am?" Cash looked into her eyes. The young sheriff was so kind, and spoke so softly. She looked back into his eyes then looked out toward the road. Pointing she told him in a voice barely above a whisper that he'd headed north; in the direction of the line.

"The West Virginia state line."

Henry woke early. He sat up on the bed and looked around the room. Scratching his head he struggled to remember where he was. Oh yeah, he remembered. Quickly he went into the room where the baby slept. She was sound asleep still, so he made his way out to the kitchen hoping to find some coffee in the cabin. Yanking open cabinet doors he was pleasantly surprised to find a can of coffee, and other cans of food as well. Just like someone left this place in a hurry and didn't take time to pack up. Henry was not sure who owned the cabin, but he knew they had not been here in a long time. The place was too overgrown and unkempt, at least on the outside.

He found a drip pot and soon had some decent coffee. He carried a mug outside and stood on the porch. Setting the mug on the railing he lit a cigarette. The sun was coming up and the air was warm and moist. Maybe it would rain today. He had a lot to do today. Finding a phone and putting in a call to the baby's Momma was his first priority. Yeah, he thought, the baby should be worth way more money to its Momma than to them crazies in New Orleans. Instead of 10 grand he was gonna ask for 100,000. He smiled exposing long neglected teeth. Then he spoke out loud to the wind. "Look out Paradise, Henry's on his way." Smiling big he puffed his cigarette, and sipped his coffee. His thoughts were already in Paradise…just waiting for Henry's body to get there.

Angelina stood in front of the mirror brushing her hair. Her hands shook and her arms felt heavy as she brought the brush down the long thick locks. She felt old. She looked old.

The stress of Audreigh's kidnapping had taken its toll on her face. New lines and puffy eyes. When and how would this all end? Angelina was tired. She wanted to go to sleep and never wake up again. Too much had happened in too little time. There was no time to grieve for her parents. No time to recover from her accident. No time. She felt as if she were out of time. If her baby were gone forever, then she wanted to be gone too. But how? That was the question on her mind this morning. How could she make it all go away forever? Will did not love her, and never would. Audreigh bonded with her nanny not realizing Angelina was her mother. Cash was the real father, and sooner or later Will would leave her because of that. The only reason he married her was because she was pregnant. He would leave and go to Nola. Deep down she knew he loved Nola. He loved Nola, not her. That knowledge made Angelina feel…less than. She felt less than. Tired of brushing she sat the brush down and walked to the window. She had been forming a plan and tonight if her courage did not fail she would put the plan in action. Feeling as if she had nothing to live for she decided to end it all in a place where no one would find her. Will could go on with his life with Nola. Perhaps Arlyn could raise Audreigh. Cash could finally claim his daughter. Yes, they would all be better off without her. Angelina knew just the place.

A secluded cabin. A place where tragedy at the hands of a mad man had once struck. No one would think of looking there. Lightning never strikes the same place twice. Glancing at the bottle of pills on her nightstand, she thought for a moment of how it would feel to swallow them all. To go to sleep and never wake again. Tonight she would know. Tonight she would sneak away and never return. The cabin in the woods seemed to call out to her. Angelina sighed. Deep and shaky her breath seemed sharp, labored, and she trembled. Looking out the window at the dark clouds she watched the storm rolling in. It was going to rain. Let it rain she thought. Let tears fall from heaven. Tears fell from her dark troubled eyes as she prayed for rain. She prayed for courage to do what she felt she must do. "Lord," she whispered, "I am drowning. Lord, save me from myself." She bowed her head and sobbed, as huge drops of rain began a steady pelting against the window pane.

The baby cried for two hours solid. Henry was ready to pull his hair out. He tried feeding her, changing her, he even tried singing some silly song he remembered from his childhood. The singing turned her cries into screams. Finally exhausted, and angry, he lay her in the middle of the bed and walked out of the cabin. Mumbling and stumbling across the yard he thought about leaving her there in the cabin and going home to his farm. Standing among the weeds he could still hear her crying, but after a few minutes of thinking hard about leaving he realized all was quiet. Audreigh stopped crying. Must have worn herself out Henry thought, or at least he hoped.

Peering around the yard he noticed a path leading down to the woods. Walking aimlessly trying to imagine Paradise and all that he would do there, Henry's mood lightened a bit.

He was walking through the tall grass and being careful of every step. Snakes loved tall grass. Having been bitten a few times by snakes, and knowing how extremely painful that was, he was always glancing around for the nasty creatures. Rat snakes were populous in this area and they were nasty, aggressive creepers.

Noticing a break in the grass he could make the outline of two rectangles ahead surrounded by tall weeds. He left the path and took a chance walking in the tall grass over to see what the strange bare spots were. Henry was shocked and curious to see what appeared to be side by side graves. Grass grew sparsely over the dirt mounds but it was obvious to him that the graves were only a couple of years old. Maybe that was why no one occupied the cabin anymore. Some old couple must have died and their kin buried them here. Henry snorted. How sweet he thought as he kicked at a clod of dirt. Turning to head back to the path movement caught his eye from the edge of the woods. Henry dropped to his knees trying to hide in the grass. His breathing sped up, and sweat broke out on his brow as he scanned the woods. He rubbed his eyes. A woman. A black woman. Someone from New Orleans he thought. They had found him. His eyes slowly focused. Squinting he peered as far into the dark woods as he could. Seeing no one he wondered if he imagined the woman.

After all those people wouldn't know about this place. He doubted whether more than a couple of people knew about this place as secluded as it was. Looking back at the graves he knew at least two who had known, but they weren't gonna tell anyone anything.

Henry chuckled and stood to his feet. He was tired and seeing things. "Your eyes is playin tricks on you Hennie Boy," he heard his Momma say. He heard his Momma in his head. Hearing his Momma made tears spring to his eyes. Wiping at them with the back of his hand he heard her again. This time he thought he heard her out loud. Glancing around Henry called out. "Momma," his breathing sped up again. "Momma," he spoke a little louder. Feeling foolish he walked quickly to the cabin. Every few steps he glanced over his shoulder as if expecting to see his Momma or the Orleans woman. Just as he reached the steps to the cabin he heard his Momma again.

"Big boys don't cry Hennie Boy. Big boys don't cry."

The sun was still high in the sky as Angelina headed her truck out on the road heading to the cabin. She felt numb and unemotional. It was almost as if she were outside of her body watching as she took all the steps needed to end the pain of living. She had the pills. She grabbed a pistol at the last minute. If the pills failed she wanted a backup plan. A good plan requires a "just in case." The "just in case" lay beside her in a small leather bag along with a bottle of pills. The pills were prescribed by the doctor, taken to put her to sleep when she became overwhelmed. She was sure if she took enough of them she would sleep forever. She drove.

Where was the turn off road? Her memory was fuzzy lately. A sign of stress she was told. There was the road just ahead. Turning on it quickly made her tires squeal a little. Unfazed, and operating in a robotic controlled manner, she continued on the narrow dirt road. She stopped the truck in the field just beyond the woods. She could not see the cabin. Sitting in the car with the engine running, both hands on the wheel; she stared at the woods. Scanning her mind she searched the dark recesses of her thoughts looking, almost hoping, for one shred of doubt. Was there anything, any reason to turn the car around, and go home? With eyes closed and steady breaths she searched, but after a while opened her eyes and put the car in park. She turned off the engine and grabbed the bag. "No reason…no reason at all…" she whispered.

Angelina began what would be the last walk of her journey. "No reason…no reason…" she said over, and over, as she struggled through the tall weeds making her way to the cabin.

Tilly knocked lightly on Angelina's bedroom door. It was afternoon and she had not come down for breakfast. Tilly thought she might be sleeping, so she did not bother her until now. There was no answer. She turned the knob to the door while balancing a tray with the other hand and entered the room. Calling out she sat the tray of food down on a small table by the sofa. The room was dark. Tilly continued to call out to Angelina as she crossed the room to open the curtains. Light flooded in to the dim room. Turning, she noticed the bed was neatly made. Thinking she might be in the bath she crossed over the room and tapped lightly on the door. No answer. She opened the door, but Angelina was not there. Concern started to rise up in Tilly. Rushing down the stairs she made her way to the garage where the cars, and trucks were housed. She met the head driver coming out of the garage and she stopped to ask if he had seen Missy Angelina. When the driver told her he saw her driving away almost an hour ago Tilly's stomach turned. She caught her breath and put her hand to her mouth to stifle a scream. The driver reached out to steady her asking what was wrong. Saying nothing she turned and ran to the house. Tilly needed to get the sheriff on the phone. Tilly knew Angelina. Tilly raised that child and she knew her. Tilly knew she was going to go somewhere and do something bad. The old woman couldn't let her mind think about what the bad thing was. She knew she needed to get help finding her. With shaking fingers she dialed the sheriff's number and started to pray as she heard the phone ring over, and over. Answer Cash, she prayed, please answer.

Cash and Will heard the phone ringing as they walked into the office. Picking the phone up Will could hear Cash asking questions. "How long has she been gone? Is anyone else missing? Did she have a gun with her?" Will stood by trying to interrupt and find out who they were talking about. Cash kept holding his hand up to silence Will, which irritated him and made him scowl.

Hanging up the phone Cash grabbed his keys to the cruiser and shouted at Will, "Angelina is missing....come on man." He headed out the office door with Will on his heels.

"What are you talking about Cash? What is going on? Cash…"

"I'll explain on the way. Hurry up and get in the car." Cash barely let Will close the door before he peeled off driving at break neck speed toward Pine Point. Like Tilly, Cash knew Angelina was going somewhere to do something unthinkable. He prayed he would be able to find her in time to stop her. Even with all that lay between them, he loved her. Driving as fast as he could and trying to calmly explain to Will what Tilly told him, he silently prayed to God to let him find Angelina. He prayed to find Angelina....alive.

TWENTY FIVE

Nola looked around sadly. The barn was falling down; boards were missing and the tin room was partially caved in. A faded, chipped sign, "Pleasant Ridge Farm" sarcastically declared the name of the property. The farm was in such a state of neglect that it was the complete opposite of pleasant. The words seemed vulgar, taunting, as they hung over the barn door sideways. One rusty nail left the sign dangling, and swaying sadly with the wind. The bones of a tractor sat in what used to be a crop field. Abandoned. Left right in the spot where it stopped running. No one cared enough to repair what broke, and get it running again. That was exactly how this place looked. No one cared. It made Nola at the same time uneasy, and curious to know what happened here. The two story wood farm house was probably quite splendid in the days when someone did care. She could see gingham curtains faded now and tattered, hanging from what must be the kitchen windows. Stepping up on the porch she was careful and walked gently. The boards were rotted. Some were lose. She hoped she didn't fall through the floor. Knocking heartily on the door of the house she knew she was wasting her time. It was obvious no one was here. But she had to try. The Benning's were her only link to what happened years ago with Mundy.

Mundy had fathered a child and these people were the link. That child came up missing and Tilly's beau hanged for the kidnapping. Like Tilly, Nola did not believe that Jessie Porter had anything to do with the missing baby.

Nola stood on the porch for a few moments wondering what to do next. She bravely drove herself here this morning, refusing to let Naomi, or Joseph, accompany her. She decided after the way Dave behaved at the creek she was not going to ask for his help anymore. His behavior bordered on rude, and she was just starting to open up to him. She was just starting to trust him and consider him a friend, maybe moving toward something more than a friend. He hurt her feelings. She was close to kissing him, and he shut her down. Hard. Her wall went back up. Dave would never be anything more than her employee. Her farm manager. By his choice that was all he would be. She shook her head to clear her thoughts. Close to lunchtime and hungry, she thought she would go into the town of Louisa, and get something to eat. Worried about her parking skills, she decided to take a chance on finding somewhere easy to park her car. Her driving skills were not good, and her parking skills worse than that. Maybe with some food in her belly she could think about what more she could do to figure out this mystery. It was haunting her not knowing. She had to know about Mundy's child. She had to know. Nola pulled away from the farm and drove toward Louisa. For now the only thing on her mind was putting something in her growling stomach.

Angelina slowly made her way across the field. Unaware of the rain that had started falling softly, it was now coming down harder. Soaked to the skin she kept walking, unaware of anything. She had only one goal. Getting to the cabin and getting to this one final task was all that was on her mind. No thought of Audreigh now, or Will, nothing was going to change her course, no reason. Making it to the cabin she found the path leading past the graves and she glanced at them as she passed. Her mind fought to take her back to that night. She would not allow any thoughts of the past or the future, choosing to remain in this moment and what she needed to do. Up the steps quickly, and with her hand on the door knob she was just about to enter when heard a baby cry. Freezing in place, with her hand on the knob, she thought she must be losing what mind she had left. Then she heard it again. Quickly she turned the knob and moved into the cabin hurrying down the hall toward the now constant cries. Stopping in the doorway of one of the bedrooms she saw her. She could not believe her eyes. Audreigh Rose lay upon the bed. Silent now, and no longer crying, the baby looked at her Mother. A smile slowly spread across the beautiful little face as she recognized Angelina. Tears hot, and heavy, fell from her eyes as Angelina moved slowly toward the bed. Feeling as if what she were seeing was a dream and the baby might disappear, she slowly inched toward the child. Standing at the side of the bed she picked her up and held her to her chest. "Audreigh...my little Audreigh Rose...," she whispered.

Something struck the back of her head. Instinctively she tried to hold on to Audreigh, but the baby slipped from her grasp and fell onto the bed. Unhurt, but startled, the child began to wail. Angelina grabbed the back of her head where the pain was, and tried to sort her scrambled thoughts to comprehend what just happened. Turning toward the place where the blow came from she saw a man. He was smiling. Smiling a huge smile with ugly teeth, he kept smiling as he struck the front of her head. His ugly smiling teeth were the last image she had before her world went black. Angelina sunk to the bedroom floor still holding her head. Henry grabbed her by her arms dragging her down the hall and out of the cabin. Breathing hard, he drug her across the field stopping every few feet, until he made it to his car. He couldn't leave her here at the cabin. Henry was afraid that others would come. Someone may know where she went. Maybe this place was not as secluded, and unused, as he first thought. She was thin, but tall and not light. It took all his strength to get her to where the car was parked. He would have to go back for the baby. Finally getting her body in the back seat, he brushed the hair from her face looking at her. Like a light bulb suddenly switching on in his brain; Henry recognized the woman. Angelina Oliver. This was the baby's mother. He smiled. Well now. Don't this beat all? Seems like this was Henry's lucky day. Now he had two bargaining chips. Surely Missy Oliver-Biggs husband would pay double to get his baby and his wife back. Henry almost danced back to the cabin to fetch the baby. Paradise was closer and closer.

Paradise was becoming more and more real. "PARADISE!" Henry shouted.

Nola grabbed a sandwich at the grocery in Louisa. The meat case was brimming with an assortment of fresh luncheon meat, and she chose a ham and swiss cheese on thick slices of fresh white bread. She bought a bottle of orange soda and ate slowly in her car. Looking up and down the streets of Louisa made her feel a bit homesick. She thought of the old house on the hill, and Dominy Brooks. Thinking of Dominy still caused tears to sting her eyes. She looked out toward the edge of town where the cemetery lay and thought of Milo, and her baby. Buried there together, she knew she should go visit their graves. She also knew she would not go there. Not today. She simply was not ready. Finishing her sandwich and drink, Nola thought of going home to her babies. She was tired, and had not accomplished anything on this trip. She found no one to talk to at the Benning's about what happened all those years ago. Maybe someone was there now. Perhaps the Benning's were shopping, picking up supplies, and they had returned home now. She knew it was a long shot. Reality told her no one was living at the farm, but she could not go home without one more try. The engine roared to life and she made a turn in the street and drove out of town to the Benning farm. Pleasant Ridge, she thought. Someone should definitely take the sign down. Pleasant it was not.

Angelina tried to open her eyes. She felt something hard beneath her body. It was the floor. She was on a floor. Her eyes fluttered and finally she was able to open them a sliver. She didn't realize they were swollen shut. The severe blow to her head blacked her eyes, and made them swell. Trying to speak and sit up at the same time made her cry out in pain. "You shut up now...else I will hit you again. You hear?" Angelina couldn't see, but she could hear. Remembering the man made her wince in pain. The man. Bad teeth. Smiling at her with those teeth. She remembered him smiling at her before she blacked out. He must have hit her, but why? She wanted to ask him why but she knew not to say anything. He would kill her. She didn't know much at this moment, but she was sure he would kill her. Then she heard the sound that made her blood run cold. It started out as a small whimper and in her confused state she thought the sound came from her own mouth. But no. Wait. She couldn't see her, but she knew the sound came from her baby.

The whimper became a cry. A baby crying. Audreigh. It was Audreigh. She heard someone screaming AUDREIGH...AUDREIGH...She was screaming. The man began shrieking at Angelina to shut up. "Both of you be still. Shut up or I will shut you up. You ...hear me?" Angelina's head fell back on the floor when Henry's hand landed across her cheek. The only sound was ragged breathing. Was it hers? She couldn't decide. Silent now she stopped screaming for Audreigh. Her mind was trying to cut through the fog, and she knew she must do whatever this man wanted to save her baby.

She found her baby. God had led her to Audreigh. Now she just had to get her away from this mad man. She lay on the floor not moving. She prayed for God to open her eyes so she could see. She prayed and she waited. Audreigh stopped crying. She thought she could hear her sucking a bottle. Praying harder she opened her eyes a little wider. Joy, pure joy entered her body when she saw her baby lying on a sofa taking a bottle. Audreigh turned her tiny head, and looked into her mother's eyes.

Pulling the bottle out of her mouth she smiled at her mother. Angelina could barely contain her joy. Quickly she tried looking around the room to find the man. He was not in the room. Where was he?

Nola turned the car onto the narrow drive way that led to the Benning's farm. Thinking about the people who once lived there she was a bit puzzled as to why she didn't have some recollection of their farm or family. Although Mother kept her isolated she was acquainted with most of the folks in Louisa. Not so the Benning's. Their farm was not so far from the hill where Nola spent the biggest part of her life. A lifetime ago it seemed. How much had changed since she left the hill. She had changed. She was stronger, less vulnerable. More determined than ever before, Nola was going to live life her own way. Slowly bringing the car to a stop in front of the barn she knew instantly something was different. Thinking, and glancing around, there wasn't any sign of a car or truck. No sign that someone had returned to the farm from a trip to town. Still, something was different. The barn.

Staring hard at the door on the barn, it dawned on her slowly that it was now open. That's what was different. Thinking hard Nola knew it was closed when she was here earlier. Opening the door and getting out she called out as she walked to the front of the barn. No one answered and it was dark inside the barn from where she stood. She walked slowly closer, calling "Hello…anyone here? Hello…"

"Stay right where you are Missy." Henry's voice was low.

Nola started to turn toward the voice behind her. "Wha…?"

"Don't turn around." Henry yelled.

Nola froze. She was confused and started to speak again. "Mr.Benning? I…I…am sso…sorry…I"

"Shut up. You be quiet." Henry was rattled. How did this woman know his name? Shoving her hard he pushed her toward the house. He didn't speak, but he grunted and continued moving Nola to the house. She tried to calm her mind. Confused, she wanted to explain that she only came to talk with him about Mundy. Somehow she knew to keep quiet. Somehow her instincts told her she was in grave danger. She fought the panic that was rising, knowing that panic would prevent her from forming a plan to get out of this. Her mind continued to swirl with questions. Who was this man? Why was he taking her to the house?

A few feet from the steps she heard the sound that caused her to inhale sharply, and stop walking. It was the cry of a baby. There was a baby in the house. Without thinking she turned to question the man, but before she could make a complete turn to face him he struck her. Hard. He struck her with something made of wood. The butt of a gun she thought. That was her last thought. She thought he struck her with a gun. Her knees buckled, and Nola Rain's world went dark.

TWENTY SIX

Cash, and Will, stood questioning a distraught Tilly. The driver stood nearby listening intently. Angelina drove off in the opposite direction of town. Cash was listening to Tilly, but thinking at the same time. Where would she be going? Who did she know that lived in that direction? Like a sudden slap to the face he knew where she went. Running to his cruiser Will stood watching until Cash yelled over his shoulder. "Come on man… the cabin."

"What cabin Cash?" Will yelled as he too ran for the cruiser.

"Riley Todd's cabin." Cash peeled out toward the road as Will stared at him in disbelief from the passenger seat.

Searching the cabin they found evidence that someone had been staying there. Finding an empty baby bottle, and soiled diapers, made both men stare in concern and confusion. Was Angelina behind the kidnapping of the baby? Will wondered, but did not voice his question. He could not know Cash was chasing the same question round, and round, in his own head. Outside looking for more evidence Will spotted blood on the grass.

He bent down and touched it. Still wet and mixed with rain he stared up at Cash; as if expecting an explanation that would chase away his growing fear. Cash bent down, and looking out to where they left the cruiser he could see the drag lines. There was a definite trail where someone had dragged something, or somebody through the tall grass and weeds. They found Angelina's truck parked at the edge of the field when they arrived. Searching it they found nothing. No blood. This was definitely blood though the rain had weakened it some, and it was thin. Relatively fresh too, Cash thought. Just as they were about to walk the field to the cruiser Cash heard some crackling noises in the woods not far from where they stood. Daylight was fading, and in the dusk he could make out a dark figure. Standing still he put his hand on his gun. Will stood silent and still. The figure moved out into the fading light and they could see that it was Maclaine Moreaux. Will relaxed and let out a sigh, but Cash remained on guard. His hand never left his gun. "Move on over here Moreaux." Cash said. "You move real slowly now." Maclaine slowly walked up to the men. "What are you doing here?" Cash asked.

"There is no time to explain why I am here sheriff." Maclaine glared at Cash.

"I am fixin to haul you in, if for no other reason than trespassing…you…"

"Henry Benning took Angelina, and the baby….if I were you I would be worried about finding them before that crazy kills em both."

Maclaine abruptly turned and walked away disappearing into the dark woods. Cash and Will stood frozen, as if in a trance. The spell broke and they ran across the field using the path that was made by Angelina's dragged body. Within minutes they were in the cruiser headed to Louisa. Both of them prayed they would find Angelina, and Audreigh, alive at the Benning farm.

The stars were beginning to appear in the nearly black sky. The clouds and rain from earlier in the day moved on. The night was clear, and cool. Naomi got the twins ready for bed with the help of the girls then tossing a shawl across her shoulders she walked to the bunkhouse. Dave was standing outside. Naomi called out to him. When she explained that Nola hadn't come home, or called, Dave didn't hesitate. He knew she would never leave her boys this long and something must be wrong. Naomi found the directions to Pleasant Ridge. Nola had written down the directions, and left a copy for Naomi just in case something happened with her boys. She knew Naomi would send someone to get her. Those boys were her world. Nola tucked them into bed, and kissed them goodnight, every night. She should have been home hours ago. Dave and Naomi knew something was terribly wrong. Dave found himself more than a little angry at Naomi for not coming to him sooner. He was also angry at Nola, for going there alone. Naomi thought of calling the sheriff, but she reasoned Dave could go find Nola quicker. Dave left quickly, and Naomi headed back to the house to wait. It would be a long night she feared.

The farm looked dark and deserted when Dave pulled down the long drive leading to the barn yard. He turned his lights off and drove at a crawl. His skin prickled and the hair on his neck stood up. Dave's senses were on high alert. He could smell trouble, and this smelled really bad. He turned the truck off and eased over to the barn. The door was open and when he looked inside he could see Nola's car. It was backed up in the barn nearly to the back. He could tell there was another car parked behind Nola's. Not recognizing it he left the barn and made his way to the old house. Nola was here somewhere, and she was in trouble. Suddenly Dave wished he had brought his gun. He felt vulnerable, and unprepared for what he knew he was going to encounter. Stopping for a moment he thought of going back to get his gun, but he was too afraid that whatever was going on might get worse while he was gone. Whoever had Nola might take her from here, and he would have no shot at finding her. He moved on to the house trying to get under the windows of what looked like the kitchen.

Crouching under the window of the old house Dave eased his body up to peer inside. There was a faint glow coming through the glass so he was fairly certain someone was in there. The window he was under was as he thought, the kitchen. He could barely make out the cook stove and a table. Beyond the kitchen a light shone from another room. The room must be on the other side of the house he thought. Easing his way around to the back he tried to look in every window he passed. All the rooms were dark. He couldn't see anything.

252

As he came around the corner to the far side of the house he saw headlights coming down the drive. The lights went out and he backed up peering around the corner. When he saw the cruiser and watched as Cash, and Will parked and got out, he exhaled. The sound of his own breath startled him. He continued to watch as they came toward the house almost in a run. Dave stayed in his spot. He knew not to call out to them, but he was afraid. Fear of not knowing who was in there and knowing that Nola's car was in the barn. There was no way to let them know at this point.

They disappeared from his sight but he heard their footsteps as they went up the steps and across the porch. He listened as they pounded on the door. Cash was yelling Angelina's name. Dave heard Will yell something he couldn't make out… and then a loud pop. A second later another loud pop. Screams were coming from the house. A baby began to cry. In all the chaos Dave stood frozen. When he heard Nola's voice he felt his feet began to move. He was running toward the sound. He could hear Nola screaming over, and over, "No…NO…NOOOO!" When Dave made the last corner he stopped, and jumped back for cover as Henry brought the gun around to shoot him. Henry fired off a shot missing him. Dave stood breathing hard. He was trying to sort out all that his eyes had seen. Nola stood over Will. Cash was lying on the porch steps. Breathing hard he knew he had to do something. The guy with the gun was crazed, and Dave knew there was not much time before he killed Nola.

Running around to the other side of the house his only idea was to try to sneak up behind the crazy man. He stopped running and looked around for a weapon. A rock, a stick, anything.

Henry shoved Nola back inside. She was huddled on the floor with Angelina. The soft sounds of Audriegh's cries were coming from the sofa where she lay. Nola was shivering, but trying to speak words of comfort to Angelina who was mumbling something over and over. Nola never took her eyes off Henry. He was pacing. Back and forth, back and forth. Talking to himself and pacing, Henry was trying to decide his next move. He tried to search his mind for options. He shot the Sheriff and that other feller. There was another one out there somewhere. They all wanted to keep him away from Paradise. Henry couldn't stand the thought of losing Paradise. Henry spent his entire life trying to get to Paradise. Henry stopped pacing, and closed his eyes.

"Hennie Boy?"

Henry jerked his head around. He spun in a circle. "Momma...is that you Momma?"

"Hennie Boy....you in trouble Hennie. You in trouble with a capitol T....you is."

Henry kept jerking his head searching every inch of the room. "Where you at Momma? Momma?"

"Finish what you started Hennie Boy. You best finish what you started. Paradise is waitin..."

Tears began to make their way down Nola's face. She could not take her eyes off of Henry. She tried to look away, but she could not. Henry was breaking down moment by moment. Any sanity that existed in Henry Benning was swallowed up by years of torment. Pity was all Nola felt staring at him now. Though he was going to kill her, all she felt for him in that moment was pity. No fear. Nola was not afraid for herself. She thought about her sons, and was saddened that they would have to grow up without her. She thought of Angelina, who thankfully would not see what was getting ready to happen. Audreigh was an innocent baby, blissfully unaware of the madness in the room. Nola steeled herself as she watched Henry bring the gun around. When the barrel reached her Henry stopped, and brought the gun up to his shoulder.

Nola looked him square in the eye. In her mind she suddenly heard Dominy's voice. Nola was not alone. God, and her dear sweet friend, were with her, sustaining her in the final moments of her life. Her old friend was reciting the Lord's Prayer. Nola began repeating Dominy's words line, by line. Lifting her chin and in a calm clear voice she followed Dominy's leading. "Our Father"…Henry had the gun to his shoulder now…."Who art in Heaven"…Henry looked into Nola's eyes…"Hallowed be thy name." Henry swung the gun suddenly away from Nola, moving his body with the gun he aimed at the baby…at little Audreigh Rose. Nola could not watch him kill Audreigh. She could not. She would not. He would have to kill her first.

Nola leapt to her feet, and in one swift movement was on Henry's back screaming as loud as her lungs would let her. She was screaming the rest of the prayer. "THY KINGDOM COME….THY WILL BE DONE"…Henry was trying to get her off his back. He spun in circles, holding on to the gun.

"I'm… a… gonna… KILL… KILL YOU!" Henry shouted.

Nola pounded her small fists into Henry's head while reciting the prayer. Henry finally backed into the wall. Nola's back hit the wall. Breathless, she slid off his back and down the wall. She lay there dazed. Air began to fill her lungs. Immediately she whispered the words of her prayer.

"On Earth as it is in Heaven." Nola could hear Angelina repeating her words. Angelina's voice was faint, but she was praying with Nola.

"I am gonna kill you…." Henry lowered the barrel.

"Forgive us this day….our trespasses…"

"Shut up….SHUT UP…" Finger on the trigger.

"As we forgive those who trespass against us…"

"On my way to Paradise…Paradise…PARADISE…" Henry smiled.

"Deliver us from evil…" Angelina whispered.

"Deliver us from evil…" Nola sobbed.

She heard the blast and instinctively squeezed her eyes shut at the sound. Expecting pain, or the darkness she anticipated would come with death, she could hear. How could she hear? The dead don't hear. Do they? The sound of her own voice seemed far away, but it was her voice repeating the words "deliver us from evil." Henry was silent. Opening her eyes she saw Henry lying on the floor. Still clutching his gun. A puddle of blood was oozing from under his body. In the door way stood Arlyn, shotgun still at her shoulder. Nanny Arlyn fired a single shot ending Henry's madness. Dave Grimm stood behind Arlyn. No one moved, no one breathed, as if life was on pause waiting for reality to resume.

Awakening from her nightmare, Nola sat up, and forcefully exhaled. Dave was by her side holding her, and whispering shushing sounds. In shock, she was unaware that she was still repeating, "Deliver us from evil…deliver us from evil."

TWENTY SEVEN

Nola sat by the creek with the metal box on her lap. A year ago
today Dave handed her the plain gray box. After a thorough search
of Riley Todd's cabin the box had been found. The authorities
opened it, and handed it over to Dave Grimm, stating it belonged to
Nola Todd. For a year it sat in her bedroom. For a year she had
looked at it every day, waiting for just the right day to open it. Nola
knew the box belonged to Mother, as she remembered seeing it
when she was a little girl. How, and why Riley came to be in
possession of it, Nola did not know. Nor did she care. So much
changed for her in a year, but not just for her. The tragedy at the

Benning farm took its toll on all involved. By the time the authorities arrived Arlyn, was gone. Slipped away unnoticed. There was a search for her, and Maclaine Moreaux, but they were not to be found. It was rumored they went back where they came from. Back to living and practicing their strange rituals in the swamps, and bayous, of Louisiana. Angelina survived, but lost the love she fought so hard to steal from Nola. She became a widow that night at the Benning farm. Positive outcomes do rise from the embers of great tragedy. Angelina was living proof. She tried to end her life that night, and found a life worth living.

The Lord took Will, but gave her back her child. God gives. God takes. No longer bitter, Angelina would give Him praise for all the days she had left. Cash lived despite horrific wounds inflicted from Henry's shot gun. He married the prettiest woman he ever laid eyes on. The wedding took place in the little white church that Angelina attended as a child. In the good years, her young years, when Angelina was a trusting sweet child, she and her Mother held hands on the steps of the old country church. Standing on those steps with Cash, a lifetime later; Angelina looked up at the steeple shaped like a hand. The finger pointing upwards to heaven was a sign that God was showing her where to look to find her way. Where to turn when she was lost. Up. Always up. Always look heavenward to God who will point the way. Audreigh was walking, and beginning to talk. Her first word was "Momma," as she reached out for Angelina. Cash gave up the sheriff position to run Pine Point. Life was good again for Cash, and Angelina, and sweet Audreigh Rose. The future would hold more children. Cash was secretly hoping for a son, someday.

Nola stared out at the gently flowing creek. The sun danced on the water making it sparkle, golden, dream like. The death of Will nearly drained the life out of her. If not for her sons, she would not have pulled through. They would never know their father. That brutal fact of life would always haunt her. Nola understood the misery of not knowing who you really were, or where you came from. Her sons were a part of her. She was strong. Will had been strong. They would be strong too.

They would grow, and live, and love. They would make their own way. She and Dave were close, but she could not find any space in her heart for another man. She buried the love of her life, and though fond of Dave, she doubted their relationship would ever go beyond fondness, or friendship. Nola had her sons, and for that she was grateful. She had Fair Meadows, and Naomi. She missed Mundy some days almost more than she could bare. On those days she heard Dominy Brooks gently reminding her "God never gives us more than we can bare child...no he sure don't. He don't never give us more than we can handle. You is a strong woman Nola Rain...yes you are." So she wrapped herself in the memory of the love they shared and made it through those days. Mundy often told her she could "Do anything for one day." That is how she lived, one day at a time.

Looking down at the box on her lap she ran her hand across the smooth cold metal. Grasping the latch she pulled it open. There was a locket she recognized as Mother's. A picture of her, and Mother, when Nola was small. Holding it up she guessed she must have been about five years old. She ran a finger across the face of the sad little child. She would love to be able to tell that her everything turned out all right. She picked up another picture, and gasped. She recognized the woman in the picture. She was standing with Henry Benning, and perhaps Henry's mother. The young woman was the same young woman in the picture belonging to Mundy. Her mind tried to put this all together, and she turned the picture over. The words jumped out at her. "Felice...Nola's Mother, at Pleasant

Ridge." Nola dropped the picture, and it fell back in the box. She shut the lid quickly as if to conceal the secret inside.

Mundy…Mundy was her father. He had a baby with Felice and someone took the baby. The law hung Jessie Porter, believing he had kidnapped and killed the baby. But the baby was alive. Very much alive. Nola was that baby. Her mother, and father, were Mundy, and Felice. She tried to steady her breathing. Tears stung her eyes. She wept for the little girl in the picture who spent her life wondering who she was. She had dreamed of this moment all her life. And she wept, for the little girl Nola, who felt unloved and abandoned. Her heart broke for Mundy, who spent his life believing his child was dead, and then dying not ever knowing that his Nola was with him. Mostly she cried for Felice… for her mother that was sentenced to a lifetime of never knowing what happened to her child. Sobbing now she was crying out for what might have been. She was sobbing for what she knew would never be.

The sky was bathed in colors of orange, and red, as the sun dipped below the horizon. Nola walked slowly home to her boys. Home to Naomi. Home to Joseph. Vowing to keep what she discovered to herself at least for now, she felt lighter on her feet. The weight of wondering, vanished. The baggage she carried all her life of not knowing who she was, gone. She was Mundy's child. Brushing a tear away, she thought of how grateful she was. Grateful for the time she had with her father. For now she would keep the secret.

Someday she would tell her sons about their grandfather. Someday she would tell them what a wonderful, loving man he was. Smiling now through tears, she walked home to the people who loved her. Clutching the box to her chest she stopped on the trail, and looking up toward heaven she whispered, "Someday…someday…"

260

TWENTY EIGHT

Deep in the swamp where the snakes hang in the cypress trees, and alligators live and glide through the murky waters of the bayou, stories old and ancient live, and breathe, and be. Legends, rituals, practices, old as dirt...old as time. They exist in places of darkness, deep in the swamp where the sun cannot be found. It has been passed down that the queen cannot die until a child is born to take her place. The new one must be accepted by the "olds," and be a descendant of the King.

On this day deep in the swamp, Mother lies upon her death bed. The shack is small, and dim, the heat in the room unbearable. Her eyes are closed, and the only sound she makes is labored breathing.

Across the tiny room Gabrielle is laboring to breathe as well. She is not dying. She is about to give birth. Jolene, and Maclaine, stand by. Waiting…waiting…Mother takes one final breath, and does not exhale.

As Mother draws her last breath, the baby takes her first, and she cries. A Queen dies…a Queen is born. The deity lives on. The "olds" smile, and plan a celebration…deep in the swamp where the sun cannot be found.

Deep in the swamp

Where the sun it no shine

It be best if you stay away.

Stay out of the swamp

Don't go poking round

Where evil finds places to play.

Lynda C. Yeates is the author of Nola Rain, and this novel; a sequel, Angelina Marie. A seasoned writer of short stories, poetry, songs, and novels, creating is her passion. Whether singing, painting or writing, expressing who she is, and sharing a part of herself, has brought immeasurable joy to her life. Lynda lives in Deer Park, Texas with her husband Donald. They enjoy travelling and spending time with family. Together they make trips to Ohio to visit her sons, mother, and other family members. You may contact her through her website www.lyndayeatesauthor.com.